Fleur McDonald has lived and worked on farms for much of her life. After growing up in the small town of Orroroo in South Australia, she went jillarooing, eventually co-owning an eight-thousand-acre property in regional Western Australia.

Fleur likes to write about strong women overcoming adversity, drawing inspiration from her own experiences in rural Australia. She is the bestselling author of *Red Dust*, *Blue Skies*, *Purple Roads*, *Silver Clouds*, *Crimson Dawn* and *Emerald Springs*. She has two children and a Jack Russell Terrier, and is secretary of the Esperance & Districts Agricultural Society.

Also by Fleur McDonald
Red Dust
Blue Skies
Purple Roads
Silver Clouds
Crimson Dawn
Emerald Springs

FLEUR McDONALD

Indigo Storm

Dear Mary
A little piece of Australia
for you! MS

ARENA
ALLEN&UNWIN

My sister Suz—you are my inspiration

Precious strong hands hold me up, even when they're not seen or nearby. These hands will always hold my heart and never go out of style. Nothing will ever change.

First published in 2016

Arena Books, an imprint of
Allen & Unwin
83 Alexander Street
Crows Nest NSW 2065
Australia
Phone:(61 2) 8425 0100
Email:info@allenandunwin.com
Web:www.allenandunwin.com

Cataloguing-in-Publication details are available
from the National Library of Australia
www.trove.nla.gov.au

ISBN 978 1 76011 261 5

Set in 13/17.5 pt Garamond by Post Pre-press Group, Australia
Printed and bound in Australia by Griffin Press
10 9 8 7 6 5 4 3 2 1

MIX
Paper from
responsible sources
FSC® C009448
www.fsc.org

The paper in this book is FSC® certified.
FSC® promotes environmentally responsible,
socially beneficial and economically viable
management of the world's forests.

Chapter 1

Ashleigh looked out of the window. Through the heavy clouds that were threatening snow at one thousand feet, a sliver of sunlight was peeking. It was the first time the sun had shone in a week and she could see the tell-tale smudge of a rainbow.

Putting her *OUTBACK* magazine down, she stood up and walked to the window. Lake Jindabyne was flat and a lone yacht was moored in the grey, unreflective waters.

She sighed, feeling a restlessness stirring inside her. Her eyes searched the tree-covered mountains, as if the answer might be found in the landscape. She knew it wouldn't be, but the view usually calmed her.

Today it didn't. Her heart beat a little faster, the knot in her stomach making her feel sick.

Ashleigh held her hands level with her eyes and could see them shaking. Letting out an angry cry, she threw back her head and stomped her foot, before spinning around and pacing over to the wall where her wedding photo hung.

Dominic, her husband, was strikingly good-looking—tall and dark, with small flecks of grey in his sideburns. He was much taller than Ashleigh, and she could remember how she had felt that day, two years before. In the photo, they were a happy couple, madly in love. Dominic was looking down at her and she up at him, as if they were about to kiss.

'You're mine now,' he'd said quietly, just before the photo was taken. Briefly, she'd smiled, thinking how romantic he was, but then she'd realised that the possessive look on his face and the pressure of his hand on her waist told a different story.

Ashleigh had told no one (after all, who did she have to tell?) that seconds after the click of the camera, he held her with a force that had startled her and said: 'Don't ever think about leaving me. You won't get far.' Then he'd smiled, the intensity on his face vanishing, and looked out at their guests, raising his hand as if in victory. The crowd had cheered and she'd been left wondering what had just happened.

Now though she turned away from the photo and noticed the fire had burned low. Ashleigh threw another log on it and then made her way back to the couch. If she kept busy and could lose herself in someone else's world, she would forget about the knot in her gut. She flicked the pages until she came to a large photo. Staring at it for a few moments, she slowly drew the magazine closer.

A couple stood in front of a stone ruin. Behind them was a creek bed, covered in stones, and along the bank grew many large gum trees. There were a couple of other photos, of a lonely cemetery and a high, mountainous range. Both places were covered in blue and red flowers and low, prickly grey shrubs.

Goosebumps rose on Ashleigh's arms and a shiver went through her. She narrowed her eyes and studied the picture. The scenery was breathtaking. Suddenly she felt a sense of déjà vu. Why, she didn't know; she'd certainly never been to the north of South Australia. It was a strange and unsettling feeling.

She quickly ran her eyes over the story. None of the names of the places or people rang any bells with her, but why would they? As Dominic loved reminding her, she was an orphan. She had no one but him.

The door banged shut and Ashleigh jumped as Dominic came into the room, shaking the rain from his hair.

'Hi,' he said as he peeled off his coat and bent down to take off his boots.

'Hi back at you,' Ashleigh said, getting up from the couch. 'How's your day been so far?'

'Fine. Lunch ready?'

A sliver of apprehension slid through her as she realised the hour. 'Um, no. But it won't take me two minutes to heat up the meatballs. Sorry. I lost track of time.' She rushed into the kitchen without looking at him.

Banging the pot onto the stove, Ashleigh opened the fridge and grabbed the plastic container that held the spaghetti and meatballs in tomato sauce she'd made yesterday. Dom loved Italian food. He said it reminded him of his heritage. Not that he needed reminding; the little gang he had was almost Mafia-like.

'Damn,' she swore quietly. Her hands were shaking and she'd spilled some of the food onto the naked gas flame. It hissed before sending up a terrible burned odour.

'Careful,' he said.

Ashleigh froze for a second. She hadn't heard him enter the kitchen. 'Sorry,' she muttered, hating the fear he aroused in her.

Dominic came up behind her and put his hands on her shoulders. 'Can't have you getting hurt,' he said, kissing her neck.

Still wary, but hopeful now, she turned to face him, lifting her mouth for a kiss.

When he was like this, he was more than nice. He was the man she fell in love with. She wondered how on earth she could ever think of leaving him. He was attentive, loving and kind. Dominic ran his hands down the sides of her body and gently tapped her hips. 'What have you been doing this morning?' he asked as he moved to the counter and got out the crockery and cutlery.

Ashleigh stirred the sauce and turned on the oven, so she could heat the bread rolls.

'Just the normal type of things,' she answered. 'I've washed and cleaned. Had all of that done by nine-ish, so I walked down the street, did a bit of shopping and came home.'

'You walked? It's all of three degrees outside.'

'I know but I like the cold. It clears my head.'

The rich tomato sauce began to boil, so she took it off the heat and ladled it into two bowls.

'Who did you see down the street?' he asked casually, but Ashleigh could tell it was a loaded question. If her answer displeased him, well . . . Like the weather in the Snowy Mountains, he could change within minutes.

'No one really. I didn't talk to anyone,' she answered. 'I saw Mrs Harper from a distance. There's lots of blow-ins, though. Heaps of people combing the clothes stores. Must be a bit colder than some of the tourists expected.'

4

'Crazy, they are,' Dominic answered as he sat down at the table. 'They don't realise that buying the clothes up here is three times more expensive than if they'd bought them before they came.'

Ashleigh said nothing as she placed his meal in front of him and then sat down with her own bowl.

'Still, it's good for the town's economy.' Dominic plunged his fork in, winding the spaghetti around it, and smiled at her across the table. 'So, what do you have in mind for this afternoon?'

The picture from the magazine flashed into her mind. She really wanted to research the little town of Blinman. 'I'm not sure,' she answered. She stopped talking, wondering if this were the right time. It was clear he was in a good mood. 'Dominic . . .' She paused, about to tell him about the photo and the magazine article—how she had felt instantly drawn to what she had seen but couldn't understand why. Something inside her made her stop.

He looked expectantly at her, his fork halfway to his mouth. When it was clear she wasn't going to say anything more, he frowned, before raising his eyebrows in encouragement.

'No, it doesn't matter,' she said, shaking her head. 'I've forgotten what I was going to say.' Flicking her hand dismissively, she deliberately made her tone light, even though her stomach was in knots.

Dominic narrowed his eyes and continued to watch her while he swallowed another mouthful.

'Something on your mind?' he asked quietly.

'No,' she answered firmly.

They finished the rest of their meal in silence but when Ashleigh got up to clear the plates, Dominic grabbed hold of her wrist.

'Is there something you're not telling me?' he asked, in a low menacing voice.

Ashleigh tried to twist herself away, but realised there was no point. He had a tight grip and, once again, like the weather, he'd changed.

'Who did you speak to downtown this morning? You're not usually secretive.'

'I'm not being secretive,' Ashleigh protested. 'I just forgot what I was going to say.'

'I don't believe you.'

Somehow, she found her courage. 'Well, I can't help that,' she retorted.

'Don't you forget,' Dominic continued as if he hadn't heard her, 'you have nothing without me. I'm your everything. You had no identity, no family history, when you met me. That's what being an orphan is. I made you someone. I gave you that history. Don't make me take it away from you.'

Ashleigh swallowed before nodding.

'Right, we've got that clear. Again!' It was as if Dominic was speaking to a small child.

The anger in Ashleigh was overwhelming but she knew she couldn't react.

Chapter 2

All the websites about domestic violence that Ashleigh had looked at said there would be a time she'd reach her breaking point. She had never believed this. In fact, she hadn't even been sure she was in a situation like the one they were talking about. Dominic had never hit her. There were times she'd thought he was going to but then she'd seen something in his face change, like he was reigning himself back in.

So, she hadn't been sure, but then she'd seen a diagram of the domestic violence cycle. She hadn't realised being kept away from people, or put down all the time, was classified as abuse. Nor had she known that intimidation, humiliation or power trips were classed as abuse. There didn't have to be bruises.

The cycle for Ashleigh had mirrored the diagram. There was the honeymoon period, when everything was rosy and beautiful. He'd bring her flowers, tell her how important she was to him, to his world, his happiness. Then ever so gradually it began to change.

When the snide comments started, the threats weren't far away. She could feel the darkness building inside him.

When it happened, it usually started over something minor. She would be yelled at for burning the dinner or talking to someone she shouldn't have. Maybe the bed hadn't been made neatly or the bathroom wasn't clean enough. Or maybe she hadn't done anything at all. He just wouldn't speak to her, for days or weeks. Among his friends, and out in public, Dominic was the perfect husband. He was attentive and caring, but was capable of making a touch look loving when, in fact, he was hurting her. He could pinch her waist while he was resting his hand on her hip, or crunch her fingers while he was holding her hand. Then, without warning, he would change back into the gentle, warm man he could be.

The only difference between her experience and what the domestic violence websites discussed was that most men promised they would change, but never did. Dominic, though, never said he wouldn't do it again. Did he even realise that what he was doing was wrong?, Ashleigh wondered.

For her, seeing the photograph in *OUTBACK* that day had been a turning point. The couple in it seemed gentle and loving. It looked so peaceful in that little country town.

She wasn't having much peace at the moment.

Lunch had ended with Dominic throwing his empty bowl at the wall. Then he had grabbed her shoulders and bent down to stare her in the eye.

'Keeping secrets from your husband isn't a good thing to do,' he said menacingly. 'Don't do it, because I'll always find out. Don't ever doubt that.'

All this because he thought Ashleigh was holding something back from him. She supposed she was. Her reaction to the *OUTBACK* article would stay her secret, at least for the time being.

ℰᴖ

Later that afternoon, while bringing in the washing, Ashleigh daydreamed about how to escape her dark and loveless life. As she folded the sheets and towels, she fantasised about heading north to get a job, about travelling on endless roads, stopping only when she felt like it. Getting a job. Being independent and answerable to no one but herself. She thought about changing her hair, gaining weight; hopefully, he would never come looking for her. Ashleigh knew that Dominic wouldn't let her go that easily. She was his possession. But she also knew that escaping was her only chance of getting out of this marriage.

It would have to be done perfectly.

She'd torn out the *OUTBACK* article and hidden it between the mattresses in the spare room. Maybe because the day she read it she decided she was going to leave. Or maybe because something kept bringing her back to the photo of the couple. Their faces seemed familiar. She'd also been drawn to the beauty and ruggedness of the background.

By the end of the day, Ashleigh had made her decision. It wouldn't just be a beautiful daydream to help her get through the bad times. She would make it a reality.

ℰᴖ

Over the next twelve months, she researched how to change her identity. She reread the *OUTBACK* article, the symbol of her escape plan, so many times that it became creased and fragile.

While Dominic wasn't home, she stood in front of the mirror practising her new name.

'Hi,' she would say, 'I'm Eliza Norwood.'

'Eliza Norwood, Eliza Norwood, Eliza Norwood,' she chanted silently at night while she was lying beside Dominic.

Eliza was her middle name and she'd chosen Norwood after looking through the phone book and thinking it sounded nice. Having been abandoned as a baby on the steps of a church, she didn't even know what her mother's name had been.

She grew her hair. Ate a lot and put on a few kilos. That had caused more than one name-calling session. But she found she could silently deflect Dominic's abuse now she had a goal. It was like a callus had grown over her heart. She only knew she had to leave.

Syphoning money from her shopping allowance became some kind of normality. Ashleigh bought non-perishable items. Extra female hygiene products. She stored them carefully in the only place she knew was safe from him—the spare tyre well of her car.

Later she would cut her hair, dye it, and start wearing glasses. One website had suggested putting a stone in your shoes, so you could walk with a different gait. Another suggested looking for headstones in cemeteries for people of similar ages to those of your new identity's parents, siblings and children. Having details such as names and death dates would give her story authenticity. Another piece of advice was to choose a close friend's childhood story to use as her own.

That would have been fine if she'd had a childhood friend.

Every time she bought something a little different from normal, she worried that someone would pick up on what she was planning. After all, Jindabyne was a small town. Everyone knew everyone and, mostly, everyone's business. All she needed was someone to mention to Dominic that she'd bought hair dye even though her hair hadn't changed colour, or bought glasses when she didn't wear them, and he would be on high alert.

She was so grateful they didn't have any children. There was no way she could escape if there had been little ones involved.

One day, when Ashleigh had served his eggs soft instead of hard, Dominic had picked up the plate, food and all, then thrown it in her direction.

And then there were the two weeks when he didn't speak a word to her.

His behaviour had filled her with such rage, she'd almost flung herself at him, wanting to pound him as hard as she could, so he understood how it felt. She'd wanted to scream and yell while pummelling her fists against his chest. But she'd held herself back, knowing that leaving was getting closer.

Ashleigh was patient and would wait until the time was right.

Chapter 3

There were two dark streaks against the light salmon pink on the horizon, which, Eliza thought, looked like her streaked mascara. Taking her hand off the steering wheel, she swiped her throbbing face again and instantly sucked in a breath. She kept forgetting the cut that ran the length of her cheek and touched it too hard every time she tried to wipe her tears away.

Bastard!

Five hours before, Dominic had hit her. But it would be for the first and last time.

'Never again,' she muttered as she straightened her back and lifted her head with a defiance no one else could see.

The fight the previous evening had brought her plans forward. As she saw it, she didn't have a choice.

She was Eliza now.

She'd turned into Eliza the minute she'd lifted her head and seen the pure hatred in his eyes.

'I saw you smile at him,' Dominic had growled as she'd come out of the bathroom, wrapped in a towel.

She hadn't known what he meant.

In one swift movement, he'd yanked her towel away, leaving her feeling vulnerable and exposed. Ashleigh had tried to cover herself but that had made him angrier.

'Why did you look at him like that? Every bit of you is mine. I don't take you to functions to flirt with investors in my business!'

'What are you talking about?' she asked, near tears.

Then he'd pushed her down and climbed on top of her. She'd tried to fight him, to wriggle out from under him, but he held her tight. He grabbed a handful of her hair and wound it around his fingers as he lifted his other hand. With her face raised to him, she gazed in disbelief as he slapped her across the cheek.

Her head felt as if it would explode with the pain.

When she let out a scream he immediately let go of her hair, clamping his hand over her mouth and pushing down with all his strength. All Ashleigh wanted to do was bite him. Hard.

She could feel something warm running down her cheek. Tears or blood, she couldn't be sure.

With a final shake, he let go. Ashleigh scrambled away, grabbing the doona for cover and security, her breathing ragged. She watched through tear-filled eyes as he left the room without a backward glance.

She heard the front door slam, the car engine start and the wheels give a short, sharp, high-pitched screech as Dominic pulled away from the curb.

She knew what would happen next. He would go to the pub and get his little gang to join him—the local policeman, the doctor. Respectable members of the community, who had secrets that Dominic knew they wouldn't want anyone else to know about. These were people who rarely saw his dark side and would protect him from anything because they had to. They were all people who broke the law from time to time and covered for each other. They were the untouchables and Dominic was their chief.

They would sit in a small room out the back, drink grappa and whisky. Smoke cigars, play cards and laugh. Tell dirty stories about which young girl they had picked up during the weekend or which prostitute they had bedded when they were last in the city, and not think of anything else.

This was her chance! He would be gone for hours. She quickly gathered her things and threw them into the car. She didn't have much, just her clothes and some jewellery she planned to hock when she arrived in a city.

Now she was Eliza, she did not hesitate to raid the cash that Dominic kept in the top drawer of his desk. Quickly counting it, she was relieved to find there was four thousand dollars. She would add it to the two thousand she'd managed to skim from the housekeeping money over the last year.

She knew the combination of the safe and opened it, grabbing a few items and throwing them into her handbag.

The last thing Eliza had to do before leaving Jindabyne forever was to change the numberplates on her car. Deftly, she replaced them with the plates she'd stolen four months ago, from a car parked on the side of the road with a defect sticker on it.

With the new numberplates on, she climbed into the driver's seat and drove out of town without a backward glance.

⁓

Eliza focused on the white lines, her eyes flicking from side to side, looking out for wildlife. The kangaroos and wombats were thick on the ground at this time of the night and she didn't want to hit anything.

The road from Canberra to Jindabyne carried long lines of cars. Mostly city drivers. Ones who had their minds on the day of skiing ahead, not the fact that random wildlife could hop or crawl onto the road in front of a moving car. Eliza had passed two police cars and an ambulance, and her stomach had constricted at the sight. She'd watched in the rear-view mirror to see if the police turned around or put their lights on, and breathed a sigh of relief when neither of these things had happened. Eliza knew that the police would be picking up people for speeding and the ambulance would be taking a few to hospital to be checked out after small accidents. She wondered how there weren't worse ones. The sheer cliff drops close to Jindabyne would be a killer if a car accidentally drove off the edge of one.

Her thoughts returned to Dominic. The wildness in his eyes flashed before her and she shuddered, which made her accidentally turn the wheel slightly. Instantly she corrected and steadied the car.

'Be careful,' Eliza muttered to herself. 'Don't call attention to yourself.'

Dominic had contacts everywhere. He was so powerful. She was sure the first thing he would do would be to call

Simon McCullen, his copper mate, and get him to put a watch out for the car.

She hoped the different numberplates would throw everyone off until she got across the border.

There were still hours of driving before that would happen.

With any luck, Eliza thought as she glanced down at the clock on the dash, *he wouldn't be home yet*. The gang get-togethers could go until the very early hours of the morning, and Simon would be hung-over, so he wouldn't be much use for a while.

Glancing down at the fuel gauge, she saw she only had a quarter of a tank. Not knowing when she'd been going to run had meant that she'd left without a full tank of fuel.

'Damn,' Eliza muttered, scanning the side of the road for a sign that would tell her how far away Cooma was.

All she saw were headlights reflecting off the stark white bones of dead kangaroos which had been hit by cars many months before.

Shouldn't be too far, she thought. *Maybe another twenty minutes. Should be okay.*

Even so, she watched the fuel gauge closely until she drove into a servo on the outskirts of Cooma.

She pulled up next to a bowser and got out, holding her mobile phone close to her side. Before she started to refuel, she placed the phone in a bin. She'd turned it off before she'd got out of the car, so he wouldn't be able to track her. That had been another piece of advice from the websites she'd been reading: the GPS in her phone could give away her location. Eliza couldn't risk that. She smiled grimly, knowing that it could only lead Dominic as far as this rubbish bin.

Eliza scanned the area.

The air was as frigid as it had been when she'd fled Jindabyne and she felt exposed under the harsh fluorescent lights. Her breath came in short white puffs and her cold fingers struggled to undo the fuel cap.

The black cap she'd bought a few weeks ago was pulled down tightly over her blond hair and she wished she could have worn her sunglasses, but that would have drawn more attention to her, since it wasn't light yet.

Out of the corner of her eye, she saw a police car turn the corner and drive slowly down the road.

She ducked her head as it drove past her, so she had no idea if the policemen were looking out the window at her. As she hung up the hose, she saw their brake lights go on.

A breath caught sharply in her throat and she threw open the car door to find her purse. Quickly, she walked into the station, and stood waiting to pay.

The sleepy clerk looked up, becoming more alert as he noticed her face but, just as quickly, his eyes slid away.

'Sixty bucks eighty,' he muttered, still not looking at her.

Eliza, having forgotten about her face, fumbled for the money, handing over a hundred-dollar note. She wanted to drop her head forward and cover her cheek but, instead, pulled her hair down over the injured side of her face and waited impatiently for her change. All the while, she tried inconspicuously to see if the police car had turned around.

'Have a nice day,' the man said to her, again without looking at her.

Obviously, a beaten woman's too confronting to look at, she thought bitterly. She hurried out the door to her car. The police car wasn't in sight and she breathed a sigh of relief.

Keeping her cap on, she drove out of town, still undecided about where she was going.

&

Eliza pulled into a small town off the main highway just as the sun was setting.

Cruising down the main street, she noted a deli, a small supermarket and a chemist and, further down, a pub. She parked over by the chemist and went in.

'We're just closing,' a young girl whose name badge read 'Jessie' said as she pushed a trolley of nail polish inside the door.

Eliza felt herself sag. After a day's driving she was exhausted and didn't need any complications. 'I won't be long,' she answered. 'Just a couple of quick things. Do you mind? It's a bit urgent.'

Jessie sighed. 'I guess.' Her tone indicated it was an inconvenience.

Eliza quickly found scissors, non-prescription glasses, foundation with sunscreen and nail polish. Gathering her purchases, she went to the counter.

'Is this all?' Jessie asked, looking straight at Eliza's bruise.

'Yes, thanks,' Eliza answered, trying to resist the urge to look over her shoulder.

'Not much that's urgent in here, if you ask me,' said the girl in a sullen tone.

'No,' Eliza agreed, thinking, *Certainly not to you, but to me they are.* Out loud, she said, 'Um, can you tell me if there's somewhere to stay in town? A motel or something?'

Jessie scoffed. 'Not in this one-horse town.'

'Right. And you live here because . . .?' Eliza's patience was wearing thin. A bad headache was forming behind her eyes and her jaw ached. 'I'll have a packet of Panadol too, please.'

'I'm not staying here long,' Jessie answered and Eliza stifled a sigh, knowing she was about to hear a life story she had no interest in. 'I'm going to Sydney real soon, to try out for *X Factor*,' Jessie continued proudly as she twirled some hair around her finger and cracked her gum.

'That's great. I'm sure you'll do very well. Um . . . somewhere to stay?'

'There's only the pub.' Jessie rang up the purchases and held her hand out for the money. Then she added, 'Your old man knock you around or somethin'?'

A shiver ran through Eliza. 'Uh, no. No. Just had a little accident.' She handed over the money, desperate to be out of the tiny shop that no longer seemed to have any oxygen.

'Yeah, right. You're still in the denial stage,' Jessie said, handing back the change. 'My mum looked like that all the time after me dad had finished w'her,' she went on, oblivious to the look of shock on Eliza's face. 'Blokes suck, hey? That's why I'm a lesbian.'

'Oh. Ah, well, that's one way around it,' Eliza groped for words. If it was so obvious to a young girl, who couldn't be more than sixteen or seventeen, it would be clear to everyone she came in contact with. 'So, the pub?' She had to get out of this shop. She had to hide.

'Oh yeah, the pub. I'm sure Sal will have a room clean enough for you.' Jessie paused for a moment, then continued: 'Make sure you ask for one with a bathroom. There's a few rooms that you have to share the loo down the end of the passageway. Still, it's not like there's going to be a heap of people staying there.'

'Sounds fabulous,' Eliza muttered sarcastically. 'Thanks again.'

She turned to leave but Jessie had one more thing to say.

'If you're running, good on ya.' She slammed the till shut and turned the key, before flicking the light switches and throwing the shop into darkness.

Chapter 4

The front bar of the pub was clean enough but it smelled like spilled beer and vomit. Sal had handed over the room key with nicotine-stained fingers and a toss of her head in the direction Eliza needed to go.

Jessie had been right on two points—Sal had a room that was clean enough and there weren't many people staying in the pub. In fact she was the only guest and had managed to get a room that had its own bathroom. That was one small mercy.

Eliza let herself into the small, dark room and groped for the light switches. A bare bulb hanging on a piece of electrical wire dimly lit the space and revealed brown curtains covering the window. The bed had a distinct sag in the middle and the room had obviously last been occupied by a smoker.

Throwing her bag on the bed, Eliza felt tears sting her eyes. She wondered how she had got into this situation. A woman on the run, from a man who supposedly loved her.

Flopping onto the bed, she let the tears run down her cheeks. Exhaustion, fear and sadness slid onto the pillow.

ɐ

Eliza realised she had drifted off to sleep, because when she opened her eyes, it was dark outside.

She didn't move. She just kept lying there and thinking. Slowly, a plan came to her. A couple of frights she'd had yesterday had caused her to get off the highway and take some less busy roads.

First, the police she had seen when she'd stopped for petrol had followed her. In the rear-view mirror, she'd seen one of the policemen talking into the radio—she was sure they were doing numberplate checks. If they were, she was stuffed. The plates she was using would have been reported by now, surely, and they wouldn't match the description of the car they were attached to.

Her heart had thudded hard and perspiration beaded across her top lip. Then, for no apparent reason, the police car had pulled out and overtaken her. Within a few minutes, it was out of sight.

The second scare had been when she pulled in at another roadhouse for more fuel and something to eat. A lady had baled her up in the toilets and insisted she go to the police about her face.

'Whoever did this to you needs to be held accountable,' she'd said, shaking her finger at Eliza as if she were the one who had caused the injuries.

'Thanks very much, but I'm fine,' Eliza had answered, trying to move past her supposed good Samaritan.

'No you're not. I can see it in your face. I knew I'd meet you today. I dreamed about you, I just didn't know it was you. I've been sent to help you.'

Eliza had finally lost her temper, and pushed past the crazy woman, before racing to her car and driving off.

Getting off the bed, she went into the bathroom and leaned against the vanity, staring at her reflection. She gathered her hair and held it back, before bunching it up in a bob-like look. Which changed her face more?, she wondered.

Having decided the bob might be an easier style to cut without any experience, she got the scissors and started hacking. As her long blond locks hit the floor, she could feel the last traces of Ashleigh leaving her.

Two hours later, she was staring at a different person. Her hair was black and the glasses were in place. Practising with the foundation, she patted it on, and paid particular attention to her cheek. The make-up didn't completely cover the bruising, but it certainly reduced the colour. The cut was still very obvious.

Still, it would fade with time. That was something Eliza had lots of.

Eliza stared at her reflection, hoping the changes were enough. Fingering her shortened hair, she decided she would get a proper cut when she got to a city.

A city! Now—where was she headed?

What was she going to do? She needed a job. And there was another question—what could she do? The woman she now was, Eliza, didn't have any qualifications. All she had was a love of animals and kids and a good work ethic. This work ethic had come from a desperation to get away from the house on the outskirts of Adelaide she had shared with an old couple who should never have been allowed to be foster parents. The house had been small and cramped; her foster parents had smelt like mothballs and the carpet of cat pee. They hadn't cared for Ashleigh or nurtured her in any way. They had only been in it for the money.

She had been okay at school—finishing somewhere in the middle of the class—and had gone on to study teaching. Dominic had made her give it up when they got married, insinuating they would have children right away. Having been madly in love, she hadn't initially had a problem with his demand, but, as time had gone on, the situation had upset her more and more. She missed the kids and their constant laughter and chatter, and she wasn't going to have a child with a man who behaved the way Dominic did.

Teaching was actually how she'd met Dominic. He was a major donor to the local school in Jindabyne, and was asked to attend prize nights and sports days to hand out the trophies and awards. As the year-eight coordinator, she called out the names of the children who had won, while he stood alongside her and shook hands with the kids.

He asked her on a date at the end-of-year school concert. Ashleigh had been wearing a knee-length sleeveless black and white dress with a belt at the waist, and red shoes.

She'd noticed Dominic staring at her legs before his eyes travelled up her body to find her eyes. Ashleigh had half-smiled at him and he'd moved towards her, his intent plain on his face.

The principal had intercepted his first attempt, stepping into his path and offering his hand and thanks for the support Dominic gave the school. But then, while they were up on stage, in between the giving of prizes, he'd whispered he'd like to take her out to dinner.

With a coy smile, she'd accepted. After all, Dominic was the most sought-after, eligible man in Jindabyne. It was well known that he was wealthy—a ski resort owner—and he gave generously to all the worthy causes in town. Mostly, though, Ashleigh liked the way he laughed easily and gave his full attention to whoever he was speaking to. He made her feel as if she was the only person in the world.

There had been plenty of women who had tried to get his attention but none had succeeded. That's where Ashleigh had been different. She hadn't chased him or tried to get him to notice her.

She didn't need anyone. Having basically raised herself, she was happy in her own company and didn't want to rely on other people.

He'd wooed and courted her, lavished her with gifts and, for the first time in her life, Ashleigh had felt an aching need to belong somewhere. Being alongside Dominic meant being home. She'd fallen deeply for this handsome man, who seemed to regard her as the best thing that had ever happened to him.

It hadn't mattered to her that he had rushed things and wanted to be married as soon as possible—in fact, she had encouraged it. They didn't want anything to delay their happiness, so why wait? Later, when she wished she'd put the brakes on, she realised that back then she wouldn't have changed anything. She was blinded by love and her need to be part of Dominic's life. Her need to belong somewhere.

But it all changed the minute the golden wedding band had been slipped onto her finger. Her life became all about domination, control and verbal abuse. No one in the town could have guessed, or would have believed, what went on behind closed doors. It had taken even her so long to see it, or at least understand his behaviour for what it was.

Now, here, in the shabby hotel room, staring at her changed reflection, she wondered how she hadn't seen before what he was like. How had he managed to keep his true self so well hidden?

And why had she accepted it was normal to be treated that way?

Eliza kicked in. There was no point in feeling sad and sorry for herself.

'Come on,' she said sternly. 'Pull yourself together. It's always been just you. This is no different. You will not be the victim. Start putting a plan together. Rely on the strength you used to have. Focus on the future, not on what has been.'

She turned abruptly from the mirror and went back into the bedroom. Pulling a map and a packet of chips from one of her bags, she sat cross-legged on the bed, tracing roads with her fingers while she munched.

Freedom opened up before her and Eliza breathed deeply. A movie played in her head: long open roads, sunshine and independence. She could do what she liked, when she liked. To make decisions that were best for her, and her alone. Unimpeded, liberated and, well, just that. Free.

Freedom, what a beautiful-sounding word. Although, deep down, she knew she would have to hang onto that word and what she was feeling now, for when things got tough. Which she knew they would.

❧

As she came out of a deep sleep, Eliza couldn't work out where she was. Heavy blankets, not the doona on her bed at home, weighed her down. Then it all came flooding back to her. The fight, the punch, the drive.

She sat up, touched her short hair and looked around. She found the remote for the TV and turned it on, checking her watch to see what the time was. Eight-fifteen a.m. She would have to get a move on if she were going to make it to Adelaide by evening, she thought.

Last night, she'd decided she would drive to Blinman. She still had no idea why the article in *OUTBACK* had resonated with her, but she felt drawn towards the town. The country looked amazing, with its razorback mountains and purple–pink colouring. It was worth visiting for that, if nothing else.

She was starting to pack her belongings when the top-of-the-hour news came on the TV.

'Ashleigh Eliza Alberto has been missing from Jindabyne since early yesterday morning,' the announcer said. 'The police are extremely concerned for her welfare, as Mrs Alberto is mentally unstable. Her husband, Dominic Alberto, has made an impassioned plea for his wife to return home safely. Tara Brown reports.'

Eliza froze as Dominic's tear-stained face flashed up on the screen. He was unshaven and looked like he hadn't slept the whole time she'd been gone.

'Please, if anyone knows where she is, can you call Crime Stoppers,' he asked in a broken voice. A photo of the two of them on their wedding day accompanied the footage of Dominic. 'I want my wife back. Honey, if you're watching this, please get in contact with the police or me. I just need to know that you're safe.' He broke down in a fresh flood of tears and the cameras zoomed in close.

For a moment, Eliza wondered if he actually meant what he was saying. Did he really miss her? A pang of regret and guilt shot through her before something flickered in her mind.

Mentally unstable! What?

'You bastard,' she muttered, sinking onto the bed.

Aiming the remote at the TV, she snapped it off. There was no way she could go out now. The only option was to stay put in the hotel for the next few days. Or travel at night, when there were fewer people around.

Or both.

Eliza drew in a breath and let it out gradually. Her hands at her mouth, she forced herself to think slowly.

After a while, she got up and showered, washed her hair, put on her glasses and went downstairs.

'Help you?' Sal asked without looking away from the TV she was watching.

With growing fear, Eliza realised it was tuned to the same channel she'd been watching in her room.

'Yes, please,' she answered, her heart thumping. 'I'd like to stay here for a few more days. Do you think I could pay for another four nights?'

Sal looked up slowly and Eliza met her eyes with a steady gaze. Inside, she was chanting, *Please don't recognise me, please don't recognise me.*

'Sure thing,' said Sal and made a note in the register. 'Pay for three nights and get the fourth one free. Need anything else?' She held out her hand for the money and Eliza passed it over. Sal stared at it for a moment, then back at Eliza.

'No, thanks. I'll be okay. And thanks for the discount.'

'Quietest time around here is about four-thirty in the afternoon. Not much happens in the supermarket or down the main street after that, if you need to get out and pick up some food or fuel, or something.' Sal turned back to the TV after putting the money in the till. 'And if you want to put your car in the garage, it's around the side. The door's open. Just pull it down after you put it in there.'

⁊

Eliza paced her small room, ten steps towards the window, ten steps back towards the door. She was buzzing with adrenalin from more feelings than she could name. She was frightened and nervous. But there were also traces of triumph and elation. And determination.

She had got this far—she wouldn't be caught now.

Chapter 5

The sky was a blanket of stars as Eliza left the hotel for the last time, a week after she'd seen the news report of Ashleigh's disappearance.

She'd kept herself hidden, venturing out only for food. Her bruise was nearly gone, and while the cut was taking a little longer to heal, she could hide it all with make-up. The air was cold as she carted her bags to the car.

The hotel room had been her sanctuary for the past week. She'd again extended her stay, as the hunt for her had heated up. Sal had taken her under her wing—Eliza assumed it was because she'd suspected Eliza was actually Ashleigh. Maybe Sal had been in an abusive situation at some time in her life and wanted to help. Whatever the reason, Sal obviously hadn't believed the reports of her guest being mentally unstable. Although she hadn't spoken more than a few words to Sal, Eliza would find parcels of food and drink outside her door in the early morning.

It was time to move on, though.

Eliza had planned the next part of her journey with precision. She would only be travelling at night and would be sleeping during the day. She wouldn't be following the straightest route to Blinman, but would zigzag over the country.

The first port of call would be Broken Hill, which was well and truly out of her way. As it was a mining town, Eliza hoped people there would mind their own business.

She turned the key and the engine kicked into life, setting off a round of barking from nearby dogs. It sounded so loud in the still of the night. Eliza put the car into gear and drove away.

ও৲

Eliza was getting excited. She was almost at Blinman. Another hour and she would be able to get out, stretch and unpack. Start her new life. From her reading about Blinman, she knew she'd be able to rent a room from the general store. Getting a job might be an issue, but she'd deal with that when it came up.

In the back of the car the swag and camping gear she'd bought at Broken Hill were jolting as she went over the bumps. She'd also bought a new mobile phone—a prepaid, so it couldn't be tracked, and a new computer. She had to get some papers for her new identity. That was a task for when she was settled and had time to research it.

Driving slowly so she could take in the scenery, she marvelled at the hills jutting against the vividly blue sky. There had been rain overnight and the bitumen was still wet in some spots.

Eliza pulled over into a tourist bay and sat in silence, looking at the scenery. The hill in front of her was in a perfect volcano formation, covered in vegetation. Perfectly spaced little gorges showed where the water had once run down to the bottom.

In the background was a higher range of hills, blue in the distance, and at the bottom was a deep creek and flood plain, covered in native pines. The native grasses were flourishing, while a few scattered white-coloured flowers, which Eliza assumed were some kind of daisy, bloomed across the landscape.

Leaning against the bonnet of the car, she took a deep breath and felt contentment settle across her. This land had a spirituality about it. It felt ancient and wild. It was isolated and harsh—she could only imagine how hot it would be up here during the summer months.

A flock of white corellas lifted from the distant creek and soared towards the sun. Their cries reached her and she shivered. There was no doubt this place was special, and she felt connected and grounded here.

ం

Eliza drove slowly, looking out the window as she went. She was getting very close now.

The road was winding, and the countryside alternated between small shrubby bushes and rocks, deep ravines lined with river red gums, grainy creek sand, and flats with pine and acacia trees.

Occasionally, she saw wedge-tailed eagles soaring on the thermals or sitting on the side of the road, picking at roadkill.

They're such majestic creatures of the air, she thought as she leaned forward, staring up at one of the eagles through her windscreen. Accidentally, she twisted the steering wheel and ran off the road into the gravel. She overcorrected and her car shot across the road. Again, she yanked the steering wheel back, but the car was on a course of its own.

Eliza gave a high-pitched scream full of fear as the red rock wall bordering the road came hurtling towards her.

There was a tearing sound of metal and the car came to a sudden, jarring halt, throwing Eliza forward in her seat.

'Oh, my God!' She stayed where she was, stunned.

After a little while, she gingerly tried to get out of the car. The door needed firm pressure from her shoulder to open it, and the metal creaked in protest.

She stood there for a moment, looking around, trying to process what had just happened.

Cautiously, she took a few steps towards the front of the car, testing that her body was working as it should.

She could see the headlight was smashed and the tyre flat. The front of the car was caved in.

'Bloody hell,' Eliza spat as she started to shake. She walked up and down the road for a while, her gaze always ending back at the crumpled front end of the car.

Looking wildly around, she tried to work out what she should do. *Wait for someone to come along. That's what Ashleigh would have done.*

Eliza, though, would take her destiny into her own hands.

She checked her mobile phone and found she didn't have any coverage. Who would she call, anyway?

Did she wait until someone came along or did she walk? Blinman wasn't that far away, but she was sure she remembered hearing that in this sort of situation you should never leave your car. But did that apply to cars on bitumen roads or only when you were lost in the bush?

Still breathing fast, she tried to make a decision. There were too many things flooding into her mind.

Her head snapped up as she heard the sound of an engine. *Which way was it coming from?*

The south. The way she'd come from. She hoped it was a local who would know what to do or who to call.

Eliza heard the car slow as it approached the bend.

Flicking the hazard lights on, she stood next to her own car, waving madly. 'Please stop, please stop,' she said to herself.

A dirty white ute came around the corner, the tray rattling. The driver gunned the engine and started to speed up, then slammed his foot on the brakes.

Eliza ran across to the ute and smiled gratefully at the man who got out. She judged him to be in his early forties, the stubble on his face having a hint of grey in it. His hat was stained with grease and dirt.

'Thanks for stopping,' she said.

'Got yourself in a bit of trouble, have you?' The man looked her over and Eliza assumed he was working out if she was okay. 'Are you all right?'

'I'm fine,' she answered. 'Are you able to help me?'

'Where you headed?' he asked as he went over to the front of the car and inspected it.

'Blinman—' She stopped as he looked up.

'Know someone there, do you?'

'Um, no.' Eliza realised how strange her plan must sound, so she stayed silent.

'Ah, a tourist, then. This isn't really the sort of car for touring.' He reached down and pulled off the fender. Eliza jumped at the noise it made.

'Maybe not,' she said defensively, 'but I have just driven halfway across Australia in it and it hasn't missed a beat.'

The man turned to face her with a grin, pushing up his hat as he did so. 'It has now.' His manner turned serious. 'Look, there's some major damage. You'll be stuck here for a bit. If you were a bloke, I'd say you've got your dick caught in a mincer, but since you're not, I'll just let you know that you're up shit creek without a paddle. Going to take a while to fix. If, in fact, it is fixable.'

Eliza opened her mouth to say something, but nothing came out. The man continued to look at her and finally she felt a bubble welling in her chest.

She opened her mouth and giggled until it became a full-blown laugh. The man stared at her bemused, then started to laugh himself.

'Wasn't expecting you to do that, lady,' he said when they had both stopped.

'No, me either,' she admitted. She wanted to say that there were too many different emotions running around inside her at the moment and humour was the last one she had expected to come out. But that would be giving too much away, so instead she held out her hand and said, 'I'm Eliza.' The words sounded forced and practised to her ears, and she hoped he didn't notice.

'I'm Chris.'

They shook hands.

'I'd better get on the two-way and call the tow truck. Have you got roadside assistance or anything?'

Eliza started to say yes, but realised she couldn't. *Bloody hell.* Dollar signs flashed before her eyes as she managed to utter 'No'.

'Ah well, Cauly will work something out with you. Can't leave you sitting here on the side of the road with strangers passing by, can we?' Chris walked back over to his ute. 'Grab what you need and lock it up. It'll take him a few hours to get out here.'

Eliza watched as he reached in through the window and pulled the mic off its holder. He called Cauley on the two-way but didn't get any answer.

'Hmm, hope he hasn't gone on another bender,' Chris muttered. 'Got everything?' he asked, turning back to her.

Eliza put her suitcase on the back of the ute and looked over at her car. 'If I lock it, will everything be okay?' She had visions of cars left on the side of the road in places she'd travelled through. All of them had been stripped down to nothing.

Chris paused. 'I'd grab everything you want to keep. It'll probably be all right but you can never tell who'll be passin'. What're your thoughts? You want to stay at Blinman, or get in the truck with Cauley and go back to Port Augusta? You're gonna be pretty stuck for a bit without a car and he'll have to tow it over there to get it fixed.'

'Blinman,' she replied immediately.

Chris looked at her strangely. 'You sure? There's no mobile reception, wi-fi, or anything fancy there. It's a town with a main street, a pub, a small shop and that's about it, if you don't take into account the town hall and tennis courts. What are you gonna do for all that time?'

Eliza shrugged. 'I don't know. Walk, read, relax.' Mentally, she added *Heal*.

Chris looked at her and she was sure he was trying to work out what she was thinking. He made a swift movement with his arm towards the car. 'Righto, you'd better grab your gear, then. I'll give you a hand.'

Together, they emptied the car and put everything in the tray of the ute.

'Let's get going,' Chris said. 'I'll drop you off at the store. Reckon Maureen should be able to find you a room out the back.'

'I'd really appreciate that.' Eliza got in, banged the ute door shut and peered out of the window. Even though she was still feeling shaken, she couldn't pull her gaze away from the scenery. Now she could look at it and take everything in.

Chris didn't seem to be interested in making conversation and Eliza was glad. Even with all the practising, she was worried she would muck up telling him her story.

The green signs that indicated the number of kilometres to the next town were counting down.

B 30. B 25. B 20.

Suddenly the sign for Blinman appeared and she caught her first glimpse of the place that was pulling her so strongly.

Chapter 6

One morning, a month after Eliza arrived in Blinman, the sun was just rising over the hills as she pulled on her sturdy walking boots, and grabbed her hat and camera, before heading out the door of the room she rented at the back of the general store.

She loved this time of day. It was still and cool, the quiet shattered only by the screams of galahs, crows and other birds. Even though there was a chill in the air now, Eliza knew that by lunchtime she would be in a T-shirt and shorts, swatting the flies away.

She was heading out on her morning walk to the old copper mine. It was up a steep, stony hill, and was her favourite place to watch the sunrise.

The rising sun made her feel reborn every morning. She wallowed in the pinks and reds that it threw onto the ranges, and found peace in the whisper of soft breezes and the gentle light of dawn.

Often, she'd stand where the fences protected the deep openings in the hills and stare down into the mine. She marvelled at the depth of the water, and the trees that somehow managed to grow below the earth's surface. Their tall branches, stretching up towards the surface, to the sunlight, held her attention.

To her, they represented something beautiful and strong that could grow in the darkness.

Today, she stood staring, lost in the beauty of the land and its colours. Then she heard someone behind her and she half turned, knowing who it was before she heard his voice.

'Mornin', Eliza.'

She paused before answering, 'Morning, Chris.'

'It's a lovely one.'

'It's one of the best sunrises I've seen since I arrived,' she said, raising her camera, trying to capture a permanent memory of what she was seeing today.

Click.

'Kangaroos to the left,' Chris murmured at her shoulder.

She turned gently and there, silhouetted against the rising sun, were five kangaroos munching on native grasses.

She reached into her camera bag to grab the zoom lens, then knelt to get a better angle.

Click.

Click.

Click.

She checked the display screen and adjusted the setting before trying again.

'That's better,' she said softly. The latest photo showed the darkened shape of one kangaroo, his paws to his mouth. Around him, the sky was a vivid red, and above that, it faded into blue.

Photography was a newfound hobby for Eliza since she'd arrived in Blinman. It was something she had always been interested in, but she'd never acted on it. The new Eliza could do what she wanted and the area was too beautiful not to capture with a camera. On a trip to Port Augusta, she'd spent some of her savings on a good-quality one and started to learn the art, reading magazines and following blogs on photography. Her plan was to take pictures and sell them to passing tourists. To her delight, some of her photos had already been shared by the popular Outback Paparazzi Facebook page. Reen had offered her wall space in the general store, and the tour operator across the road had done the same. She would be another in the long line of photographers in the area, but she hoped somehow she could get an edge and that people would buy her prints.

'I brought you a coffee,' Chris said, putting down his backpack and pulling out a thermos and two mugs.

Eliza turned around to look at him, feeling nervous. 'Did you? That's nice. Thanks.'

Ever since Chris had first dropped her at the general store, he'd called in to check on her every time he was passing. Eliza found it very unsettling.

Maureen had elbowed her in the ribs the third time he'd come in.

'Reckon he's got the hots for you, love,' she grinned.

Eliza had shaken her head. 'Not interested, Reen. I've told you. I've sworn off men. For good!'

'Ah, come on now. Man's not a camel.'

'Huh?'

'Well, I don't know the female version of that saying,'

Maureen had grinned. 'Surely you know it means that a man can't go without a drink?'

Eliza laughed and again shook her head at her friend.

'You shouldn't let that one get away,' Maureen said. 'He's a lovely bloke, got a steady job. Hell, being a park ranger, he'll never be out of work, since he's paid by the government! And there's those two kids of his. Nothing but cuties, if you ask me. Don't know why that wife of his did what she did.'

'Not interested, Reen,' Eliza said again.

A man was the last thing on her mind. Even if he was good-looking, and kind, and intelligent . . . and had the cutest smile!

Eliza reminded herself again. She was living a lie.

'Take a seat,' said Chris as he squatted to pour the coffees.

'Few and far between out here,' Eliza answered and stayed standing.

'Geez, anyone would think you were frightened of me,' he said, handing her the cup.

Eliza said nothing, but blew on the steaming liquid and looked out over the roofs of the Blinman township.

Chris came and stood next to her.

'So, you've decided to hang around?' he asked.

'Yeah. I seem to be the odd-job girl at the moment. Reen says I can work in the shop for a few hours every day, and Stu and Stacey are going away for a week or so and have asked me to feed their dogs and horses. Keep an eye on the place, so I'll do that.' Stu and Stacey were a young couple who lived just outside Blinman, and were about to go on their honeymoon. Their animals needed tending and Eliza loved animals. She continued, 'So, yeah, I'll hang around for a bit. Might even learn to pull a beer or two at the pub!'

'You'd be better off on the other side of the bar,' Chris said, but Eliza shook her head.

All the websites she'd consulted about how to change your identity had said to avoid alcohol. It loosened tongues, and she couldn't afford to let anything slip.

One issue with being in the northern Flinders Ranges was that there was limited mobile coverage and the internet was spasmodic at best. She had no idea where Dominic was searching for her and had no intention of finding out. She avoided the news and TV when she could.

'Why not?' Chris asked, taking a sip of his coffee.

A crow flew over and squawked as it hunted for something to eat.

'I don't drink,' she said.

Chris was silent for a moment, digesting that fact.

'Hmm, you might have a hard time fitting in here, then.'

'I haven't so far. Everyone's been really kind and accepting. I've become pretty settled, even in the short time I've been here.'

'That's good, because I've got a proposition for you.'

Eliza's stomach curled and she held her coffee cup a little tighter as she answered, 'Really?'

'Yeah, really.'

She waited, but Chris didn't say anything more. The silence reverberated around them.

'Well, are you going to tell me or not?' she finally asked.

He grinned. 'Oh, so you want to know. I wasn't getting the feeling you did!'

Eliza couldn't help smiling back.

'All right, I'll put you out of your misery. You know I've got two girls, Heidi and Tilly?'

Eliza nodded.

'They need a bit more of a woman's touch than I can give them. So, I was wondering if you'd consider coming to the park and being their governess. Supervising the School of the Air work, taking them on a few excursions, reading to them, all that sort of thing. It's the tourist season and that makes me extra busy. I'm battling to find time to do everything and it's always the girls who miss out. I don't want that for them.' He paused to take another sip of coffee. 'Now, I know you're not experienced in teaching, but you don't really need to be—just a bit switched on. All the work is supplied by the School of the Air and you can talk to them any time you need to. At least, if the bloody internet is working or hasn't slowed down to a snail's pace.' Chris turned to look at her. 'What do you think?'

Eliza didn't need to think.

'When do you want me to start?'

⁊

Eliza opened up the general store and started putting the home-made Cornish pasties into the warmer. Hopefully, Gillian, who made the iconic pasties and pies, would swing by today with some more homemade quandong pies. They were running low.

Traditional Cornish pasties, with apple in one end and meat in the other, and the quandong pies were the two most ordered things on the menu. There were some talented cooks in the town, and the general store gave the pub, with its great burgers and other meals, a bit of a run for its money.

She thought back on her conversation with Chris that morning. If she hadn't needed the money, she would have said no. But her finances were looking decidedly lean, and the few

43

dollars she made working at the general store and being the odd-job girl around town weren't going to keep her in food, clothes and lodgings for long. She was slowly paying off the bill for the repairs to her car too. It was a matter of pride that she was able to look after herself.

'Morning, Eliza,' Maureen said as she shuffled in.

'How are you today, Reen?' Eliza asked, stopping to look concernedly at Maureen's doubled-up frame.

'Top of the world, love, top of the world,' Maureen answered with a wink. Her back injury from a car accident ten years before had left her in constant pain and there were days she couldn't stand upright.

Eliza knew better than to comment or make any offers of help. Instead, she asked, 'Is Gillian bringing more pies today?'

'She should be over fairly soon. Did you get out for your morning walk?'

'Yep, and guess who turned up?'

'Wouldn't be some hunky park ranger, would it?'

Eliza laughed. 'So hard to trick you,' she said, her tone laced with sarcasm.

'I keep telling you and you keep not listening. He has more on his mind than just being friends.'

'You know what, Reen?' Eliza stopped stacking the drinks fridge and turned to face her.

'What?'

'I don't think he has. He asked me this morning if I'd be a governess for his girls. I think he's just been sizing me up to see if I'd be suitable for that.'

Maureen paused for a second before responding, 'You are either naïve, silly or blind, and you won't convince me otherwise.'

'Okay, let me put this to you. How long has it been since his wife left?'

'Claire left three years ago. How she could leave those little girls behind, I just don't know.'

Eliza butted in before she heard a full rant from Maureen about her anger towards Claire. She'd heard it all before. 'Such a nice girl, no one would have had any idea she was going to do what she did,' Maureen always said. 'Not so nice now, you mark my words!'

'And, in all those years, he's never chased another woman, has he?' Eliza asked.

'Lovey, if you take a look around, you'll see there's not a lot of choice out here.'

'Puts me in a good category, doesn't it?' Eliza teased.

'That's not what I meant and you know it. Good Lord, girl, sometimes you can be infuriating!'

'Seriously, what I'm trying to say, Reen, is that I might be the first girl he's shown any interest in, but only because he needs help with his daughters. I get the feeling he's struggling a bit. The conversation was all business, I can promise you! Besides, people who've been hurt are usually scared of getting involved with anyone again, aren't they? I'm pretty sure he's wary of getting close to any woman.'

Maureen eyed Eliza closely. 'You know what?' She crossed her arms. 'I think, without knowing much about you, I could put you in the same category.'

Butterflies coursed through Eliza's stomach at her friend's words and she tried hard not to show her shock. She grabbed a soft drink in each hand and stacked them neatly in the fridge.

'Don't know what you're talking about,' she said lightly.

Chapter 7

'This is the schoolroom.' Chris pushed open a screen door so Eliza could peer in.

The room was basic, with two desks pushed together, and a computer in the middle. On one wall was a blackboard, and on the other a window, which looked out over a small patio. There were papers spread across the desks, and a few drawings by the girls Blu-Tacked to the wall.

Chris gestured for her to walk in. 'There's only an hour or so a day actually spent on the computer with their teacher. The rest of the lessons are done out of these workbooks.' He handed her a thick paperback and she started flicking through it.

Hmm, the handwriting could do with a bit of work, she thought.

'Their lessons from this,' he tapped what she was holding, 'are what I was wanting help with. I'm their dad, not their teacher. I know plenty of parents do teach their kids, but I'm not one of them. I'm an outside, hands-on sort of bloke, not a classroom one.'

Eliza looked up from the workbook, and saw guilt and sorrow in his face. She understood it wasn't that he didn't want to teach his daughters. It was that he couldn't. Her heart went out to him.

'That's no problem. Kids tend to learn better from someone other than their parents, anyway,' Eliza said. 'In another life, I worked with kids, and dealing with only two in a classroom situation will be much easier than managing twenty.' She realised Chris was about to ask her a question, so she rushed on with the first thing that popped into her head: 'And the girls, where are they now?'

'They'll be over at the camp sites, talking to the tourists,' he answered.

She looked at him in horror. 'You let them go and talk to strangers by themselves?' Who knew what sort of people were camped at the park? The next David and Catherine Birnie could be over there, with two unsupervised young girls wandering around. It sent a shudder of disbelief through her.

Chris looked surprised. 'Yeah. It's mostly the grey nomads around here. During the school holidays, there's plenty of families. It's good for them to meet people and talk to them. And there's lots of people around. It's not like they're completely by themselves.'

'Right.' Eliza still couldn't comprehend it.

'I'll take you to meet them, but first let me show you how to use the computer and hook up with Port Augusta.' He hit a few buttons and explained as he went. Eliza whipped a notepad out of her backpack and started writing.

'Their teacher is Mr Goldsworth. He's really approachable,

so if you've got any problems, he's the one to go to.' He paused before saying, 'It's a bugger but I'm sure they're both behind where they should be.'

Eliza thought, then said: 'Unfortunately, we're all victims of our own circumstances, Chris. We can't change that. Just have to do the best we can with what we're given.' She changed the subject quickly. 'So, Heidi is in year four and Tilly's in year one?'

'Yep. Nine and five. They're polar opposites! Heidi is a little go-getter. She could pick out native animals and track kangaroos before she went to school. Tilly's a bit different. Quiet and measured. Always thinks before talking. She loves animals and can raise as many joeys as I bring home.' He smiled and Eliza could see how much he adored his children.

'Well, they had to learn those skills from someone and I'm guessing that someone was you. So, see? You do make a good teacher!' She threw a quick smile at him. 'I'll look forward to meeting them.'

'Do you want a cup of coffee? I can make one and call the girls back.'

'That would be great. I'll just have a quick look through these books, so I know what I'm doing, and be right out.'

After Chris left the room, she stood for a moment taking everything in. It was clear that for some time there had only been a man's touch in there.

She walked over and sat at one of the desks, before picking up Heidi's workbook and turning to halfway through it. There was the normal 'look, say, cover, write, check' and short stories that kids of that age did, along with addition, subtraction and multiplication.

At a glance, Eliza could see that Heidi was struggling with her maths as well as her handwriting. *Two things to work on straightaway*, she thought as she read a story Heidi had written.

'There was an echidna that lived in a hole. He was very prickly, so it was hard to make friends . . .'

Even though her handwriting was awful, the punctuation and sentence structure were fine. 'Okay, that'll be easy enough to deal with,' she said to herself.

Eliza put down Heidi's book and picked up Tilly's. Numbers and sentences being matched to pictures were featured heavily. She flicked through a few pages and something caught her eye.

'Project: Interview an older person on what it was like to live a long time ago.'

That's interesting, she thought.

A siren sounded, and Eliza jumped and looked up. She automatically thought it was a fire siren, calling in all the volunteers, as happened in country towns, but quickly realised it couldn't be. This wasn't a town, it was a park. Maybe it was some kind of alarm system.

She went in search of Chris, who was standing in the kitchen, pouring cups of cordial.

'Everything okay?' she asked.

'Don't worry,' he said. 'That's just the way I call the girls in. I rigged this up when I thought they were old enough to head out by themselves. They could be a couple of kilometres away, but they know to come straight back when they hear it.'

Eliza shook her head. She still found it hard to understand how Chris could let young kids wander around in the bush and talk to strangers. That never would have happened in Jindabyne or out on the snowfields, no matter the time of the year. Even in the short time she'd lived at Blinman, she'd noticed the differences between the two places—everyone here was very laid-back and casual. There was a fiercely strong sense of community, independence, and everyone's spirit was equally strong.

'When I was a kid, Mum had a cowbell she would ring to get us to come back,' Chris said. 'We'd be miles away, out on the station, riding the horses or up to mischief of some sort, and we'd hear the bell and have to head straight home. She'd give us half an hour and if we weren't back in that time and she had to come looking for us, Dad would tan our arses.'

Just as he finished, there was a clattering of feet and two small humans tumbled through the door, chattering over the top of one another.

'Dad, we found a goanna's nest!'

'I found the goanna's nest, not you.'

'It's over at the bottom of Bailey's hill.'

'No, it's not, it's more towards the creek on the other side.'

The babbling stopped as soon as they saw a strange woman standing in the kitchen.

Two sets of wide brown eyes looked curiously at Eliza, and wild, tangled hair tumbled out from dusty caps. Both girls were wearing sturdy boots, jeans and T-shirts.

'Hello,' the older one said. 'I'm Heidi.'

Chris calmly pushed over the drinks and a plate of biscuits.

'Hello, Heidi, I'm Eliza,' she responded and put out her hand so Heidi could shake it if she wanted to. She was pleased when the little girl slipped her hand into hers.

Turning towards Tilly, she smiled at her inquisitive look. 'Hello, Tilly, I'm Eliza.'

Shyly, Tilly extended her hand. Eliza assumed it was one

50

thing to talk to strangers outdoors and another to have one inside her own home. A female stranger, at that.

Chris finally spoke. 'Girls, Eliza is coming to give you a hand with your schoolwork.'

'Ugh, Daaadd,' Heidi groaned. 'You know I want to be outside with you.'

'I know, princess, but you've got to do your schoolwork if you want to be a park ranger too. I had to do mine when I was growing up. It's a right bugger, but you have to be able to write to fill in all the forms and documentation there are.'

Heidi sighed before looking back at Eliza.

'Are you a teacher?'

Eliza caught herself before she said yes and coughed slightly to cover it. 'Sort of,' she said. 'I've worked with children, so I know how to help you with all of your lessons.'

'Can you do maths?' Tilly asked.

Smiling, Eliza nodded. 'Although it's not my favourite subject. What's yours, Tilly?'

'I like the singing and rhyming.'

'I see from your book you've got a really interesting project coming up, about interviewing an older person. Who do you think you might talk to?'

'My nana,' Tilly said proudly. 'She's so old. Nana's nearly ninety!' she chanted and Eliza laughed.

'Is she really?'

'It's a chant I made up. Is Nana nearly ninety, Dad?'

'Not for a while yet, honey, but you're right. She's quite old.'

Eliza took a sip of the coffee Chris put in front of her.

'Where are you going to sleep?' Heidi asked as she pushed a biscuit into her mouth.

Eliza fought the urge to take her hand gently and ask her to take smaller mouthfuls.

'I'm going to be driving down from Blinman a couple of days a week. Do you think that will be okay?'

'I guess so.'

'Tell me about this goanna nest you found,' Chris said, looking at the two girls.

'Oh, it's really cool, Dad. I found it in a hollow log. I could see there were tracks going into it, so I had a look.'

'Did you actually bend down and look in it?' Eliza asked, trying to keep the alarm out of her voice. 'Aren't they dangerous? What about snakes?'

'Only if you don't know how to deal with them,' Heidi answered scornfully. Then she looked at Chris and rolled her eyes. 'It's too cold in the early morning for snakes yet, but,' she conceded, 'it'd be a good place for them to hibernate during winter.'

Eliza could almost hear her thinking *Where did you find this one, Dad?* She made a mental note not to question Heidi about any of her antics. Or at least not to show she was concerned.

'There were a couple of eggs in the nest.'

'Were there?' Chris asked. 'Are you sure they were good? It's quite late in the season for them.'

'I think so. Plus, the tracks were fresh, Dad. Why would they be going in there unless the eggs were okay?'

'Good point.'

Eliza turned to Chris as she put down her empty coffee cup. 'What time would you like me to be here?'

'The lessons start about nine-thirty, so before then. I won't be around. Tomorrow is the day I've gotta empty all the rubbish bins and clean up the camping sites.' Chris made a face.

'Ah, the glamorous life of a park ranger.'

'Something like that. Usually, I take these two twerps with me, but,' he turned to the girls, 'you'll both be head down, bum up, working really hard on your schoolwork, won't you?'

Heidi rolled her eyes. 'Okay, Dad. But you know I don't like school.'

'I know, honey.' He reached over and ruffled her hair.

Tilly moved closer to Eliza. 'I like school,' she said in a quiet voice.

Eliza turned to her. 'You and I will get along really well, then. I like school too.'

Chapter 8

Dominic stared into the fire, his fingers clenched around a glass of red wine. It was taking all his self-control to sit there like nothing was churning inside him, that he wasn't burning with anger and hurt pride.

Taking another swig, he threw himself out of the chair and paced the length of the room. His eyes never strayed from the wedding photo that hung on the wall.

He remembered clearly how he'd told her she was his now and warned her never to try to leave him.

Damn! The small amount of love he'd felt for this woman had made him give her a hint of what could happen. He didn't want to be in a situation where he had to hurt her, dammit.

'Fucking hell, Ashleigh,' he almost whined. 'Why didn't you listen to me?'

How had she managed it without him realising? Why hadn't she been as frightened of him as she should have been? That was how he controlled all the people he needed. There was a skeleton in every closet, and skeletons, as he'd found, were very useful tools to have.

Ashleigh must have planned it, he'd decided. *It must have been in the wind for some time before she actually left, but how was she surviving? And money? Staying hidden cost money. She couldn't work, unless she had false papers.* None of it made any sense to him. The money she had stolen from his top drawer wouldn't have kept her going for very long.

He squeezed the glass tighter, then stared at it as it shattered in his grip. Blood and red wine mingled, and dripped from his fingers.

'Bitch!' exploded from his mouth.

He went to the kitchen, deposited what was left of the glass in the bin and rinsed his hand in the kitchen sink. Though the darkened window had spots of rain on it, he could see his reflection. He stared at himself, knowing how much he looked like his father.

His Italian heritage was strong in his features—wavy dark hair and eyes that were almost black.

The reflection stared back at him, the eyes never leaving his. He knew the coldness in them; he'd seen it before.

When he found Ashleigh, he would make her regret leaving him—that he was sure of.

When Dominic was growing up, he had idolised his father, Nunzio. It had been ingrained in him that he would take over Nunzio's business interests once he became too old to manage them, or died. Much to Dominic's ire, his sister had been installed as the caretaker of the business until he proved himself.

Having a devious streak, he'd explored options and businesses that had taken him in a different direction from his father's. He would let nothing get in the way of building his empire. He was ruthless and had no problems breaking the law. In the old country, that was accepted.

To do that, he'd needed a beautiful wife at his side. After all, if he wasn't married, people might wonder why, and being unattached also brought unwanted attention from single women. As an upstanding member of the community, it was useful for him to have someone to take to dinners and other events.

However, he needed a wife who was submissive, silent—and loyal. The only way Dominic knew how to make people stay true to him was to hold something over them. Ashleigh had been taught that right from the start but, to his surprise, he'd underestimated her.

For that, Ashleigh would pay.

He heard a knock and tore himself away from the window. Wrapping a towel around his hand, he went to answer the door.

Simon stood there, rain dripping from his hat. 'G'day, Dom,' he said, before stopping and looking down at Dominic's hand.

'It's nothing,' said Dominic, dismissing his inquisitive look. 'Don't stand out there on the street. Hurry, come inside. What have you found out?' He shut the door firmly behind the policeman.

Dominic noted Simon looked nervous as he followed him into the lounge room, and how he stared at the glass fragments and blood on the floor.

'Do you have any news?'

'No. I'm sorry, Dom, there's nothing. It's like she's disappeared off the face of the earth.'

Dominic straightened and sharply drew in a breath. 'That can't be. She can't outsmart us.'

'Every police officer in Australia knows she's missing. They know not to approach her, just as you asked, because of her mental instability.' He stopped for a moment. 'Dom, I don't know how you're going to prove that, when you do find her. Ashleigh's stable. There isn't a doctor in this country who would say otherwise.'

'I'll find someone who'll say that she isn't,' Dominic answered. 'Our friend the local doctor should have already modified her medical records.'

Simon nodded. He took a breath, then asked: 'Are you sure there isn't any family she knows about? Somewhere safe she could have run to?'

'I've told you. She has no one. I have personally gone back through her history. She was dropped at the church with nothing but her name. That was why she was perfect. No family, and her foster family don't have anything to do with her. The mother is dead now, anyway. She was a loner. A few friends, but ones who wouldn't be hard to get her to lose contact with; I made that happen. No one was going to miss her. The only information I found on her—her birth certificate—I've got under lock and key. Not that it will tell her anything. There's no names on it at all.' Dominic strode over to the bar and poured himself another glass of wine. 'Want one?' he asked, the bottle hovering over an empty glass.

Simon accepted.

'What about some other identifying factor? A tattoo or jewellery, or something. Give me something else I can look for. It's easy to change your appearance, but not tattoos or birthmarks. Not without money.'

Dominic stared into the fire, his mind racing. 'Do you think she was smart enough to change her appearance?' he asked.

'Yeah, I do. If there was anyone around who even slightly resembled her, there would have been a sighting somewhere. We get sightings of people all the time and it turns out just to be someone who resembles the person who's missing.

'I really thought we were going to be able to follow her when the cops from Cooma reported her refuelling. If she's clever enough to change her numberplates, she's certainly clever enough to change the way she looks.'

Dom's eyes narrowed at the thought he'd been outsmarted. He whirled around to face Simon.

'Okay, do a composite drawing of her with different-coloured hair, shorter hair, longer hair. Fatter, thinner. That sort of shit. Whatever it takes.'

Simon shrugged helplessly. 'I can't. You'll have to go higher than me if you want to do that. It's been over two months, Dom. You know the search has been scaled down. We've been through everything—her computer, her phone records, bank accounts. She obviously knows to use cash wherever she is. I've investigated the option that she was talking to someone online who may have helped her, but that hasn't paid off. She can't be working unless it's for cash or she's got false papers, but no one I know who makes false papers has heard of her. It was another dead end.'

'I'll *pay* for another TV appearance.'

'You can try. But it won't make any difference to the police department.'

'Then I'll pay for a private investigator and more investigative work than you can do. He can work without restrictions.' Dominic knew he sounded desperate but he didn't care.

Simon nodded. 'You can try that too. But whoever you get won't have as much pull as I do. They won't have a badge. But, sure, he can knock on doors in other towns. I can't, because I have to be here.'

Dominic couldn't hold back his anger anymore. He threw his glass at the stone wall. Flames hissed and flared as the drops of alcohol splashed onto the hearth and fuelled the fire.

'Fucking bitch, how dare she? She's brought my name into disgrace.'

Dominic spun around, his face still red with fury. He could feel the blood seeping from the cut on his hand, but he didn't take any notice.

'Jewellery,' Dominic rasped, so furious he was barely able to speak.

Simon waited.

'She has my mother's engagement ring. It's an heirloom and very distinctive.'

'Okay. That's a good idea,' the policeman answered calmly. 'We probably should've looked at that first off.' He paused. 'I'm pretty sure she wouldn't be wearing it, though.'

Dominic clenched his fists and drew a deep, fuming breath.

'But,' Simon continued, 'she might pawn it. Have you got a photo? I'll alert the pawn dealers across the country. Hopefully, she hasn't done it already.'

'I'll find one.' Dominic stomped off to his office. There was a photo in the safe for insurance purposes. 'She's got to be living off something because I made sure she didn't have any money of her own except for shopping. I invested her savings in shares in both our names so she couldn't touch it without my approval.'

Dominic entered the code and pulled out a fire-safe box, then flicked through the photos and documents inside it.

He stopped as he came across one of Nunzio and himself on his twenty-first birthday. It was taken only a week before his father was killed in a car accident, although Dominic knew it wasn't an accident. It had taken four years for him to track down his father's killer and avenge his death. It had been a slow and agonising punishment, with Dominic using pruning shears to chop off his toes one by one. He was about to start on the man's hands before he got an admission that he had killed Nunzio. But the man's confession hadn't saved him. It hadn't been hard to pile the body parts into a hollowed tree and pour acid over the remains. This was Dominic's first murder.

It had all been done deep in the Kosciuszko National Park. The killer's body had never been found and Dominic slept easily at night. After all, it did say in the Bible, *'An eye for an eye and a tooth for a tooth.'*

Now, though, he paid people to kill for him instead.

His mother, Maria, had died when he was three. His father had loved her so much he'd never looked at another woman, and had put all his efforts into raising the strongest son he could. He raised his daughter to be strong too, but Dominic preferred not to think about that.

His only aim was to keep making his papa happy, but things hadn't worked out the way he'd thought they would.

Now his chest tightened as he looked at the photo of his father. They were smiling, arms around each other's shoulders, and Dominic knew how proud Nunzio was of him that day.

'My boy,' he'd said when they were alone in his office, 'my boy, you are the image of me and my father. You have honoured our family tradition by being proud and strong. You will succeed in anything you try. I am more than satisfied with you.' He'd clapped him on the shoulder and handed him the pocket watch that was always pinned inside his suit coat.

Dominic's throat tightened at the memory. That had been before his sister had interfered.

His fingers searched through the box for the pocket watch. He kept it there, away from prying eyes. That was the trouble with living in a tourist town. There were plenty of people with light fingers.

He liked to hold the watch every so often and think of his father. It calmed him and, by hell, he needed calming at the moment.

What? It should be in between the share documents and birth certificates.

Wrinkling his brow, he searched again.

It wasn't there.

Dominic reached inside the safe, pushing aside the gun and bullets. There was another box towards the back that held more family heirlooms.

He came up empty.

'No,' he muttered quietly. It was one thing to run from him, but another altogether to steal from him.

With a roar that brought Simon running, he emptied the safe onto the ground and searched through it.

'That fucking slut,' he snarled as he held up her engagement and wedding rings. 'She's taken my pocket watch and left her rings. '

He looked up at Simon in shock. It was the final 'fuck you'.

A thought hit him like a lightning bolt. He grabbed the box and started rifling through the papers in it. Ashleigh's birth certificate, which he'd hidden for the past two years, had gone too.

Chapter 9

Maureen shut the door of the general store, locked it and gave a huge sigh. Her body ached and she was bone tired.

She hadn't been able to believe her luck when Chris had brought Eliza in after she had crashed her car. Eliza's help, in return for minimal board, meant Maureen could rest every afternoon. Her inability to get through a day without feeling like she needed to curl up and sleep was frustrating. At only forty-five, she still wanted to be out playing netball and walking, but that was only a distant dream. Maureen dragged her useless body over to a chair and sat down. Sometimes, during her darkest moments, when her body hurt more than she thought she could endure, she wished she'd just been killed in the car accident, along with her husband, Mike. Then Hamish would smile at her and all those thoughts would disappear.

Thinking of Hamish, she looked at her watch. He'd be at footy practice now. She hated sending him away to boarding school, but there wasn't any choice out here. She'd taught him for as long as she could, in conjunction with the School of the Air, but first-year high school had come around far too quickly. She still felt so much pride when she saw him standing there in his school uniform. He was a young man now, and looked so much like his father.

Memories of Mike—like the way he would hold Hamish when he was a baby—still brought her to tears. Maureen had always thought there was nothing sexier than a man who loved his children and Mike had done that so well.

A banging on the door interrupted her thoughts.

'Bloody good thing too,' she said to herself as she got up to answer it. 'Could've got all twisted up there.' She tapped her chest over her heart a couple of times as she limped over to the door.

'We're closed,' she said, pulling the door open, but her jaw dropped when she saw who was standing on the verandah. 'Kim! Dave!'

She threw open her arms and Kim, one of her dearest friends, fell into them. Reen didn't see anywhere near as much of her and Dave as she'd have liked to, since his work kept them in the small town of Barker. 'What are you doing up here?' Maureen asked.

Kim laughed. 'Oh, Reen, it's so good to see you. How are you?'

Dave leaned over and gave Maureen a kiss on the cheek. 'How you going? Still coping?'

'Of course,' Maureen answered indignantly. 'Don't be cheeky! Come in, come in,' she added, holding the door open and waving them inside. 'Do you want a drink or coffee? Something to eat?'

'We're taking you out to tea at the pub,' Kim said.

'You're staying overnight? I'll make up one of the rooms. I've got a full-time lodger now, so you can't have your normal room, but . . .'

Dave held up his hand. 'Steady on there! This is us you're talking to. We've brought the swag, we just need somewhere to roll it out.'

Maureen took a breath as a lump appeared in her throat from nowhere. 'It's so good to see you both,' she said with a wobbly smile. She took a breath. 'Why are you up this way, anyway?' she asked.

'I had a couple of things I had to check out, so we thought we'd just keep on coming. My cousin Kate and her family are camping at Wilpena, and we stayed last night with them. Now here we are,' Dave answered.

'Well, I've got to say it's bloody good to see you both.' She was about to say more when Eliza popped her head in.

'There you are, I've been over at your place looking for you. Oh, sorry to interrupt,' Eliza said, noticing the couple.

'Don't you go anywhere,' Maureen instructed her. 'Come in here and meet two of my best mates. Eliza, this is Dave and Kim. Dave's a detective with the SA police and Kim's his wife.' She paused as she watched Eliza's expression change to one of fear, then her attempt to hide it.

'Hi,' Eliza said in a slightly higher octave than her normal one. 'Good to meet you. If you'll excuse me, I've just got a couple of things to do.'

Maureen narrowed her eyes and watched as Eliza hurried from the room. *Interesting.*

'Did we frighten her?' Kim asked.

'Nah, I wouldn't have thought so. Just doesn't want to

64

intrude, knowing Eliza.' She focused on Kim and Dave. 'So, come on, out with all the news.'

'Tell you what, why don't we head over to the pub and then we can have a drink and catch up,' Dave suggested.

'Hang on a sec.' Maureen limped over to the counter and reached behind it, bringing out a key. 'Make yourselves comfortable in room five. I'll just have a shower and I'll see you over there—how does that sound?'

'Great idea,' Kim beamed. 'See you soon.'

∽

Maureen went to Eliza's room and knocked on the door.

'Hey,' Eliza smiled when she opened it.

'Can I come in?'

'Sure, I'm just editing some photos.' Eliza cleared some photography magazines off a chair so Maureen could sit down. 'Nice to see your friends?' she asked.

'Always,' Maureen answered. 'Dave is the one I've told you about, the one who pulled me out when we had the accident.'

'Oh.' Eliza nodded in understanding. Maureen talked openly about that terrible night.

She'd known Mike was dead, as she'd hung upside down inside the car, her seatbelt trapping her. The Blinman to Parachilna road was full of twists and turns, and deep drop-offs. Kangaroos and goats were rife. What had made Mike take that route home in the middle of the night, Maureen would never know, as she hadn't had time to ask him before the collision—and she certainly couldn't ask him now. It had been three hours before another vehicle had come along, and another two before she'd been able to get out of the car.

Dave, who'd been out on an investigation, had arrived first on the scene, and stayed, talking to her and calming her. Having known Dave for many years through their membership of the cricket club, she would be forever grateful for the comfort he gave her during those five hours that had felt more like a lifetime. Kim had come and visited her in the hospital, well and truly cementing their friendship.

'So, you acted like you'd seen a ghost when I introduced you and then you took off like you had a red-hot poker up your bum. What's that all about?' Maureen asked.

Eliza laughed at the description, then became serious. 'Nothing, Reen, honestly. I've had a long day and I didn't want to interrupt. That's all.'

'Excuse me if I don't believe you.' Maureen held Eliza's eyes steadily. 'Now, I'm going to tell you this once. I'm really happy to have you here—I like you. I don't need to know about your past, and I won't interfere or pry when it comes to that. But if you've done anything illegal, or you're on the run from the police—and the way you scarpered back there made me think you were—then we need to have a chat. I will not hide a criminal or criminal activities.' She paused. 'And, to be honest, Eliza, the fact that you just turned up here, out of the blue, with no links to Bliman, not knowing anyone, it sort of reeks of hiding out. I'm not the only one who's thought this but we're genuine people out here. We don't pry and we accept people the way they are. But not lawbreakers. It's not like you've told us much about where you were before.'

Eliza, who had been swallowing nervously while Maureen spoke, licked her lips a couple of times before she got up and went to a box in the corner. Dragging out a tattered page, she held it out to Maureen.

'I can't tell you why I ended up here, but I saw this story and I somehow felt drawn to Blinman. I don't know if it's this couple or it's the country. I just knew I had to come.' She rushed on. 'And I'm sure that sounds really stupid and fanciful, but that's just the way it was.'

Maureen glanced at the picture and skimmed the article. 'That's John and Mary Caulder. They've got a station east of here. They don't get off it much.' She looked up at Eliza. 'Have you made contact with them yet?'

'No. How can I do that? It was just a stupid feeling I had. I can't ring them up and say, "Hey, I've lobbed into Blinman because I felt connected to this story."'

Maureen was silent for a long while. 'All right,' she said, getting up. 'If you're not in any trouble, you won't mind coming and having dinner with Dave, Kim and me tonight. We'll all be at the pub in about half an hour. It'll give you an opportunity to meet a few more of the locals too. See you there.' With that challenge, she left the room.

છ૭

The pub was crowded with tourists when Maureen arrived, happy at the thought of having dinner with Dave and Kim. A hot shower and a couple of painkillers later, she felt like a new woman.

She smiled and nodded to a few people at the bar, but made a beeline for her friends, who were sitting next to the fire, nursing drinks and talking.

'Hope you don't mind but I asked Eliza to come and eat

with us tonight. She's only been here a couple of months and she's still getting to know people.'

'That'll be lovely,' Kim said. She leaned forward and put her hand on Maureen's knee. 'Now, tell us about you. How are you?'

'I'm fine,' Maureen answered and proceeded to bring them up to date on what had been happening since they'd seen each other last.

Between the chatter and the warm glow of the fire, Maureen began to relax.

'Dave, I've got something to ask you,' she said after a while. 'Why would someone come to Blinman to try and hide?'

The detective raised his eyebrows. 'Talking about anyone in particular?'

'Just a question.'

Dave thought for a while. 'Could be any number of reasons,' he answered. 'Trying to dry out from drugs, make a clean start. Debts, bad marriages, maybe there's a warrant out for their arrest. If it was a bloke, he could be running from paying child support. Or they could've lost their memory and feel comfortable here, for some reason. Blinman is fairly out of the way and not many people have heard of it but, on the other hand, the trouble with hiding out here is that it's so small. Someone new coming into town'll be the centre of attention.' He looked at her levelly. 'Funny question, Reen.'

'Just working out a few things.' She smiled. 'Oh look, here comes Eliza. You'll love her—such a beautiful, gentle soul. Amazing photographer. Just started to teach herself since she arrived.'

'But you can't help feeling there's a lot more to her than she's told you?' Dave asked.

Maureen pointed a finger at him. 'Spot on.'

Chapter 10

Eliza loaded everything she thought she would need for the day's teaching into the dual cab ute she'd borrowed from Stu and Stacey.

It had done a lot of kilometres and hit a few kangaroos in its time—there were a few dents to prove it, along with a bit of rust. Stu had promised her it was reliable, and was happy for her, as their 'go-to' girl, to use it while they were away.

'All organised?' Reen called out as she walked across the road.

Eliza looked around at the sound of her voice. 'Yep, I think so. I might pop into the shop and grab a couple of chocolate bars to sweeten the deal when I have to lock them in the schoolroom.' She threw her backpack on the front seat and straightened up. 'I have a feeling that Heidi might be a slight handful until we get a routine happening.'

'She's one switched-on kid, that's for sure,' Maureen agreed. 'Tell me what you want and I'll put them on the counter for you.'

'Oh, just a couple of Flakes or something.'

Maureen leaned against the side of the car and looked at Eliza.

'What?' Eliza asked.

'That's a big job you've undertaken with those kids.'

Eliza looked at her friend, feeling she was fishing for information, before nodding. 'Yeah, it is. But I think I'll be okay. I'm pretty clued in when it comes to maths and English. I mean, how hard can it be? It's only year one and year four. I should be able to manage it.'

There was silence between them for a while. A magpie flew down from a tree and started bathing in a puddle from the showers overnight. It must have been the joy of bathing in fresh water that made the magpie warble, a low, musical sound.

Finally, Maureen spoke. 'I'm sure you'll do brilliantly.'

⁊

'Girls, you need to come and sit down,' Eliza encouraged Heidi and Tilly. 'Your teacher is going to be on the computer in about three minutes.' She'd read up on the way this computer-ised teaching worked, and learned that video cameras and the internet were used. It was like watching live TV—the teacher was beamed all the way to classrooms across the state. As well, two-way audio made interaction between teacher and students possible. Eliza was keen to see it up close and how class control would be maintained.

'But I need to check that goanna nest,' Heidi whined.

'No, Heidi, you need to sit at your desk and get ready.' Teaching had come back to Eliza like she'd never stopped doing it. By staying firm but kind and not letting either of the girls get away with anything, she felt alive. How lucky she'd been that Chris had asked her to be their governess.

'I like the songs we get to sing with Mr Goldsworth,' Tilly said, her large eyes on Eliza.

'We can sing some more after you've finished, if you like,' Eliza answered. 'Oh, here you go. Heidi. Bottom on your chair, please. Now.'

Heidi sat down, a pout playing on her face, but it disappeared within seconds as the call came over the computer, followed by the roll being read.

Eliza sat back and listened as the lesson was conducted. She flicked through Heidi's workbook and made some marks next to maths questions that she wanted the little girl to attempt. Then she took some paper and drew lines across it, and wrote some basic sentences for Heidi to copy—it would be good handwriting practice.

'Okay,' Eliza said, when the School of the Air lessons had finished. 'Let's have a little break, then come back here. Heidi, would you like to show me where the goanna's nest is?'

'Yeah!' Heidi was up and out the door before Eliza could give any other instructions.

'Let's go, Tilly,' Eliza said. 'We might lose her scent otherwise!'

'What do you mean? Does she smell?' Tilly sniffed the air.

'Oh, it's a little joke. When someone moves as fast as your sister just did, the only way to follow her is by her scent, or smell. A bit like following a trail. Have you ever read *Hansel and Gretel*?'

Tilly shook her head and, leading the way, walked out the door.

'It's a story about two young children who get lost in a forest, but the boy cleverly left a trail of breadcrumbs to follow home again.' *That's the short version*, she thought as she trailed behind.

'Are you two coming?' Heidi called.

'We're following your, um, smell!' Tilly called back.

Eliza bit back a giggle.

'I don't smell!'

'You do if you go too fast. That's how we get to follow you. Eliza said so.'

'Okay, okay. I tell you what,' Eliza broke in. 'What about we take a thermos and some sandwiches, so we can have a picnic out in the bush? Maybe you could show me your favourite spots to visit.'

'I want to take you up to the top of Hunter's Ridge,' Tilly immediately said.

Heidi screwed up her nose. 'No, you don't. That's just boring. You need to go where no one else goes. They're the best bits of the park because they're lonely. That's what Dad says, anyway.'

'We can go to both places,' Eliza intervened. 'We'll just do one per day, how does that sound?'

'Sounds better than doing schoolwork,' Heidi answered, bouncing off.

Eliza closed her eyes and smiled. She sounded just like Chris.

␣

'This is where the tourists camp,' Tilly explained.

'Do lots of people stay here?' Eliza glanced around at the tidy camp sites. She counted eight caravans. Outside one, a

73

woman was sitting reading a book, and cooking smells came from within another.

A crow was perched on the top of a rubbish bin, its head deep inside.

'Bloody crows.' Heidi made a move to scare it off. 'They take the rubbish and spread it around the park. Dad's always complaining about them.'

'Does he complain about your language?' Eliza asked mildly and watched a blush rise on Heidi's cheeks.

'Heaps of people stay,' Tilly answered Eliza's earlier question. 'There's always people here. Even when it's really cold and raining. Sometimes they come more than once.'

'Yeah,' Heidi chimed in. 'Nana and Pop Taggart come quite a few times every year.'

'Oh, it's nice you get to see your grandparents so often. Are they your mum's or your dad's parents?'

Heidi continued to lead the way towards a line of gum trees, which, Eliza now knew from her numerous walks, would lead to a gorge.

'Mum's. We don't see that much of them, though. They're not really kid people. Come this way.' Heidi picked out a path that Eliza couldn't see. She watched, in awe, the sure-footedness of the young girl. She was sure that the sisters knew more about the park, and about nature and animals, than she could ever hope to. It was clear that Chris had often taken them with him when he'd been out and about, and taught them well.

Eliza wanted to ask more about their grandparents, but thought better of it when she saw Tilly's face. Her little lips were jutting out as if she might cry. Eliza didn't know much about Claire, but wanted to give her a piece of her mind for just up and leaving these two beautiful little girls. She would never understand how a mother could do that.

'Just through here.' Heidi wound her way between shrubby trees and clumps of grasses, before jumping down the bank and landing on the gravelly bed of the creek.

Eliza had walked many gorges since she'd arrived in Blinman but she never lost her wonder at the scenery. River red gums were dotted along the ragged creek edge. From the last flood, branches intertwined with leaves and bushes were tumbled against thick-trunked trees and there were deep puddles in the crevices.

'Along here.' Heidi kept walking.

'Where are you taking us?'

'To a spot that only Dad, Tilly and I know about. It's just up here.' She pointed to where the creek split into two.

With a hill edge high on one side and a line of gum trees on the other bank, they trekked in, listening to magpies singing and crows calling. The gentle, pale sunlight was warm enough for Eliza to think about taking off her jumper, but the wind had a brass monkeys chill factor.

Finally, Heidi stopped. 'Here,' she said and pointed to where a cliff overhung the creek. 'You can shelter when it's raining or get out of the hot sun in here. We've had lots of picnics here, haven't we, Tilly?'

'Yeah. I don't like coming here.'

'Oh, really?' Eliza looked at her, puzzled. 'Why would you not like it here? It's so beautiful and peaceful.'

The two girls looked at each other before Tilly looked up at Eliza. 'We came here when Mum still lived with us.'

Eliza swallowed. 'Let's set up the picnic,' she suggested, shrugging her backpack from her shoulders. 'Now, I brought a couple of special treats. Who likes chocolate?'

'Me!'

Eliza laughed as they answered at the same time. She handed out the chocolate bars and poured water into the plastic cups she'd brought.

She asked questions about the park and the girls answered every one she threw at them. They were hungry for female company, she realised, and both of them were extremely clever.

When they had eaten their fill, they all lay on their backs, looking at the blue sky.

'Okay,' said Eliza. 'What rhymes with "tree"?'

'Bee!' called Tilly.

'Great, now let's spell it. B. E. E,' Eliza led off and the girls joined in. *These two are going to learn better outside*, she thought. *This is where they're both comfortable.*

Without warning, Tilly leaned over to Eliza, who was still lying on her back, and reached out a finger. Eliza froze as she felt the gentle touch on her cheek.

'How did you get this?' Tilly asked.

Eliza felt her hand go to the scar and was instantly transported back to Dominic looming above her. When he had pulled her hair she'd had tears in her eyes from the pain and her chest had felt tight. Now, concentrating hard, she tried to get her feelings under control.

'Eliza?'

She realised both children had sat up and were staring at her. 'Um,' she took a shaky breath. 'I had an accident and I got cut.'

'How?'

'Oh, it was just a silly accident. It was so long ago now, I've forgotten. Now, how about we pack up and head back to the house, so we can do a bit more schoolwork? We've had such a lovely break. Thank you for showing me this beautiful spot.'

Playing follow-the-leader, the three of them walked back towards the house, Eliza trying to still her heart and furious with herself for reacting the way that she did.

She was not a victim anymore. How could she allow Dominic to still have any power over her? It was something she'd thought a lot about and worked really hard on since she'd left him. There was no way she wanted him to have any influence over her life and that included her reactions.

She recalled that not long after she'd first arrived in Blinman, she'd woken one night to the sound of a vehicle.

Breaking out in a sweat, the fear she'd felt and the knots in her stomach had been testament to the fact she still had a way to go when it came to Dominic having no power over her. It had been the sound of the engine.

It was the same as the one in the vehicle Dominic drove.

Tilly's voice broke through her thoughts.

'Here comes the policeman again.'

Eliza looked in the direction she was pointing.

'What policeman?' she asked. She glanced towards the house, trying to work out how long it would take her to get there. She wanted to usher the kids inside, so she could stay hidden in the schoolroom.

'He visits every so often,' Heidi said. 'His name is Dave.'

Eliza watched with trepidation as a white station wagon drew to a halt in the middle of the road. She had enjoyed his and his wife's company when they'd had dinner together, but she preferred to keep a very safe distance from Dave, no matter how nice he was. She imagined that, being a detective, he would have some kind of sixth sense about things not being quite right.

Dave Burrows' friendly face stared out at them and he broke into a smile.

'Hello there, you two,' he said. 'Are you showing your new teacher the ropes?'

Eliza stood back from the car as Heidi launched into great detail about their stroll and what they had been doing.

She could see Dave listening intently, his eyes never leaving Heidi's face—which she was grateful for. He asked a few questions, engaging both children, then opened the glove box and handed over two Kit Kats.

'Now, you make sure you're not too hard on Eliza,' he instructed. 'She's new here, you know, and you wouldn't want to scare her too much. She might run away.'

Eliza felt her face flush and she looked down, too frightened to see the expression on his face. She hoped that his choice of words was just that—and didn't mean he knew who she was.

Chapter 11

The door of the shop flew open and a man rushed in.

'Reen!' he called. 'Hey, Reen!'

Eliza came out from the kitchen, where she'd been reading a photography magazine. 'She's not here. Sorry. Can I help?'

The man looked at her, puzzled. 'Sorry, I don't know you.'

'No, and I guess I don't know you either,' Eliza quipped. 'But, despite all of that, can I help you at all? I promise I can cook, pack up the pasties and pies, work the till, charge you correctly and clean.'

'Good. I'll marry you then,' he shot back at her with a grin.

Eliza raised her eyebrows, a small smile crossing her lips. 'I don't think that's an offer I'll take up. But thanks anyway.' She stood there and waited for him to tell her what he wanted.

'So, where is Maureen?' he asked as he went across to the drinks cabinet and pulled out a Coke.

'Gone to Port Augusta to get some supplies.'

'Can I get a Cornish pasty and a quandong pie to take away, please?'

'Sure.' She grabbed a paper bag and a pair of tongs before sliding open the warmer. The man leaned against the bench, pushing his hat back on his head, and looked at her.

'I think I know you,' he said.

'I'm sure you don't.' A nervous feeling crept through her stomach.

'You look familiar.'

Concentrating on keeping her face impassive, she answered: 'Oh, I just have one of those faces. Everyone says that to me.' She shrugged. 'I don't take any notice of it anymore.'

'You didn't tell me your name.'

Eliza stopped what she was doing and eyed him. 'You didn't tell me yours. Or why you came rushing in looking for Reen.'

'Fair call. I'm Jacob. Station owner.' He held out his hand and Eliza took it.

'I'm Eliza. General dogsbody.'

'Oh, yeah, I've heard about you. From Stu. I'd forgotten. Sorry.'

'I help out with the house animals while they're away. Where's your station?'

''bout twenty k west of here. Out on the Parachilna road.'

'Oh, okay—have you got that windmill and sheep yards on the creek there? I was out there the other day and saw some goats.'

'Yep, that's mine.'

There was a silence that Eliza felt the need to fill. 'Well, that's got that sorted. Anything else I can get you?'

'Nope.' He held out a fifty-dollar note and waited while Eliza rang up the sale on the till and gave him the change. 'So, where have you arrived from?'

'Oh, here and there,' she answered vaguely. 'I've been travelling a fair bit, so I don't really come from anywhere.'

'Interesting.'

'You didn't say why you were in a rush.'

'I just like to stir up Reen. Run in here and pretend I'm in a hell of a hurry, and then sit and yarn to her for a while. She doesn't ever take me seriously. I've been on holidays for the last couple of weeks and so it's been a while since we caught up.

'So, since she's not here, I'll sit and talk to you.'

Eliza shook her head. 'Sorry, I can't. I've got vegetables to cut up and another batch of scones to make.' Jacob was making her nervous, with his brown eyes regarding her steadily. In the five minutes he'd been in the shop, he'd asked her more questions than anyone else had in the whole time she'd been in Blinman.

'Oh, come on now. Surely you've got time to chat to a lonely bachelor who only gets any company when he comes to town to have a beer?'

'No, I've really got to get all of this done before Reen comes back. Otherwise, she'll be wondering why I haven't finished.'

'Actually, I did have an idea I wanted to talk through with Reen, but how about I run it past you?'

Eliza, making a show of being busy, started to walk back into the kitchen. 'Make it quick.' *And stay out there*, she thought.

But Jacob followed her through the door and hefted himself up onto the counter.

'Not sure that'd adhere to health and hygiene standards,' Eliza said dryly as she watched his boots leave a trail of red mud behind him.

'Oh shit. Sorry.' He glanced around and leaned over to pick up the magazine Eliza had been reading. 'Uh-huh,' he muttered in a sarcastic tone. 'Real busy, I can tell.' Jacob shot her an amused look before putting it down.

Ignoring him, Eliza grabbed a handful of carrots out of the fridge and started peeling them. She decided to steer the direction of the conversation.

'So, what's happening on the station for you at the moment?'

'Been mustering, getting the sheep closer to the yards, so we can start lamb marking,' he answered. 'Know much about farming?'

Eliza shook her head. 'I know about a few basic things like shearing, but not the details.'

Jacob nodded. 'So, what do you do other than help out Reen? Do you want a hand to peel all of those?'

'I'm fine. But thanks. I've started helping out Chris Maynard, by governessing his girls. I go down there a couple of days a week and supervise their schoolwork.'

'Keep you out of mischief.'

'Those girls keep me on my toes, that's for sure.' She smiled and grabbed a knife out of the drawer to dice the carrots.

She lifted her head as she heard the front door bell ring.

'It's only me,' Reen called out. 'And if that Jacob Maynard is spreading mud or dust around my kitchen, there'll be hell to pay!'

Eliza raised her eyebrows and Jacob spread out his hands in a 'who, me?' gesture.

'Maynard?' she asked.

'Yeah, Maynard. I'm Chris's brother.'

Reen came into the kitchen, shopping bags spilling out of her hands. 'Oh, there you are. Chatting up my kitchen hand, are you?'

Jacob assumed a look of complete innocence. 'Never.'

'No, of course not. Make yourself useful, can you? There's still some more shopping out in my car.'

'Anything for you, Reen.'

'Yeah, yeah. Get away with you.'

'You never told me Chris had a brother,' Eliza said after Jacob had headed out for the shopping. She started to unpack the bags Reen had put on the floor.

'I don't suppose it came up. I'm not the genealogy society of Blinman, you know.'

'Of course you are! You know everything about everybody.' Eliza saw pain in Reen's face. 'Long day?'

'Yeah, but a good one. I'm exhausted now.'

'I've cooked tea for you. It's in the fridge. Save you having to do it.'

'You're a gem. That's the last thing I feel like doing. I want to curl up in my bed with a whisky and my electric blanket. And perhaps a few painkillers too.'

Jacob returned and put some more bags on the bench. 'I actually came to talk to you about an idea I had,' he said seriously.

Reen pulled out a chair and sat down heavily on it. 'Fire away, then.'

'I've been thinking about this year's cook-off.'

'Not far away now. Have I told you about it, Eliza?' Reen asked.

Eliza shook her head. 'I've read about it—just what was in the magazine. I know it's fairly popular.'

'It's huge! We get hundreds of people up here for it. They've got to cook over coals in a camp oven. It's amazing what people produce. Curries, cakes, roasts. The smell is divine!'

'Can't wait.'

'And it's not just camp oven cooking,' Jacob broke in. 'We have a few other events too. Damper throwing and swag rolling—that's always a good one.'

'It's a fun weekend,' Reen remarked.

'But, Reen, I was talking to Mary Caulder and she was saying that the Frontier Services are running fairly low on funds. Can we do some sort of fundraising for them? I thought the cook-off might be the best bet.'

Eliza opened the freezer and placed the loaves of bread inside, then started stacking the bacon and meat patties along-side them.

'Really?' Reen leaned forward and put her chin on the heel of her palm. 'I wouldn't have thought they'd have problems. The church usually props them up, doesn't it?'

Jacob nodded. 'Along with fundraising and donations from the public. But there's not enough of either at the moment. You know how tight things are around here, with the last few years being so bad.'

'I tell you what, you couldn't have got a better service from them up here during the drought years,' Reen said. 'I reckon there would've been a lot more suicides if they hadn't been around.'

'Absolutely,' Jacob said. 'And you know I would have been one of them.'

Silence filled the shop and Eliza froze, not knowing how to react. She looked over at this strong-looking man, who had an easy smile and kind eyes. He'd done nothing but joke with her since he'd arrived and there was no way she would have guessed that he'd ever had suicidal thoughts.

Jacob turned around and caught her looking at him. 'True story,' he said. 'Dessie, he's the chaplain, drove into Manalinga—that's my station—just at the right time. It was like he knew he had to come and see me. I'd just thrown the rope over the shearing shed rafter.' Jacob looked down and swallowed.

Eliza, overcome with emotion, reached out and touched his arm. 'It's okay, you don't have to tell me.'

'It's good to talk about it,' he answered, not looking up. 'I was trying to work out if I should take my dog with me. Except I would have had to shoot him and I didn't think I could do that. Strange, isn't it? Didn't think I could shoot my best mate, but I thought I could hang myself. Anyway, old Dessie sat with me in that stinking hot shearing shed. It was about forty-seven degrees and the wind was howling—moaning around the openings of the shed. It was so hot and dry, even the flies were sitting down somewhere.'

Eliza slowly lowered herself to the floor, transfixed by what she was hearing. Reen had reached out and was holding Jacob's hand in support.

'We sat like that for hours. He didn't try and talk me into going into the house, or anything, to get me away from the rope. We just stayed as he found me. I talked. He listened. Then he talked and I listened. Finally, I stood up and we went back to the house.' He gave a sad smile. 'I would have been stuffed if he hadn't come by that day and, I tell you what, I'll never know how he came straight to the shearing shed instead of going to the house first. I hadn't left my ute outside—it was at the house. He just knew.'

'He's saved loads of people,' Reen said, patting Jacob's hand. She grinned widely. 'And he's married a few too.'

'As well as christened the babies and buried the dead.'

'We need to keep Dessie coming out here, that's for sure. Reckon the community would be lost without him.' Reen continued, 'So, what sort of fundraiser did you have in mind?'

'I've got an idea,' Eliza said. 'What about a selfie trail?'

They both looked at her, puzzled.

'What do you mean?' Reen asked.

'Okay—say we make up a list of places people have to visit while they're in Blinman: the mine, Parachilna Gorge, places in the national park. They have to take a selfie to prove they've been there. It's a great way to get people to see parts they otherwise wouldn't go to.'

'Where does the fundraising come into it?' Jacob asked.

'They have to pay an entry fee. Either per person or per carload, or something like that. We can work out the details later.' Eliza felt a bubble of excitement building inside her. 'Pick some places that are out of the way; unusual spots that are beautiful or different, and people don't usually go to. Someone's homestead, a cemetery, that type of thing. The first person back with all of the places documented in selfies is the winner. They get a prize of some sort.'

Jacob nodded. 'Yeah, like Forget-me-not Well or the Wilson cemetery. Hey, I like this idea! What about you, Reen?'

'It's certainly got merit, but are you going to get older people taking selfies, do you think? Some of them find it hard just to use a mobile phone.'

'From what I've seen at the park, most of the caravaners there have got iPads, but they could take photos on their cameras and show us. All we need to see is the photo on the display screen. And everyone has digital cameras these days.'

'Yeah, absolutely they do,' Jacob agreed.

'Let's get some other heads together on it,' Reen said. 'It'll take more than us three to get it organised and we'll have to thrash out the details. Eliza, I think you should be in charge, don't you, Jacob?'

'Her idea. She's in charge,' Jacob said, with a wink in Eliza's direction.

His enthusiasm was infectious but Eliza was torn. Part of her was worried about drawing attention to herself, and the other part wanted to be involved in this tight-knit community.

'I think I can do that,' she answered, trying to ignore the nervousness threatening to overtake her.

Chapter 12

'*Wife disappears without a trace*', Dominic read in the local paper. He'd tried to place the article in a national magazine, but even with his contacts and money, he hadn't been able to get it into *Woman's Day* or *New Idea*.

He was convinced that if he could do that, he'd find Ashleigh. Those magazines had readerships in the millions, and someone, somewhere, had to have seen her, or perhaps she'd confided in someone already. Dominic was sure she couldn't keep her mouth shut for long.

Every year 35,000 Australians are reported missing. Eighty-five per cent of these are found or make contact within the first week, and it's estimated that 1,600 of these have been missing for more than six months.

Dominic Alberto's wife went missing nine weeks ago and since then there hasn't been a single sighting of her. Her husband holds grave fears for Ashleigh's safety. In this exclusive tell-all interview, he tells of the days leading up to his wife's disappearance.

'I hadn't noticed anything out of the ordinary, except that she was a little quieter than usual,' he said. 'Sometimes when her medication needed adjusting, she was like that but it always took a few days for it to become apparent. It was only after she left, I realised she hadn't been taking her medication at all. There were full packets of her pills in the bathroom, which hadn't been touched. Not taking her pills causes her to become irrational and have anger attacks.

'I plead with anyone who has seen her, or even thinks they have, to come forward to the police. I'm desperate to have her home safely, where I can look after her.'

Local policeman Simon McCullen said it's out of character for Ashleigh not to make contact with Mr Alberto. 'Well, she's a good communicator, but if she hasn't been taking her prescribed medication, she could be unpredictable.'

There was a knock at the door. Dominic threw down the paper and got up to answer it.

Simon was there, flanked by two plain-clothes detectives.

Dominic looked at Simon, a question forming on his lips, then noticed that his friend was looking very uncomfortable. He suddenly realised this wasn't going to be a pleasant visit.

'Mr Alberto, we need to come in and ask a few questions,' one of the strangers said.

Simon stepped forward. 'Dominic, meet Detectives Harry Potts and Stephen Haliday. They're both from Sydney's major crime unit and we need to ask you a few questions.'

Dominic switched on the charm. 'Come in, come in, please. Do you have news on Ashleigh? Please tell me you have.'

'No, sir, we don't. We have more questions.'

'Of course. Anything, if it helps find her. Please, sit down.' He indicated seats, then offered coffee. He hoped they would accept, so he could get Simon alone and find out what the fuck was going on here.

'No, thank you,' Haliday answered. 'We'll get straight down to business. Have you got any idea why Ashleigh may have disappeared?'

Dominic shook his head. 'No. We had a happy marriage. Or, at least, I thought we did. It was her mental health that was the problem. You see, sir, she was abandoned as a child and very insecure. It caused her to have panic attacks that would range from shaking and crying, to being so angry that she would throw things. When we met, I made sure she had the best doctor we could find and the best care. The doctor changed the medication she was on and, for a long time, Ashleigh was a completely different woman—happy and loving—but she changed when she didn't take her tablets. She was dependent on them to keep her level.'

'That must have been very hard to live with.'

'It was, but it wasn't. You see, I love her more than life itself, so it wasn't a hardship. I understood her.'

'Did she have any friends she would have confided in?'

'No. Ashleigh was very private and her panic attacks made it hard for her to go out in public. She found it easier to stay at home, rather than put herself in a situation where she might become the centre of attention.'

'Okay, but you've just told us that while she was on the medication, she was able to act normally. Why would she be afraid to go out in public or make friends? She was a very good schoolteacher before you were married, so I understand.'

'She was. That was what attracted me to her in the first place. I thought she would make a wonderful mother.' Dominic stopped. He didn't think he would answer the other questions unless the detective pressed him.

'Have you found anything missing?' Potts asked. 'Jewellery, clothes, that type of thing?'

Dominic found it hard to answer because he was engulfed in rage. The violent fury he'd felt when he found his pocket watch stolen and her wedding rings in the safe hadn't abated.

He didn't want to tell the detectives about the rings because it made it seem that Ashleigh had wanted to leave him. Or maybe they would turn it around, to make it look like he'd killed her and kept the rings.

'My pocket watch, which has been passed down for two generations, is missing,' he admitted, shoving his hands into his pockets so the detectives couldn't see they were clenched into fists.

'Is this a photo of it?' said Haliday, offering the picture to Dominic.

'That's right.' He glanced at it and kept his hands in his pockets.

'What about money?'

'What about it?'

'Did she have any?'

'Detective, I don't mean to be rude, but I've already been through this with McCullen here. Is there anything new you want to ask me?'

'Where were you on the night Ashleigh disappeared?'

Dominic eyed the detective steadily. 'I was at the pub, playing cards.'

'You can't think of a reason why Ashleigh would leave?'

'I don't think she would leave if she was of sane mind, Detective. I've given her a privileged life and she loves me.'

'Are you sure you didn't have anything to do with her disappearance, Mr Alberto?' Haliday asked, suddenly leaning forward.

'Why would I? I keep telling you, I loved my wife.'

'Did you ever hit her?'

'No.'

'Yell at and abuse her?'

'No.'

'Threaten her?'

'No! What is this? I'm the victim here and you're treating me like the criminal.'

'Really?' Haliday replied. 'Unfortunately, that contradicts the information we have.'

Silence filled the room. Dominic didn't move, although his mind was racing. What could they have on him? What hadn't Simon told him?

'Ashleigh made a complaint to the police about you, a year ago,' Haliday informed him as he dug into a folder and pulled out a piece of paper, which he waved in front of him.

'What?' Dominic's voice was low and steady. He wanted to grab that form and rip it to shreds, but he managed to stay seated, unmoving.

'It seems that she didn't feel safe enough to go to Sergeant McCullen so she made the complaint at a Canberra police station. It alleges you verbally abused her and threatened to hurt her if she didn't do what you told her to.'

'That's a load of rubbish.'

'Is it?'

'I've already told you. I loved my wife.' His voice rose, angry and indignant.

'Loved?' Potts asked. 'As in the past tense? Did you kill her, Dominic?'

'I most certainly did not,' said Dominic, shooting up from his seat and towering over the two detectives. Unable to hold his tongue, he turned to Simon. 'How dare you let them ask these types of questions!'

'Why would Sergeant McCullen be able to stop us asking you questions, Mr Alberto? Is he on your payroll? We understand you have a large one.'

'If you haven't got anything else to ask me, I suggest you leave now,' Dominic said in a low and menacing voice. 'Your boss will be hearing about this.'

'You're right,' answered Haliday, getting up. 'He will be.'

After the three men had left, Dominic paced the room, his mind whirling. He hadn't seen that line of questioning coming. Why hadn't Simon told him they were going to interview him? And why the hell hadn't he told Dominic about the report?

He was furious. He would not stop until he found Ashleigh and made her pay for bringing him to the attention of the police.

In a violent burst, he ran at the door, and hip-and-shouldered it, before punching it three or four times. Dominic let out a roar as he felt a bone shatter.

A moment later, the three men were standing in front of the broken door, staring at him.

'Bit of an anger management problem there, Mr Alberto?' asked Potts. 'Wouldn't like to see a woman on the end of that, would you, Haliday?'

'Certainly not. Never know what might happen. He might even hurt a lady so badly that she dies.'

Dominic said nothing and nursed his hand.

'Maybe you should come along with us to the hospital and have that hand looked at. Wouldn't want you to accuse us of police brutality, would we?'

There didn't seem to be any other option, so he went with them.

ℙ

At the hospital, his hand was X-rayed and he was cleared of any breakage. The nurse put some disinfectant on the cut and bandaged his hand. 'That's really quite deep and nasty, Dominic,' she said. 'Make sure you come back tomorrow, to have the dressing changed.'

Dominic jumped down from the table he was sitting on, avoiding the eyes of the detectives, who were both leaning against the wall, watching him.

'Thanks very much for your help.' He could see the nurse wanted to ask him what had happened and why the police were there. He picked up his coat and walked out, the policemen following him. He couldn't wait to be away from the bright lights that made him feel like he was under extra scrutiny.

Out in the corridor, his doctor friend stopped him. 'Ah, Dominic,' he said and offered his hand, withdrawing it quickly when he saw that Dominic's was bandaged. 'I've been meaning to call and thank you for the very generous donation you made to the mental health facility of this hospital. We appreciate it.'

'You're welcome,' Dominic responded. He had to get out of here. 'If you'll excuse me?'

As he was about to get into the car, Haliday said, 'Seems you're the big man around here.'

Dominic didn't answer.

℘

He had just poured his first drink after getting home when he received a text message from Simon: *Have been put on leave pending an internal investigation.'*

Chapter 13

Eliza made sure Heidi was busy with her sums before she turned her attention to Tilly.

'Now, Tilly, we need to organise this interview with your nana for this family history project, while they're here at the park.'

'They're going soon,' Tilly said. 'They didn't say when, but in the next few days.'

Eliza nodded. 'Yep, your nana told me this morning. It must have been nice to have them here for a few days?'

'They don't seem to like us much. We can't go into their caravan or anything like that. Dad says they're very private.'

'Some people are like that. Now, have you seen a family tree before?'

Tilly shook her head. 'It's like a tree?' she guessed.

'Sort of. It's lots of lines, all linked together. It has lots of branches, and each member of the family is on a branch each, and their kids, or the people they marry, are added to it. Here,

I'll show you.' She took a piece of paper and started drawing a diagram. 'So, we put your nana at the top and draw a line to her husband. Do you know what his name is?'

'Pop.'

Eliza suppressed a smile. 'What about his first name? Like Tilly, or mine, Eliza.'

'Oh! I don't know.'

'Okay, we'll just put "Nana" and "Pop" in the top line. Now, see? I'm drawing a line down and adding your mum's name here. Then I put an "m", which means married, and I write your dad's name.'

'She's not part of the tree,' Tilly said. 'She left us, so she doesn't get to be on here.'

Eliza paused, wondering how to answer. Her heart ached for these two girls. She knew exactly how they felt—after all, her mother hadn't wanted her either, and her foster parents hadn't cared about her.

'See, the thing is, Tilly, your mum gave birth to you. You wouldn't be here if it wasn't for her, so we do have to pop her in here. Maybe we could write her name a little smaller or something?'

Tilly shook her head, a stubborn look crossing her little face.

Eliza tried again. 'I tell you what. You and I know that you don't want your mum's name on here, and Heidi knows that too, but to make this worksheet and project the best it can be, you put her on and not take any notice of her being on there, okay? All the important people know that you don't want her on there.'

Tilly gazed out the window, her face awash with emotion,

and Eliza had to make a big effort not to give her charge a hug. That wasn't the done thing these days.

Instead, she looked at the clouds scurrying across the blue sky, and at the leaves of the gum trees along the creek streaming out in the wind. She pulled her jacket around her a little more. But even though it was cold, she wouldn't mind being outside. It would clear her head and maybe help her find the words to comfort Tilly.

'Okay.' The little girl finally tore her eyes away from the window. 'But it has to be in small letters.'

'Great idea. Okay, now we draw a line from your dad to your mum, and another downwards.' Eliza demonstrated, before writing the sisters' names. 'This is what's called a family tree.'

Tilly regarded it. 'Doesn't look much like a tree.'

'I guess it doesn't. Not like the trees you're used to.' Eliza then read out some of the questions in the workbook. 'We need to find out when everyone was born—that will help you know how old everyone is now. Then you ask about their occupation—the job they did.'

'Eliza, I need help,' said Heidi, looking up from her work.

'Sure.' She turned her attention to Heidi and worked through a couple of problems with her, and before they knew it, it was time for a break.

Eliza poured the girls and herself a drink each, and put butter and Vegemite on Sao biscuits.

'What was your mum's name, Eliza?' asked Tilly.

Unease shot through her so she took a sip of her drink to stall for a moment.

'I don't know,' she answered.

'Why not?' Heidi asked, looking interested.

'I never knew my mum.'

'So, who looked after you? Your dad, like ours does?'

Oh, this is dangerous territory, thought Eliza. 'No, I didn't know my dad either.' She changed the subject, with the first thing that came into her head. 'Now, I've heard about some ruins not far from here. The Kanyaka ruins. Do you know where they are?'

'Oh yeah,' Heidi said, getting off her chair and walking over to the large map that Chris had hung on the wall. She put her finger on it. 'Follow the road that goes to Quorn—you never actually get there,' she said, tracing the thin line downward. 'Go through Hawker, and a bit further on, and there you are.' She stabbed at a marking on the map.

'It's really not that far from here, is it?' Eliza thought for a while. 'Do you know why the town was abandoned?'

'Nah,' said Tilly. 'Maybe it got too hot.'

'Or too dry,' Heidi added.

'I've heard there were seventy families living there at one time. Can you imagine? Blinman hasn't even got seventy people living here, let alone seventy families!'

'I bet they ran out of water,' Heidi answered. 'Dad said people didn't know how to store things the way we do today.'

'They could have,' Eliza agreed. 'I tell you what. If it's okay with your dad, let's go for a drive out there tomorrow. It's good to know the history of where you live. Are you both in?'

After a chorus of 'Yes!', Eliza thought it was best to finish the school day on a high note, so she suggested they play a game of Twister.

Eliza drove out of the park, stopping briefly to say goodbye to Chris and wave to Jane and Mark, the girls' grandparents.

She knew exactly what Tilly had meant when she'd talked about her grandparents not being 'kid people'.

They weren't at all warm towards the girls—in fact, they were downright stand-offish. She hadn't seen either of them hug their granddaughters, or even squat down and look them in the eye as they talked to them.

She couldn't imagine what Claire must have been like—or what Chris might have seen in her. She sighed. People were just strange at times.

Eliza turned her thoughts to the excursion she had just suggested. She wanted to see something outside Blinman. On the other hand, the prospect of leaving this safe area made her extremely apprehensive.

☙

By the time the next day arrived, the wind had blown itself out and the sun was shining. It wasn't warm by any stretch of the imagination, but it was more pleasant than it had been.

Eliza pulled up in the dual cab and the girls came running out.

'Eliza, guess what?' the words tumbled out of Heidi's mouth.

'I don't know, but it must be exciting!'

'Remember the goanna's nest we showed you? The eggs are *gone*!'

'What? Where have they gone? Do you mean they've hatched?'

'No, silly, a fox must have got them. I went down there last night to check and they weren't there.'

'That's terrible!'

'It's life,' Tilly said as she came to stand alongside Eliza.

100

'Well, it is,' Eliza had to agree, 'but doesn't it make you sad? After all, you've been watching those eggs for a few weeks now.'

Heidi shrugged. 'It happens. Dad says it's nature.'

'It mightn't have been a fox,' Tilly said. 'It coulda been a wedge-tailed eagle, or a crow.'

Heidi paused, thinking. 'You're right,' she said, sounding surprised. 'It could have been. I didn't know you were that clever, Tilly.'

Eliza's eyes widened. A bubble of laughter escaped her but it sounded like a snort.

'Did you just *snort*?' Heidi asked incredulously.

'I may have,' Eliza agreed. 'Just a little bit. Now, are you two ready?' Just then, the door slammed behind Chris, who was carrying two small eskies and a water bottle.

'Lunch for two,' he said, putting them in the back. 'What time do you think you'll be back?'

Eliza glanced at her watch. 'Maybe three-ish. Might be a bit later. How long will it take to get there?'

They talked distances and then Chris handed over a book. 'Here's a bit of history on the places along the way, and this,' he handed over some sheets of paper, 'is a bit of info on the homestead itself.'

'Brilliant, thanks. The satellite internet was so slow last night, I couldn't download anything. I was going to do it when I got to Hawker.'

Chris tapped the information pack. 'It's all there.'

'Righto—in the car, you two,' commanded Eliza. 'Let's get going.'

'Try not to have an accident with my kids in the car,' Chris said, as he tapped the roof of the ute and waved them goodbye.

'I'll do my best.'

'Bye, Dad.'

'See you, Dad.'

On the way down, they played I Spy and numberplate bingo. Eliza stopped at Hawker and bought them each an ice-cream.

A couple of hours later, they arrived at the Wilson cemetery and got out.

Eliza shivered, even though the sun was shining. The cemetery was on a wide open plain between two sets of ranges and clearly hadn't been tended in many years.

The wind had picked up and it whistled around the headstones, making a strange moaning sound.

The girls had tumbled out of the car, pleased to be free, but they froze when they sensed the eerie atmosphere.

'I don't like this place,' Tilly said, moving alongside Eliza and slipping her hand into hers. 'It's scary.'

'It's only the wind that makes it scary,' Eliza said calmly. 'It makes horrible, creepy noises, but if it wasn't windy, there wouldn't be any noise except for the crows and magpies. I expect you'd be able to hear sheep. See, there's some over there at the bottom of that hill.' She pointed to a mob grazing. 'I'm sure there's a galah or two around to make a bit of noise too!' She stopped and looked at Heidi and Tilly. 'I bet you could hear the traffic from the road. Look, see—there's a truck.'

Tilly seemed unconvinced.

'Come on, Tilly,' her sister said impatiently and walked through the gate. 'Anyway, whoever's in here is dead and has been forever, so they can't hurt you.'

Even after reassuring the girls about the graveyard, Eliza had to admit to herself that she felt unnerved, especially after reading a sign saying there were people buried in unmarked graves. She wouldn't know if she were treading on a spot where people had stood a hundred years ago, burying a loved one.

She imagined the men, dressed in trousers with braces, and dirty shirts. The women would have worn black skirts and white shirts, perhaps with aprons. Hats would have been a must.

The burning sun would have shone down on the cracked earth where the men laboured to dig holes deep enough to bury the dead.

Maybe a horse-drawn carriage carried a plain wooden box, or maybe there was a handcrafted coffin carried by four or six men. It would have all depended on the deceased's family's money and standing in the community.

Eliza explained all this to the girls as they wandered around the graveyard, reading the engravings on the stones.

'There's so many rabbit holes,' Heidi said. 'Some of them are so deep, I wonder if you can see the coffins.' She stopped and peered down into a deep, dark one.

'I wouldn't have thought so.'

'Can we go?' Tilly asked.

'You can go and hop in the car, if you like. I just want to have a read of this sign again. Have a listen to this—it's a good example of how tough life was here back in the eighteen-hundreds.

'One family had five children die over five years and then the mum died too. Oh, look at the dates: she must have died while she was having the baby. See here? "Adelaide Frances died 1890".' Eliza checked the information Chris had given her. 'But, see here, there was a Harriet Frances born in 1890 too. I love exploring this type of family history. It's so interesting.

'And here,' she flicked over another page. 'This is a newspaper report. "*It has been so very hot these last three weeks. Two children have perished because of the heat.*"'

'That's horrible,' Heidi said, wrinkling her nose. 'Have we got any relatives in here?'

Eliza turned to the back of the book and ran her finger down the list of names of people who were buried in the Wilson cemetery.

'No, there aren't any Maynards that I can see,' she said. Her eyes flicked further down the page, to see if there were any other names that were familiar to her.

There weren't.

Chapter 14

Eliza tried to calm her racing mind as they arrived at the Kanyaka ruins.

She pulled her hat down further over her face and made sure her sunglasses were in place as she got out of the car. The car park was full of tourists towing caravans, and people were wandering about, cameras strung round their necks.

It had been easy to get complacent about her disguise while she'd been at Blinman, but now she was suddenly faced with people who could have seen her picture on the news a few months ago. They might find her face familiar. She couldn't risk it.

Along the edge of a creek were the remains of a large building and a few smaller ones. They covered such a large area that Eliza was awestruck. The chimneys towered into the sky and, although there weren't any roofs on any of the buildings, the ruins were surprisingly intact, with parts of walls having been restored. Ivy was growing up through some of the fireplaces and a lone palm tree stood outside.

'Come on, girls, let's look at the cemetery first.' She pointed to a few headstones on a flat piece of land at the base of a high hill.

'Do we have to?' Tilly asked. She hung back and looked over at the large building.

'You're such a scaredy-cat,' Heidi muttered, flouncing off down the path that led across the stony creek bed.

Eliza went to Tilly and put her hand on her shoulder. 'Honestly, there's nothing there that can hurt you. I know this is hard and a bit frightening, but it's part of your project and will help you understand something of the way people lived in the olden days.'

'Can I play in the creek while you look at it? I'll go and look at the buildings with you first, I promise.'

Eliza agreed. It was a good compromise.

As they wandered around, couples walked past and smiled while nodding hello. Both children were open and chatty with the tourists—after all, they spent most of their time in a national park, close to where people camped—but Eliza kept her distance.

'Come on, Heidi,' she called when she spotted the girl showing a woman something high in a gum tree. Looking up, she saw a bird different from any she'd seen before. She smiled to herself, realising Heidi would be giving the tourist a lecture about the bird.

Eliza waited at a distance and watched Heidi not break stride in her passionate delivery. The woman seemed impressed at her level of knowledge and asked a couple of questions.

'Come on, Heidi,' Eliza called again when she noticed her finally take a breath.

With a flick of her ponytail, Heidi ran over. 'Did you see it?'

'See what?' Eliza adjusted her sunglasses, and scanned the ruins.

'The chirruping wedgebill,' she answered in a tone suggesting Eliza was stupid not to know.

'Heidi,' Eliza said, amused, 'I don't even know what that is, so how would I have seen it?'

'It's a bird. They're really unusual here. I'll have to make sure I tell Dad about it.'

'I'm sure he'll be really interested.'

'Oh yeah! We've got to tell him whenever we see a bird or animal that's really rare. He always wants to know things like that. Then he can point tourists in the direction they were seen last.'

Tilly piped up, 'Yeah, but sometimes they go to see them and spend hours watching and they never appear.'

'That's why they're called rare. Duh.'

'Heidi, that's enough,' Eliza said sternly. She turned to Tilly. 'I guess if they're birds, they can fly to a different area.'

'Yeah, but that chirruping wedgebill will have a nest around here somewhere,' Heidi answered.

'Okay, girls, let's focus on why we're here. Have you noticed the stone wall?'

Both girls nodded.

'It was nearly forty kilometres long! Can you imagine how long that would have taken to build? And this house here . . .' she pointed to the large homestead. 'This had sixteen rooms! And later, up on the road, there was a two-storey, twenty-roomed hotel.' She shook her head incredulously. 'Wow, that's almost like a mini town.'

The three stood together and looked around. The stones that had been used were large and would have been extremely heavy to lift, and the pug to hold them together would have to have been mixed by hand.

'I can't imagine how they did this,' Eliza said quietly. 'Stables, outhouses, shearers' quarters. They had everything they could want. I bet they employed a full-time cook and maids. They would have had to grow their own food—the veggie patch would have been huge.'

Goosebumps broke out on her skin. There would have been so many stories to tell, if only these walls could speak.

ℰℕ

Eliza drove into the national park and pulled up at Chris's house. She got out and looked in wonder at the purply pink sunset reflecting off the hills. Sometimes the hills looked white, like sand dunes. Other times they were a deep blue or indigo purple. She was sure she wouldn't ever tire of that view.

Her fingers itched for her camera, but she couldn't do anything with it until she had the girls safely inside and by then the good light would be gone.

Eliza had emailed a photo of the sunset she had taken near one of the camping sites to an online competition. A towering gum was its main focus but, behind it, the evening's colours had given the tree an outline of indigo and gold.

The car door opened and Heidi appeared, rubbing her eyes, Tilly following her a few moments later.

Eliza smiled fondly at them.

Chris came out and took one look at his daughters before

saying, 'Shower time, I think.' Heading back inside, he called over his shoulder, 'Pour yourself a glass of wine.'

Eliza hoisted the eskies up and took them inside.

'I think they'll be asleep before you can feed them,' she said when Chris came into the kitchen.

'Nah, those two ferals'll be raring to go again once they've had a shower. Especially if they slept on the way back.'

'I reckon they would have had a good hour's worth.'

Chris nodded. 'Yep. I'll expect shouts, laughs and fights any time after they get out of the shower. Did you get yourself a drink?'

'No, I need to get back to Blinman. But thanks for the offer.' She turned to go but Chris put his hand on her arm.

She flinched.

'What's the hurry?' he asked.

'I'm tired too,' she said, hoping he hadn't noticed her reaction. 'Oh, but I did have one thing to ask.' She turned back to him. 'Do you have any more books on the ruins around here? I was fascinated by the history in the Wilson cemetery. So many deaths.'

'Yeah, there were. I tell you, it was tough country back then. People these days don't know how much easier it is, even if there is a drought.' He turned and walked out of the room.

Eliza raised her eyebrows at his retreating back as Jacob flashed into her mind. She wondered why Chris would say something like that when his own brother had struggled so badly.

Chris came back in, carrying another book. He waved it at her before handing it over.

'Thanks,' Eliza responded, flipping to the back, wanting to see if there was another register of people who had lived in the area. Details of names and dates were of great interest to her.

'Did you take the girls to Death Rock?'

'No, we were running out of time, so I said we'd go there another time. I really wanted to see the Kanyaka waterhole too.'

'There's lots of good history just around here,' Chris said as he went to the fridge and got out a beer. 'Sure you don't want a drink?'

Eliza hesitated. 'Something soft,' she said finally. She was torn between wanting to hear more about the history of the area and wanting to run out the door.

It wasn't that Chris frightened her—she was only as wary of him as she was of any bloke. And she was still sure he didn't have any thoughts beyond friendship. On the other hand, she wasn't going to do anything that could be misconstrued as a signal.

Chris handed her a lemonade and pulled a packet of sausages out of the fridge.

'There's plenty of iconic places around about.'

Eliza sat on a bar stool and opened her lemonade. 'Where?'

'There's the Hunter shearing shed. About twenty minutes' drive from here. Then there's Jacka's cave—it's said a drover spent the night there and was visited by a min min light, which spooked all the cattle and they ran over him. Killed him, of course.'

'Hell, that's tragic.'

'This country is full of suicides and other deaths. But that's the way life is out here.' Chris put the sausages into the frying pan and got out three plates. 'I'm betting I can't get you to stay for tea?'

Eliza shook her head. 'I actually have a meeting I need to get to a bit later.'

'Ah, what's Reen roped you into?'

'We're trying to raise money for the Frontier Services,' Eliza answered, and went on to tell him about her idea.

Chris listened as he set out salad and turned the sausages.

'What about using Forget-me-not Well, out on the boundary of the Caulders' and my brother's place?'

'Oh yeah, I meant to tell you I met Jacob. Hasn't he got a sad story? That's why we're raising money. It was his idea. He said the service is really short on funds at the moment.' Eliza saw a strange expression cross Chris's face. 'Did I say something wrong?' she asked.

'No. Not at all.' He turned off the gas and looked at her. 'My brother is pretty soft. Jacob was mollycoddled as a kid. He had a rocky start to life and Mum always wrapped him up in cottonwool. I'm not saying he didn't have a real problem back when things got a bit rough but I reckon he needs to toughen up a bit. And I'm pretty certain I won't be popular for saying that.'

'Oh.' Eliza tried to keep her face neutral as she felt shock pass through her.

'Look, I see it like this. If life throws you lemons, make lemonade. If it was such tough going, then maybe he should take himself out of the farming business and take up some-thing that doesn't stress him out. It's a choice thing. See where I'm going?'

'But, Chris, mental health is a different thing altogether. That's like saying: "Oh, if cancer slows you down, then change jobs."'

'Not at all. If you have cancer, you do something about it, don't you? You go to the doctor, have treatment. You do whatever's recommended. If you ignore the advice, you've got a fair idea that you won't like the outcome. Same with my brother. My parents asked him to sell the station quite a few years ago. He wouldn't. Too attached to it. But it's the cause of the stress and therefore the mental health issues.'

Eliza felt torn. *In one way, what he said was commonsense, but in another she knew it could never be that easy.*

She decided to change the subject.

'What was the well you were talking about? I'm sure I've heard Jacob mention it before.'

Chris gave her a look. 'Whiplash,' he muttered.

'What?'

'I'll get whiplash if you keep changing the subject as quick as that. There's so many stories about that well. It's like a little oasis in the middle of a dry and dusty landscape. There's a really nice little grove not far from it and I know people have been married there. There's been a couple of suicides and, I'm sure, in earlier times, probably people born there, but it's certainly got a lot of history.'

'You mentioned it was on the border of Jacob's property?'

Chris nodded. 'Mmm, and Mary and John Caulder's. Very old family friends of ours.'

Eliza felt a shiver of excitement run through her. She remembered that Caulder was the name of the people in the article.

'How awful about the suicides,' she said, trying to contain herself. 'Does anyone know why people killed themselves there?'

'Girls! Tea's ready. I don't know, I've just heard that there's spirits who are supposed to haunt the well. An old wives' tale, of course, I don't believe in shit like that, but some of the locals swear by it.'

'How tragic.' Eliza got up. 'I've really got to go,' she said. 'Can you just make sure that Tilly does that assignment with her grandmother before they leave? I won't be back before they do it, I don't think.'

A strange expression crossed Chris's face. 'They left today.'

'What? Just like that?' Eliza asked incredulously. 'Without saying goodbye to the girls?'

Chris shrugged. 'It's the way they are. Don't think about anyone except themselves. They turn up when they want to, expecting a free site, even though Claire isn't here anymore, then leave. Usually without saying goodbye. It suits me when they leave. They piss me off.'

Eliza wanted to ask about Claire, but didn't. He would tell her if he wanted to.

'So, what about Tilly's assignment?' she wondered out loud.

'I reckon she might as well go and talk to Mary and John. They're close enough to us to be her grandparents. I'll organise it so you can go out and see them.'

The girls appeared for dinner and Eliza said her goodbyes to them all, not understanding how people who had family could act like they didn't care about them, when there were people like her around, who wanted nothing but a family.

Chapter 15

Eliza raced into the pub, puffing hard. The night was so clear but so cold; there was sure to be frost in the morning.

'Sorry I'm late,' she said as she pulled up a chair at the meeting. Glancing around, she realised she knew only a few people. Smiling tentatively, she tried to hide the rush of adrenalin that ran through her when she saw opposite her one of the faces from the magazine article.

'Everybody, this is Eliza.' Reen waved a hand in her direction. 'She was the one who had the idea of the selfie trail.'

There was a general murmur of welcome. Reen went on to introduce everyone at the table.

'I'm not going to remember everyone's names,' Eliza admitted. 'Hope you don't mind if I ask you again if I forget?'

'You ask as many times as you need, dear,' answered Mary Caulder. Her voice had a slight English accent and, like so many of the older people in the area Eliza had met, her expression indicated a sweet nature—she was just as Eliza had imagined.

'How did you come up with the idea?' asked a man whose name, she thought, was Mark Patterson. It was apparent he was a pastoralist, with his weather-beaten face and tanned skin.

Eliza shrugged. 'I remember reading about something similar at a zoo, with kids. They had to follow a trail, taking photos of the animals, not themselves, with their iPads.

'I thought we could make money by asking for a $100 entry fee plus a gold coin donation for every person in the car, at every stop. Sort of like a Rotary fine. Then, an adjudicator assesses the photos from all the places and decides who goes into the draw to win.'

As she talked, she stared into the fire, which was roaring close by. It had been her idea to do a hide and seek trail for the kids at Jindabyne.

'Well, I reckon it's a top idea,' said Jacob, leaning forward and putting his hands on his knees. 'You're the only one here without a drink. Can I get you something?'

Eliza shook her head.

'What does everyone think?' asked Julie Nadier. 'I wondered if it might be a bit too hard for some people?' Eliza had met Julie before and hadn't liked her very much. She was loud and gossipy, and Eliza tried to stay away from her as much as possible. This was a little difficult, though, as she was Reen's next-door neighbour.

Will Jameson, the local shearing contractor, shook his head. 'I think the genius of this idea is that it takes the tourists off the beaten track. Let's get them to our stations, take them to the shearing sheds, or to the top of the highest peaks. Grey nomads talk to each other, and if people get to see some really different country and sights, they'll be telling all their friends. We'll get more people through the town and that'll bring in more money.' He scratched his grey beard and Eliza thought how much like Father Christmas he looked. Those mischievous blue eyes twinkled at her, making her smile back at him.

Everyone around the table—except Julie, who pursed her lips—nodded in agreement.

'Okay, so let's talk about where the route should go,' Reen said, pulling the meeting back into order.

'Hang on a minute. Are there any other ideas?' Mary asked.

Everyone looked at each other.

There was general chitchat, then Jacob spoke up. 'When we've got all this sorted, we should put Eliza in charge. It's her baby and she'll do a really good job of it.'

'I'm happy to do the legwork,' she agreed.

'You'll have to promote it too,' Reen said. 'You know, get the media on board and do some radio interviews, that sort of thing.'

Fear shot through Eliza's stomach. 'Um . . .' she muttered.

Mark thumped the table. 'Now, here's an idea,' he said, excitement in his voice. 'Eliza is new to Blinman. She could follow the route we set up and post every day to the town's Facebook page. We'll all share the posts and it'll get out there really quickly. I hear you're an excellent photographer.'

'No!' The word shot from Eliza's mouth before she could stop it.

Everyone turned to look at her, puzzled by her outburst.

She looked down at the table and tried to slow her heart rate, which had shot up of its own accord.

'No, I'm sorry, I can't do that. I'm not a front-of-the-camera type of girl.' She paused as she tried to think of a convincing reason for this. 'I get nervous, you know? I'd be much better off in the background, doing the legwork.'

'How can you get nervous behind a camera and a computer?' asked Julie in a condescending tone. 'You're not talking to anyone.'

Reen interrupted. 'That's fine, Eliza. It's not a problem if you want to be behind the scenes. I do most of the media anyway.' Still, Eliza saw Reen looking at her and she knew that her friend would be asking questions very soon. 'Right, now, do we have anything else to discuss?'

'Bra ping-pong,' Jacob said with a wicked grin.

'I'm sorry?' Mary looked over at him, her eyes wide. 'What are you up to this time, Jacob Maynard? I know that look.'

He grinned at Mary. 'I think this'd be a fantastic extra activity for the camp cook-off. You get a wooden board and some old bras, and attach them to it. You have to make them stick out so you can hit a ball into them; basically, the aim of the game is to hit a ping-pong ball into a cup.' He sat back and crossed his arms, looking very pleased with himself.

There was a moment's silence before everyone around the table burst out laughing.

'That sounds like a ripper,' Will said. 'Actually, I'd say more but I won't while there's ladies present.'

'Good idea, young man,' Mary said quickly, winking at Jacob. 'I'm not sure my heart could take it, though.'

'I reckon that's brilliant!' Reen leaned forward and pointed at Jacob. 'You're in charge of that.'

'No problem at all,' he answered. He shot a sideways glance at Eliza. 'Don't suppose you've got any black lacy bras you could lend me, do you?'

ᘒ

'Want a cuppa before you head to bed?' Reen asked as she limped towards her house.

Eliza, wanting to avoid her questions, yawned elaborately and said, 'I don't think so, thanks. I'm knackered from taking the kids to Kanyaka today.'

Reen stopped and turned around. 'Did you enjoy the day?'

'The kids were great and the ruins were unbelievable. I can't get over how much work went into those buildings, and it would all have been done by hand. Just unreal.' She stopped and looked up towards the hills. They were bathed in moonlight, the bush casting long shadows across the rocky ground. 'And it's amazing to think about the people who used to work in that mine.' She shook her head before looking up at the sky.

'It was certainly pretty tough back then,' Reen agreed. 'All right—well, get a good night's sleep.'

Relieved, Eliza went to her room and sat on the bed, trying to work out her feelings. For so long, she'd just been thankful to be away from Dominic. But now, she realised, she was angry.

She was lying to her friends and she hated that.

Tonight, she'd felt she looked like a fool, having to react the way she did.

Eliza threw herself backward with a deep sigh, wanting to hit something. She grabbed a pillow and threw it across the room, before stamping her feet up and down on the bed.

Feeling a tear slip down her cheek, she knew she had to

do something. She grabbed her iPod, camera and tripod, and headed out into the night.

The moon was bright enough for her to walk without a torch, and she made her way to the northern end of town before turning onto a dirt road.

From her earbuds pounded 'Fight Song' by Rachel Platten. It had become her theme song, as there was plenty of fight in Eliza yet, and she wasn't going to let Dominic beat her. But sometimes she needed to be reminded of that and this was one of those nights.

She would put 'Fight Song' on repeat, feeling the strength in the lyrics fill her being, knowing she would soon feel resilient enough to take on the world again. She reminded herself that the kowtowing, browbeaten Ashleigh was long gone, and she was Eliza now.

Eliza could stand on her own two feet. She was slowly healing, in this town whose people mostly showed only care and concern for her, a stranger who had just lobbed among them for no apparent reason.

She stopped at the edge of a creek and leaned against a gum tree. The eucalyptus scent surrounded her and the crisp, gentle breeze swept over her, lifting her hair as it passed by. As the song finished, she felt goosebumps ripple over her skin and her nipples harden.

Eliza smiled. Even on the days she thought she wasn't coping, she was stronger than she'd been before and that was all that mattered. Pulling the earbuds out, she turned to face the wind.

Then she heard it. An engine. She turned and looked around her, trying to work out which direction it was coming from. Then she saw lights coming around the corner.

She moved into the scrub, before settling behind a prickly acacia bush. In the distance a fox barked. The goosebumps were back, but for a different reason. She was frightened this time.

Cars were uncommon here in the middle of the night.

The lights came closer, and Eliza could smell dust and hear gravel flicking up and catching under the car.

The moonlight reflected off the bonnet as it passed her hiding spot. It wasn't a car she recognised, so whoever was driving it wasn't from around here. She was familiar with most of the locals' cars now.

This one looked different too. There was a small satellite dish on the roof, and the back of the roof and the bullbar were covered in aerials of all different shapes and sizes.

She squinted as dust blew over the top of her, but watched the car disappear further into the darkness.

Chapter 16

As Eliza had predicted, the next morning was frosty. On the tennis court fences, icicles followed the contours of the wire, and long spikes of ice hung from the leaves of the cypress pines in the main street.

Bundled up in a beanie and gloves, Eliza spent the first hour of the morning snapping the spectacle. It had been so cold, she hadn't been able to have a shower, because the pipes, which ran along the outside of the units, were frozen. She would have to wait until she got back from Mary Caulder's place. Chris had kept his word, and organised for Tilly to speak to Mary about her family history assignment.

She glanced at her watch, picked up her backpack and headed for the door. Then she suddenly stopped and turned back to the wardrobe. She grabbed the box she kept hidden inside, opened the lid and reached in. There was the article with the photo of the now-familiar Mary Caulder. Eliza was yet to meet John but she assumed she would today. She tucked the photo into her back pocket and headed over to the shop.

Chris would be dropping Tilly and Heidi off in about ten minutes.

'It's so good of Mary to do this for Tilly,' Eliza said to Reen, trying to hide her excitement. She felt like her whole mission in coming here was about to be accomplished by this visit.

'Mary will do anything for anyone around here,' Reen answered as she chopped vegetables. 'She is grandmother to the whole community. Tilly's grandparents on Chris's side are dead. I've only met Claire's parents, Jane and Mark, once.' She stopped and put her hands on her hips. 'Now, they're a strange family. They come and visit, but never want to get involved with things that are on or be a part of the community. Usually, when locals have family turn up, they're happy to come in and have a meal at the pub, or fill in for the cricket team—that sort of thing. But Claire's family never did, even when she lived here.' She fixed Eliza with a stare. 'And, after what you've told me about the way they left before helping Tilly with that assignment—well!' she huffed. 'I mean, they're grey nomads! They don't have to be anywhere at any given time. One more day wouldn't have hurt.'

'I know,' Eliza said softly. She hadn't been there when Chris had broken the news to Tilly, but she hoped it hadn't bothered her too much. 'I didn't know both of Chris's parents are dead.'

'Yeah, they are.'

'What happened?'

'His mother, Fiona, had cancer and died when the boys were both quite young. Mary helped raise them. Well, not really raise them, but she was always on the other side of the fence if she was needed. You get what I mean? Dean did a

122

great job as a single dad, but there were times when a woman's touch was needed with the boys. Mary took over then.

'It was funny—Chris and his mother never seemed to get along, and yet she and Jacob were inseparable. I think that's caused some tension between the boys in the last few years.'

Eliza nodded, remembering what Chris had said about his brother and how harsh she'd thought it had sounded.

'What happened to their dad?'

'That was tragic. He was mustering on a horse—you know how rugged the country is around here. We think what happened is his horse tripped, or shied, something like that. Dean took a fall and, whatever happened, the horse landed on top of him.' Reen stopped talking for a minute and fiddled with her necklace. 'Everyone just hoped he died instantly because he wasn't found for a couple of days, and the horse was still on top of him, still alive. It was pretty obvious it had been thrashing around, trying to get up, but with a broken shoulder, it couldn't.'

'Bloody hell!'

'Yeah. It was a pretty awful time.'

'I don't think I can even begin to imagine. There've been some tragedies here, haven't there?' she said quietly.

'Oh yeah, we've had more than our fair share,' Reen agreed.

There was a pause and Eliza remembered the car she'd seen the previous evening. 'Oh, by the way, I saw the weirdest-looking car last night.'

Reen looked up from the onions she was chopping. 'Last night? Did you go out after the meeting?'

'I couldn't sleep, and the night was too beautiful for me not to try to take some photos,' she answered.

Reen put down her knife and leaned against the bench as

Eliza described the vehicle she'd seen. She thought she saw recognition in Reen's eyes.

'Do you know the car?' Eliza asked.

Reen started to say something but was interrupted.

'Eliza! Are you in there?' Heidi came into the shop, Chris and Tilly following.

'Yep, here I am. Ready to go?'

There was a chorus of 'Yes!'.

'Right then, we'd better get you in the car. You'll be able to tell me the way, won't you?' She had a mud map that Reen had drawn for her folded in her top pocket, but didn't think the girls needed to know that.

'Yeah, we can,' Heidi answered.

'Cool. Well then, let's hit the frog and toad.'

'The what?' Tilly's brow crinkled in puzzlement.

'Oh, that's just a funny saying. "Hit the frog and toad" means hit the road,' Eliza explained. She turned to Chris. 'Thanks for bringing them into town.'

'No problems. Cuts down the trip for you by a fair bit.'

'We'll see you later on, then.' She turned to the girls. 'Do you need to go to the loo or have a drink before we go?'

'No way! Mary will have sponge cake for us,' Heidi said, excitement in her voice. 'She knows it's our favourite, doesn't she, Tilly?'

'Yep!'

☙

The drive to Mary and John Caulder's was short in comparison with some of those Eliza had done. The girls chatted constantly throughout, their enthusiasm obvious.

'Just round this corner,' Heidi pointed. 'The ramp is right at the bottom of the creek. Gets flooded sometimes.'

'Do you get enough rain here to flood?' Eliza asked as she took her foot off the accelerator.

'Some years,' the girl answered. 'Not very often, though. Uncle Jacob talks about one year he couldn't get around Manalinga 'cause he kept getting bogged.'

Eliza turned into the driveway, crossed the cattle grid, and followed the road as it wound along a creek bed until it went up and over the bank.

In front of them was a flood plain, covered in green grass. Woolly sheep were grazing and, in the distance, Eliza could see a homestead nestled at the base of a line of hills.

She slowed down to try to take everything in, a feeling of peace coming over her. She slowed the car to a stop.

'What's wrong?' Tilly wanted to know.

'Do you mind if I take a couple of photos?' Eliza asked, grabbing her camera bag. Without waiting for an answer, she was out of the car and scanning the view for the best angle. She stood and closed her eyes, hearing crows and magpies singing. There was an occasional bleat from a lamb and then a deeper, louder one from the mother ewe in answer.

She could hear the leaves of the trees in the creek rubbing together. A prickling sensation rippled across her skin and she opened her eyes. She'd never felt like this before.

A lone galah flew overhead, crying loudly, prompting Eliza to open her eyes. She looked straight at the homestead and realised it was pulling her towards it. Finally, she understood her reaction.

It felt like home.

⌇

'Welcome, welcome,' Mary called as she came down the steps from the verandah. 'How are my girls?' she asked, holding her arms open as Heidi and Tilly ran towards her.

'Careful!' Eliza said, frightened they'd knock the older lady off her feet.

'Hello, Eliza,' Mary smiled warmly at her. 'Come on in.'

'Thanks. How are you?'

'Fine, as always,' she answered as they walked inside, one arm firmly around each of the girls.

'Did you make the sponge cake, Mary?' Tilly asked.

'Of course I did! I can't have you two coming to visit me and not have any cake!'

'Where's John?'

'He's sitting in the sunroom, waiting for his morning cup of tea.'

When Eliza entered the house, she was surprised that it was cold and dark. As they walked down the passageway, she glanced into the lounge room. The small windows let in little light and the furniture had white sheets covering it.

Further on, though, they came to the kitchen, which was warm and welcoming. A fire burned at one end and over the mantelpiece sat a line of photos—some of them black and white, others in colour.

A large kettle hung over the fire, steam escaping from its spout, and on the table was the much-talked-about sponge cake, as well as homemade biscuits and sandwiches. To Eliza, it looked like there was enough food for a month!

'Heidi, why don't you take Eliza out to the sunroom, and Tilly and I will bring out the smoko,' Mary said as she picked up a tray with a lace doily on it.

So, this is what it's like to have a grandmother, Eliza thought as she let Heidi lead the way.

Stepping into the sunroom, she saw an old man with hunched shoulders and wispy grey hair sitting in an office chair behind a huge desk. Papers covered every inch of it. On one side there was a line of bookshelves, which ran the length of the room, sun-faded spines filling the shelves, and on the other were louvred windows, letting the sun spill across the floor. The walls were covered in more photographs.

'Hi, John,' Heidi said as she went to give the man a hug.

'Ah, you're here already,' he said as she swung the chair around. He gathered the little girl in his arms. 'And who have you brought with you?' he asked.

His eyes flickered over to her.

'I'm Eliza,' she said and held out her hand to shake his.

After a moment's pause, he took her hand in his. 'Mary has told me about you.' He seemed to be gathering himself before saying, 'It's nice to meet you, Eliza. Where are you from?'

She opened her mouth to give a well-rehearsed answer, but stopped as a rattling of tea cups sounded behind her.

'Who needs a cup of tea?' Mary asked, entering the room.

Eliza saw Mary glance at John. Mary's eyes shut very briefly and an acknowledgement seemed to pass between the two of them.

She was bubbling with questions but couldn't say anything in front of the kids. Did they recognise her? Why did she feel at home here?

'I'd love one,' she answered at last.

John cleared his throat and turned to Mary. 'Well then, dear, you'd better play Mother,' he said, hoisting Tilly onto his lap. 'Now, little lady, I need to hear all about this family history project you have going on. Which teacher asked you to do this?'

Eliza let the conversation flow around her, but her eyes were constantly moving. She looked at the photographs to see if there was anyone she recognised, but they were too far away.

She searched Mary's face for similarities to her own and couldn't see any. Then she tried the same thing with John's face. She watched as he laughed and talked with the girls.

There was a moment when he glanced over at her, catching her eye, and something like recognition flashed through her, but it was so fleeting she could have imagined it.

Or else she was looking for something that wasn't there at all.

Chapter 17

'So, Eliza, what's brought you to Blinman?' Mary asked.

The two women stood at the doorway of the sunroom and watched John dinkying the two girls on his motorbike. He'd offered to take them up to the top of the hill behind the house and show them the Sturt's desert peas that were flowering.

Eliza had wanted to go too—she hadn't yet seen the flower—but it was too good an opportunity to talk to Mary by herself to pass up.

'I had an accident coming up here,' she answered, 'and I totalled my car. While I was waiting for it to be fixed, I fell in love with the place. I enjoyed talking to Reen and I really do think this countryside is incredible. Plus, I'm paying off the repairs to my car.'

'I see. Come and have a look around outside.' Mary opened the door and indicated she should walk through. 'I spend a lot of time in my garden these days. It's a change from the dusty sheep yards.'

'Who does the work for you now?' Eliza asked, following the rocky path towards a large garden.

'We lease it to Jacob,' Mary answered. 'A couple of years ago, I was hit by a wether in the sheep yards and broke my wrist. Then, a couple of months after that, John fell off his motorbike and cracked some ribs. We thought it was time to give someone younger a bit of a go. We still have a few sheep in the paddock closest to the house and that's enough for us.'

Eliza felt the smooth leaf of a locust tree that was towering over the back fence. 'Um, I don't mean to be rude,' she said, 'but are the girls safe with him on the motorbike? It's just I'm in charge of them and I'd hate for something to happen—'

'He'll be fine,' Mary interrupted her. 'John only goes really slow these days and he's been dinkying those girls since they were born.' She smiled in the direction the motorbike had gone, looking nostalgic.

Eliza still felt uneasy. How the hell would she explain it to Chris if there was an accident? She tried to let it slide.

'I detect a slight English accent, Mary. Are you originally from England?'

'Yes, dear. John and I came out as Ten Pound Poms. We came up here to work—what an experience that was. I'd never known heat or flies or dust like it. I cried for months. All I wanted to do was get on another boat and go home, but I couldn't, and I wasn't raised to quit things. After the shock wore off, I rolled up my sleeves and made the best of what we had. I wouldn't live anywhere else now. They'll have to carry me off here in a box.'

'The flies have certainly been an experience,' Eliza agreed. 'They're nothing like this where I come from.'

'And where do you come from, dear?'

'I was leaving New South Wales when I turned up here.' She didn't elaborate.

As they wandered around the garden, Eliza exclaimed over the vivid geraniums and lavenders that were blooming. Mary told her she had planted the roses that were beginning to bud up many years ago.

Outside the fence were the pepper trees that Eliza had noticed everywhere, along with a large palm tree.

'How do you keep everything so beautiful? Surely the heat knocks the plants around.'

'Oh yes, that certainly happens at times,' Mary concurred. 'I can remember summers when the heat was so intense, babies and the elderly died because of it. We're lucky here, though, Eliza.' She pushed open the wire gate and it squeaked loudly on its hinges. 'Let's head up to the woolshed.' She pointed the way. As they walked over stony ground, Mary continued to tell her story.

'We have underground water and that's the only reason anything survives. We need the rain to bring the feed for the animals but, more importantly, we need water.'

'Did you and John come up here all by yourselves?' Eliza asked.

An indecipherable look crossed Mary's face. 'No,' she said softly. 'We came out with another couple. We thought it was going to be the adventure of a lifetime. We all wanted new challenges and experiences, and that was certainly what we got.

'Now, have you seen a shearing shed before?' she said, clearly changing the subject.

Eliza understood that was the end of the conversation, and even though she had many more questions, she listened while the old lady talked of blade shearing in the early nineteen-fifties, and told tall tales of loud and boisterous shearers, cricket matches on dusty pitches, and tennis matches that turned into sing-a-longs around the piano.

ॐ

Once they were back in the house, Mary poured more tea and Eliza asked if she could use the toilet.

On the way back from the bathroom, she stopped and looked at some of the photos on the walls. One of them showed Mary and another woman standing with John and another man, in tennis outfits. All four of them held racquets diagonally across each other.

The next one showed a much younger John, holding a cricket ball high above his head. In another were a couple of young girls, both dressed in tennis whites, and off to the side was one featuring the same two girls with a birthday cake in front of them. Their eyes were sparkling as they looked at the candles.

There were another four photos showing John and Mary and other couples in sporting outfits. In every one of them, they were smiling broadly and holding some type of trophy.

'Oh, I see you've found the brag wall,' said Mary, appearing alongside her.

'Yeah, it looks like you guys were pretty keen on sport. Had you women beaten the blokes in this one?' She pointed to the first photo she'd seen.

'Unfortunately, they were just a little too strong for Clara and me. Still, sport is huge in country areas. It's almost like the fabric that holds us all together in the tough times. Do you play anything? Our tennis team is always looking for new players.'

'I haven't played since school. I'll sign up when the season comes around. You don't still play, do you?'

'I'm a bit slow around the court, but I do have a hit now and then. Nothing competitive anymore, I'm afraid. By golly, I used to love a good final!' Mary's face lit up. 'Now, I'm sure it was 1958, and Clara and I were the defending champions. Copley—a little town just north of here—had another couple of girls who were very good, but we weren't going to let them beat us. We ended up going right to the wire. We had tiebreakers every game! In the end we won but it was a marathon. Four hours and thirty minutes and, let me tell you, dear, we were a mess at the end of it because it had been a fairly warm day. It was worth it, though.'

'And these two girls?' Eliza asked. 'They're so cute!'

'That's our daughters, Karen and Roseanna.' She looked fondly at the photo. 'Such beautiful girls.' She sighed. 'I wished they'd stayed closer.' She turned and started down the hallway. 'I'm sorry, but talking about them makes me sad. I miss them, you see. Come back into the sunroom. I like sitting in there. I can look at the garden.'

Eliza followed her, wanting to ask more questions. As she did so, she put a hand in her back pocket and pulled out the article she'd brought with her.

Waiting until they were both comfortable, she took a deep breath and held it out. 'I saw this in the R.M. Williams *OUTBACK* magazine. I know it's a year or so old, but I was immediately drawn to it. I'm not sure why. Would you have any ideas?'

Mary reached out and took the page. 'Oh, I remember that. Such a lovely young girl from Port Augusta came up to do the interview. They wanted a couple of oldies to be in the picture, and we happened to be in Blinman that day, stocking up on a few things.' She handed the page back. 'It was just by chance we were there. The story isn't about John and me, though. It's just about the township of Blinman and a bit of history.'

'Yeah, I know.' Eliza uncrossed her legs and leaned forward. 'There was just something about the photo. I never under-stood if it was the photo of you two or the other pics of the countryside that attracted me to the area.'

Mary was silent as she looked at Eliza, her eyes flicking over her face. 'The country around here is certainly beautiful,' she agreed after a while. 'I can't think it would have been John and me who attracted your attention. I don't think I've ever come across you before, have I?'

'I don't think so,' Eliza answered, feeling terribly stupid. 'Look, it doesn't matter. It was just a funny feeling I had.'

Mary sat back in her chair. 'Why don't you tell me a little about yourself? I've told you quite a lot about us.' She linked her fingers together and put them on her knee as she looked at Eliza expectantly.

'There's not really very much to tell.' Eliza was flustered. She'd felt comfortable with this woman until now.

'Oh, don't be silly! Everyone has a story. Where were you born?'

Eliza looked down. She felt the tell-tale heat of tears behind her eyes. That was not what she wanted. She started to sing 'Fight Song' silently and imagined strength radiating from her core. Not her heart, not her head, but her core, deep within her.

'Oh, my dear, I've upset you,' Mary said softly, leaning forward to put her hand on Eliza's knee. 'I'm so terribly sorry. I didn't mean to do that.'

Eliza shook her head. 'No, it's fine. I just don't know much of my history, that's why there isn't much to tell.' In one way, she wanted to tell Mary everything. To let it gush out of her and leave her, but she knew she couldn't. She would be risking everything she'd fought so hard for. Her freedom, her independence, her ability to control her own life and be happy. So she pressed her lips together, swallowed and looked up.

'I was living in New South Wales before I headed over here. Teaching at a school there. I really felt like a change, so I sold everything and left. I wanted to travel, to see Australia. So that was what I did.'

'And your family?'

'I don't have any.'

There was a pause, before Mary offered a quiet, 'I'm sorry.'

Eliza, wanting to lighten the atmosphere, smiled. 'So, I'm off on a great adventure, but I seemed to have got stuck in Blinman!'

'I don't think that's such a bad place to get stuck,' Mary answered with a smile. 'We like taking people under our wings here and that's just what we're going to do with you, my girl. We'll be your family.'

Chapter 18

Dave reread the intelligence report that he'd printed off earlier that day.

It was the second lot of information he'd received in about two weeks. The first time he'd been told animal trafficking could be going on, he'd driven up to the Flinders Ranges National Park, just to have a bit of a look around. It had been a while since he'd been up there and he needed to reacquaint himself with it. To hide what he was doing, he'd taken Kim with him, knowing they would be able to catch up with Reen during their trip.

'*We were camped in the Flinders Ranges National Park, and one evening, I was getting tea ready when I heard a conversation that I found very strange,*' Dave read. '*There were three people, two men and a woman. The conversation went something like this*:

'So, can you get them out tomorrow?'
'We'll leave tonight. Have they been packed properly?'

'What do you think I am? Of course they have.'

This man sounded very annoyed.

'Okay, we were just checking. We lost so many Flinders Rangers worm-lizards last time, we didn't get paid.'

'That wasn't my fault.'

'Have you got the equipment organised yet?'

'Yep, that's all done.'

'We need as many eggs as we can get.'

'I'm on the lookout.'

I didn't hear too much after that, as they moved away. I went out of my caravan to have a little look around, but I couldn't see anyone or hear anything. I went straight to my husband and told him what I'd heard, because we'd seen something on the news about animal trafficking recently. We decided it needed to be reported.

Dave put down the report and leaned back in his chair, thinking. It was a hearsay report—they hadn't actually seen anything, just heard it.

He'd never had to investigate anything like this before.

Glancing through the first report he'd received, he tried to see how it all fitted together. The original account had come from the New South Wales Stock Squad. There was nothing concrete in it but the word around a few country pubs near the New South Wales and South Australian borders was that a group of people was trafficking animals and reptiles from the northern Flinders Ranges area, and officers should keep an eye out for anything suspicious.

The something suspicious was this statement from Melissa and Ian Hooper, particularly the mention of the lizards and not getting paid for them. Dave thought it was worth going on another trip and having a chat with the ranger up there.

Stuffing his mobile in his pocket, he went outside and opened up the back doors of his four-wheel drive. Pulling out the trays in the back, he methodically went through the equipment, checked the spare tyre and generally made sure everything was in order for a trip.

'Hey there, you gorgeous creature,' said Kim from behind him, putting her arms around his waist and laying a kiss on his neck.

A smile broke across his face and, not for the first time, he thought how lucky he'd been to meet Kim again while investigating her niece after a money theft at the Torrica rodeo the previous year. He'd been lucky that Milly had been innocent and that Kim hadn't been angry about the investigation.

'Hey back,' he answered and turned so he could kiss her.

'What are you up to?'

'Reckon I'm going to head back up Blinman way.'

Kim stepped back and leaned against the side of the car while Dave continued his check. 'Ah.' She paused before asking, 'When are you heading off?'

'First thing in the morning, I reckon.'

'I'll have time to cook up a few yummy things for you, then.'

'Sweetheart, you know you don't have to do that,' Dave said as he opened the forensic kit and rifled through the contents.

'I know, but I like to.'

Dave gave her a gentle look. He'd never met anyone who had understood him so well or touched him so deeply. He would swear that she knew what he was thinking before he said it out loud. 'Have I told you today that I love you?' he asked.

Kim gave a grin, cocking her head to the side. Her long, curly hair tumbled over her ample breasts and Dave felt his heart start to beat faster.

'You might have told me but you haven't shown me,' she answered coyly.

He put down the kit and, with one swift movement, cupped her face with his hands and kissed her. 'How remiss of me,' he murmured. 'I'd better fix that.'

৩

When Dave arrived, the camping sites at the national park were full again and people were sitting in deckchairs outside their vans. The smell of cooking permeated the air and Dave could see a couple of crows sitting on a rubbish bin, fossicking through it, looking for something to eat.

He drove over to the ranger's house and after checking to see if the ute was in the garage, got out and knocked on the door.

'Hang on,' called a female voice.

Dave waited on the verandah until the door opened and Eliza stood there.

'Oh, hi, Eliza. Sorry, I didn't expect you. I was looking for Chris.'

Eliza looked uncomfortable before glancing over her shoulder. 'He's not here at the moment. I'm not sure when he'll be back.'

'Righto. Do you know where he is?'

She shook her head.

'No worries. I'll see if I can get hold of him.' He turned to leave, then stopped. 'How are you settling in?'

'Fine.'

'That's good. I'll catch you later.'

'Bye.'

Dave went back to his car, his mind whirling. He was sure there was more to Eliza than met the eye. He was also pretty sure he knew what it was, but he needed to talk to her alone before he did anything else. Looking back at the house, he saw she was still standing in the entrance, watching him. When she saw him looking at her, she quickly disappeared.

He recalled the earlier conversation he'd had with Reen, when she'd agreed there was a lot more to Eliza than she'd let on.

There was certainly more than one reason for him to keep coming back to the national park.

He pulled the two-way mic from its holder and called Chris. There was no answer. He waited a moment before calling again, but there was still no reply.

Maybe he'd go and chat with some of the national park visitors until Chris returned.

❧

There were plenty of people around, but no one Dave spoke to in the national park had any information about smuggling native wildlife. He had put out a few feelers but not one person picked up on them.

He was back in his car, about to head off to Blinman, when a ranger's ute came into view.

Chris pulled up next to him and wound the window down.

'G'day, Dave. What brings you up here again? It's not that long since you were here last.'

'How are you, mate?' They shook hands through their respective windows. 'There's a few things I need to talk to you about. Got a couple of minutes?'

'Yeah, no problems.' They both pulled over, then got out of their vehicles and leaned against them.

'Just wondering if you've noticed anything odd while you've been out and about? Car tracks where they shouldn't be, people where they shouldn't be, that type of thing?' Dave said. 'Hurt or injured animals?'

Chris looked at him curiously. 'That sounds a bit strange. Want to tell me anything more?'

Dave shrugged. 'I really don't have anything more to tell you. I've had a bit of intel that there might be some movement in animals from up around here. I'm just doing prelim enquiry stuff at the moment.'

Chris stared at him. 'What the hell are you talking about?'

The sun slipped below the hills and immediately the air became cool.

'Smuggling native wildlife out of the park or taking it from nearby properties.'

Dave watched a look of shock cross Chris's face. Then he leaned in through the window, took out a jacket and shrugged into it.

'Holy shit,' he said.

A vehicle started up and they both looked towards it. A woman was directing her husband as he brought their caravan back further into the bay. She was making elaborate hand signals.

141

'Keep coming, keep coming!' she called out.

'Ah, bugger,' Chris said, starting to jog over to them.

'Stop!' screamed the woman just as the van hit a marker.

Dave walked over to where Chris had stopped, with his hands in his pockets.

'Fun times,' Dave remarked.

'Mate, you wouldn't believe how many marriages split up over reversing caravans,' Chris said with a small laugh. 'Anyway, another thing to fix tomorrow.' He turned to the couple. 'You blokes right?' he called.

The man, who was out of the four-wheel drive and looking at the scratch on his caravan, gave him a thumbs up without looking over, while his wife stood there, her hands over her mouth.

Dave turned as he heard children's voices, and saw Eliza climbing into a dual cab. She waved goodbye to Heidi and Tilly, and drove out, acknowledging him with a slight nod. She stopped briefly to talk to Chris, then left, a cloud of red dust hanging above the road. The air was so still, Dave knew the dust would still be there ten minutes later.

It didn't seem like he would get anything out of Chris for now, so he decided to head to Blinman. He knew he could stay the night at the park, but he had a suspicion it might be a good idea for him to leave and come back under the cover of darkness.

'Hey, Chris, I'll leave you with it. I can see you're going to be busy,' he said. 'Catch you later, maybe tomorrow.'

'Yeah, yeah—no worries. I'll have a think and see if anything stands out, hey. Cheers.'

Driving through the shroud of dust, Dave followed the

road back to Blinman. He kept looking in his side mirrors and catching glimpses of gold, pink and red shimmering off the hills.

It was interesting, he decided, that Eliza had appeared out of the blue and suddenly he was getting reports of wildlife smuggling. Maybe she wasn't avoiding him for the reason he had thought she was. Maybe she was here on business, not hiding from a different life.

He narrowed his eyes, deep in thought.

Too late, he saw the kangaroo and slammed his foot on the brakes. There was a heartbreaking *whoomp* and a thud as the roo hit the front of the car. He saw it crash to the ground and knew at once that it was dead.

Dave groaned. 'Bloody, bloody hell.' He hit the steering wheel, and got out to make sure the roo hadn't destroyed the radiator and that his car was still drivable. If it wasn't, he was stuck—at least until he could get another car.

Chapter 19

Dominic walked down the main street of Jindabyne, ignoring all the openly curious stares.

It had been like this ever since Ashleigh had disappeared. People watched or avoided him. They talked behind his back, or whispered to each other while he was in plain view.

The man who had been known as generous and kind, and only ever held in high regard, was now the centre of another type of attention and he didn't like it one bit.

He'd heard some of the rumours through members of his entourage. No one had asked him anything outright.

'Dominic?'

He kept walking.

'Dominic!' The voice was insistent and now he could hear footsteps behind him.

He checked himself, making sure he had a smile plastered on his face as he turned around.

'Ah, Lilian, how lovely to see you,' he said, groaning on

the inside. Lilian was the Esme Watson of Jindabyne.

She went to church every Sunday without fail, mainly to see who needed prayers. She loved to speculate as to why they did, and her conclusions were usually so far from the truth, they were laughable.

'How are you holding up, love?' Lilian put her hand on his wrist, holding on fast.

'I'm managing.' He tried to move his arm away gradually, but she tightened her grip even further.

'Such a terrible tragedy. I can't believe it. And not having a body.' She tut-tutted and Dominic gritted his teeth.

'I'm hoping we'll find her alive, Lilian.'

'Yes, of course. But, as I'm sure the police would have told you, the longer there's no word, the less likely it is—'

'Yes. Yes, they have,' Dominic interrupted, desperate to be gone. He wished he'd never braved the walk from his house to his office, but he'd needed the cold, crisp air to help him think straight. 'Now, if you'll excuse me.' He made to walk forward.

'I've had an idea,' Lilian said, still hanging on.

'I'm sure you have. And I've got one too,' he growled. 'Why don't you . . .' He was tensed, ready to rip his arm away. He could feel the all-too-familiar anger welling up inside him. All he wanted to do was strike out and hit this interfering old witch. He had to get away before he did something that would completely change the community's opinion of him.

'A vigil,' Lilian said quickly.

'Sorry?' He pulled away and started to walk.

Lilian ran with little steps to keep up with his large ones. 'A vigil. To remind everyone we're looking for her. We can get newspapers and magazines to cover it.'

Dominic stopped and looked down at the wrinkled face.

'Talk,' he commanded. Media attention. That was what he really wanted. Webs that would spread across Australia to wherever she was hiding. Someone who didn't know her would go to the police, and then he'd have her.

Lilian looked affronted for a moment, then started to speak quickly. 'Oh, this must be so difficult for you. No wonder you're a little . . . um . . . tense. Not to worry, love. We want to do anything we can to help you.'

'Yes?' snapped Dominic.

'Well now, whether Ashleigh is found alive or not, we need to remind people she's still missing. We know you're not a God-fearing man, Dominic, but you've done so much to help this town, we want to try and do something to help you.'

'Very kind of you, but if the police can't do anything, I'm not sure you can.'

Lilian rushed on quickly, now wringing her hands nervously. 'We thought if we held a vigil on the edge of Lake Jindabyne. Pastor Hunter would pray for Ashleigh's safe return.'

An idea started to form in Dominic's mind but he stayed silent.

'We all miss her, you know. She was so wonderful with all the children when she was teaching. Such a beautiful, smart girl.'

Too smart for her own fucking good, thought Dominic. He stared into the distance, imagining the publicity. He could stand in front of the camera, crying. Begging for her return, like he'd done before. Her photo would be flashed across screens all over Australia. He felt a hand on his wrist again and looked down blankly. *Shit*. He'd forgotten Lilian was standing there.

'What a lovely idea,' he said softly. 'But I'm really not sure I'm up to organising it, Lilian. I'm finding it all so hard.'

'That's why we thought we'd do it for you, love. All you have to do is be there on the day. We thought next Saturday, at sundown. It'll be cold, but we can all rug up, can't we? It's not like we're not used to the cold here.'

He nodded, smiling at her. 'Well, if you insist. I'd be very appreciative.'

'Don't you worry about a thing, Dominic. We'll handle everything.' With a satisfied smile, she patted his arm once more and turned away. 'Oh,' she said, looking back over her shoulder, 'would you like some more casseroles? We can have another bake-up, if you're running low.'

Dominic shuddered at the thought. The church ladies had filled his freezer with all sorts of different meals. It was like a lucky dip—you never knew what you were going to get. In his experience, though, there were only a few worth eating.

'Thank you for such a kind offer, Lilian. But I'm coping okay. After all, while I hope I don't have to, I might have to get used to looking after myself.' He strode away quickly, before she could say anything else.

ɕɔ

'You need to alert the media,' Dominic said to Simon when they met for their usual afternoon drinks.

'I haven't got any capacity for that while they have me on leave,' Simon answered, raising a Scotch to his mouth and drinking deeply. 'I still can't believe they've done that.'

'I hope you haven't implicated me in any way?'

Simon looked scornfully over at Dominic. 'As if. You'd kill me if I had.'

'At least you know that.'

They were silent, staring into the fire. Rain hurled itself against the window.

'Where do you reckon she's gone?' Simon finally asked.

'If I knew that, she'd be dead by now.'

'Do you reckon she might be trying to track down her family? After all, she took her birth certificate with her.'

'She can try, but there's nothing for her to find.'

'How do you know that?'

Dominic stared into the fire again, wondering whether to tell Simon the story. Maybe it would stop him asking questions. He decided to tell him the basics.

'When she was dropped at the church, there was a note from her mother. She said getting pregnant had been a mistake. She didn't want the child and she wasn't going to raise a child alone. She didn't want to be found now or later. And that was it. And her foster parents didn't want anything to do with her once she'd turned eighteen and they weren't getting any money to look after her. As I said before, there weren't any names on the birth certificate, just the place where she was born and her birth date. That's why I chose her, you know that. She had nowhere to go. I thought I could control her and keep her close. I fucking hate the fact I was so wrong about her. I'm not usually wrong.' He took another sip of his wine and savoured the taste, swirling it in his mouth before he swallowed.

'Is she really worth all this? I mean, mate, she's gone. Why not just let it go? If you don't make any more noise, everything'll die down. People will forget. The police will file it as an open unsolved.' He paused and looked over at Dominic. 'Unless she's really dead, she's never going to turn up.'

'What the fuck do you mean?'

Simon looked at him steadily.

The policeman knew damn well she wasn't dead because he, Dominic, would have been the one to do it. 'You know I don't work like that,' he answered sullenly.

'Yeah, I do. But is it really worth putting yourself in the cops' line of sight, with all your other business operations? Honestly, they'll turn over everything they can until they work out why Ashleigh's run. People who are happy and content don't run for no reason. The police are looking at you first and foremost.' Simon took a breath and continued, 'Are you sure your sister'll thank you for bringing the Alberto name into the media and to the attention of the police?'

'You can shut the fuck up any time you want.'

Simon held his hands up in a peace gesture. 'Just putting it out there.'

Dominic poured another red wine. There's another shipment coming next week,' he said.

Simon shifted uncomfortably in his seat.

'It's coming the usual way,' Dominic continued, staring at the floor.

Simon stayed silent but put his drink down.

'I'll let you know where you have to meet it.'

'I can't do it.'

'Yes, you can.'

'No, I can't. I'm on leave.'

'You always do it.'

'I've never been made to go on leave before. They're going to be watching me like a hawk, Dom. I can't do it.'

'Can't or won't?'

'Jesus, Dom, which bit don't you get? If you want me to keep being useful to you, I've got to get back onto the force. At the moment, they've taken my badge away and that means I can't do anything for you. I can't get in and see reports, I have no access to the computer system, and if I use my ID to get inside and look at anything, they're going to know what I'm looking at and relate it to you. The best thing I can do is stay well clear. They might even have someone tailing me, for all I know.'

'Have you been watching out?'

'Of course I bloody have,' Simon snapped. He got up and walked over to the window to stare out into the rain-filled afternoon. 'I'm not fucking stupid.'

'That's good to know. I've been wondering.'

'Get fucked.'

Simon had been the most pliable one in the whole group and now he was making noises like he wasn't going to be so cooperative anymore.

Dominic would have to keep a close eye on him.

Chapter 20

Dominic's pocket watch was burning a hole in Eliza's side as Reen drove them to Port Augusta.

She was running out of money. But she was nervous about hocking the pocket watch. For all she knew, Dominic had discovered it was missing by now—actually, she was sure he would have—and reported it to Simon, who would have notified every pawn dealer in Australia.

She had little choice, however. The cash she got from Chris was eaten up by photography expenses and food, and she really needed her car back—the repayments were killing her. She hadn't sold any photographs yet.

'Can we just call in and see if the girls are at the park?' Eliza asked Reen. 'I tried to ring earlier and see if they wanted anything, but I couldn't get hold of them.'

'Yeah, that's fine. I've got a box of things to drop off to Chris anyway,' Reen answered. 'He rang yesterday, wanting some pies and Cornish pasties to freeze for lunches.'

Eliza looked out the window and watched the now familiar sights fly by. There was more traffic on the road than she'd ever seen—caravan after caravan was snaking its way north. More wild flowers had burst into bloom in the last couple of weeks and were brightening the countryside with every colour of the rainbow. She found it amazing that flowers could grow out of what looked to be nothing but stones. Then there were the carpets of blooms that could have been planted by hand, they were so precise: lines of red Sturt desert peas; white and blue everlastings; and many other flowers, whose names she hadn't yet learned. They stretched across the flats and under the native pines, up the sides of the hills and into the valleys, and along the banks of the creeks.

What Eliza found magical about these fields of flowers was that when she sat quietly among them, taking photos, she heard every tiny thing there was to hear. The bees, which hopped from one flower to the next, loaded with pollen, before flying away to their hive. The buzz of the flies, and the thump of kangaroos hopping.

The day before, she'd been taking photos when she'd startled five kangaroos sleeping in the shade. She'd watched as they'd sat up and looked at her, their ears and noses twitching as they tried to work out if she was an enemy or not.

Quietly, she'd sat down on the grass and aimed her camera at them. They decided, in time, that she wasn't a threat and laid back down again, using their paws to swipe at their faces when the flies annoyed them.

Her zoom lens made for beautiful close-ups. In fact, one was so clear and close, you could see flies clustering in the corners of a roo's eyes. These photos could be framed for sale.

'Eliza! Where are you? You're not in my car, listening to me, that's for sure!'

Eliza reined in her thoughts and focused on Reen.

'Sorry. I was just working out what I'm going to do with my photos,' she answered. 'What did I miss?'

'Look at that.' Reen had slowed down and was looking out the window intently, pointing to a caravan parked on the side of the road. Cardboard boxes and foam eskies were piled up next to the wheels, and two chairs and a gas stove were set up underneath a nearby tree.

'What are they doing?'

'Probably having a cuppa and repacking the caravan. But it's weird. I don't know any caravaners who travel with more than they need. Those boxes wouldn't fit into any caravan cupboards or under the bed.'

'Did you want to stop?' asked Eliza. 'To make sure they're okay?'

Reen hesitated. 'No,' she finally answered. 'If they wanted help, they would have waved us down.'

Eliza noticed her friend kept her eyes firmly on the rear-vision mirror until the couple and their caravan were out of sight.

ↄ

She had left Reen to follow up on some sponsors for the cook-off before her doctor's appointment. Eliza was going to make the most of her time alone to find a pawn shop.

A bell tinkled above her head as she walked into a dingy shop in the Port Augusta mall. Looking around, she saw all types of items that people had sold to make ends meet. She wondered briefly what stories were behind them—was the diamond engagement ring on display in the middle of the jewellery from a broken engagement? Or were the collectable coins sold because a woman couldn't buy food for her children? Surely there would be happy stories too—maybe the whitegoods and tools down the back had been sold due to an upgrade.

Eliza forced her mind back to the matter at hand.

Behind the counter sat a man whose glasses had slid down his nose. He was reading a magazine and had looked up briefly as she'd walked in.

'Can I help you at all?' he asked.

Eliza tried to fight the nervous feeling in her stomach. If she wanted to live, she needed to sell this watch.

'Um, yeah.' She walked over to the counter and placed the pocket watch in front of the man. 'I'd like to sell this, please.'

Without a word, the man picked it up and turned it over, looking at it carefully. He picked up a loupe and inspected it even more closely.

'Nice piece you've got here,' he finally said as he put it down and looked up at her. 'Where did you get it from?'

Eliza froze, then quickly reached for it. 'It was my grandfather's.'

'Any reason you want to sell it?'

Giving a sharp laugh, Eliza said, 'Oh, the same reason anyone sells anything—I need the money.'

'Family heirloom?'

'Something like that.'

'Hmm. I can give you three thousand.' The man held his hand out for the watch again, but Eliza continued to hold it.

'I was hoping for more.'

'You might have been, lady, but you won't get it from me. You can try in Adelaide or somewhere, but that's my offer.'

'Three thousand five hundred?' Eliza asked hopefully.

'Three thousand two hundred.'

'Please?'

'I'm not here to give you charity. Three thousand, two hundred, and that's my offer.'

'I'll take it.'

'Fill this in, please.' He pushed over a form and Eliza picked up a pen. Looking down, she paused, wondering what name to give.

'I need to see some ID too.'

That clinched it. She pulled out her old driver's licence, then filled in the details for Ashleigh Alberto, not Eliza Norwood.

The man looked at the picture on the licence, then back up at her, then down again.

'I've lost a bit of weight,' she blabbed.

'Dyed your hair too,' he commented and put her licence on the photocopier before Eliza could stop him.

When she walked out of the shop, her heart was beating fast. She could only hope that Dominic hadn't reported the pocket watch missing.

⁘

Eliza pushed a trolley with a dodgy wheel up and down the aisles of a Port Augusta supermarket, adding the items on Reen's list to it. Her friend had texted to say she was still waiting at the doctor's, so Eliza had offered to do the shopping.

Her heart was still beating way too fast. Maybe she should change her hair colour again? Or do something really radical and get contact lenses that change the colour of her eyes? *God, what to do?* What if Dominic worked out where she was and came looking for her?

Her mind whirled with possibilities as she packed the shopping in the car and found a public toilet. She looked at herself in the mirror and got out her old driver's licence.

Eliza had almost forgotten what she'd looked like before she left Jindabyne. Now she could see that her disguise wasn't as complete as she'd thought. And her hair was shaggy, as she'd been trimming it with nail scissors—maybe it was time to get a properly styled cut.

Once she'd washed her hands, she pulled the door open to leave and almost ran into a woman standing outside.

'I'm sorry to bother you,' Eliza said. 'Can you tell me if there's a hairdresser where I won't need an appointment?'

∾

'Reen! Over here!' Eliza called out to her friend, who was walking across the road.

She saw Reen look over at her and glance away, before doing a double-take. 'Eliza? Good God, what've you done to yourself? I didn't recognise you!' She made a beeline to her.

'Just thought I'd have a bit of a change,' Eliza said and spun around, showing off her new hairstyle: black, with purple streaks through it. 'I love it! Hasn't it given me a whole new look?'

'You can say that again.' Reen took hold of Eliza's hand and spun her around again. 'Wow,' she finally said. 'Just wow.'

'I've done the shopping and it's all packed in the car. How did you get on with the doctor? Did you get all your medication organised?'

'Oh, fine. No problems there. Just had to wait an age at the doctor's, and then he wanted to do X-rays, so there was another wait at the hospital but, then again, that's not new either.' Reen gave a dismissive wave.

'I'm starving. Have we got time to get something to eat or do you need to get going?'

'Let's get takeaway and head off. I don't want to be dodging roos on the way home.'

'Sure thing. Let's go, then. I'll bring the car to you, so you don't have to walk.' She bounced off down the street, enjoying the feel of her new hair bouncing on her shoulders.

Ten minutes later, they were on their way back to Blinman.

Reen pointed to the ranges they were following before starting through Horrocks Pass. 'When I was a kid, my mum used to tell me that part of the range was a sleeping elephant.'

Eliza looked at where she was pointing and laughed, before turning back to the road. 'Oh yeah, I can see that! And she looks like she's got a baby sleeping next to her.'

'Yeah, she does.' Reen turned to Eliza, suddenly serious. 'That's a pretty huge change you've just made, Eliza. I'm convinced you're not doing anything illegal, but I'm pretty sure you're running from someone. Someone you're really frightened of. I've seen the way you react when anyone comes into the shop and calls out when you hadn't realised they were there. I've seen the way you jump when someone puts a hand on your shoulder. I've seen the way certain vehicles make you freeze.

'I'm not sure of your story and if you don't want to tell me, that's okay. I want to help you. I want to make sure you're okay. Because, sweetheart, if I'm close to the truth in any of this, you've got to know I'll do everything to make things better.'

Eliza drew in a quick breath, wrestling with her emotions. She wanted to tell someone. To not have to cope with the fear and lies by herself. But could she trust Reen enough to tell her everything? How much would it change things between them?

She was aware that, after today, she might need people around who had her back.

Swallowing hard, she opened her mouth and began to talk.

Chapter 21

'Come on, I've got somewhere to take you,' Jacob said as he rushed through the front door and grabbed hold of Eliza's hand.

'What?' She reared back and tried to release herself from his grip. 'Where do you want to go?'

'It's a surprise. Can you spare her for a couple of hours, Reen? Wait—crap, what have you done to your hair?'

Reen stuck her head through the swinging doors that separated the kitchen and shop. 'Sure, but only if you bring her back in one piece. Looks good, doesn't it?'

'Well, it's different, that's for sure.' Jacob threw an uncertain glance Eliza's way. 'Reckon you might scare the sheep with that colour.'

Self-consciously, Eliza reached up and patted her new hairstyle, which she'd pulled back into a ponytail. 'You'll get used to it,' she said.

'I don't see that I have a choice! Anyway, are you coming

or not? Pack yourself one of Gillian's famous Cornish pasties and follow me.'

Eliza laughed. It was easy to get caught up in Jacob's enthusiasm. 'Just let me grab my camera.'

When she was settled in his ute, she asked where they were going.

'I've got some sheep work happening at Manalinga and I thought you might like to see it. And there are a couple of spots I want to take you to that we might be able to use for the selfie trail.'

'Oh, cool. I checked out one of the spots when I was with the girls at the park last week. I walked up the hill at the back of the camping ground, the one that looks out back towards Blinman.'

'Yeah.' Jacob drove through a creek a bit too fast and the ute hit the bottom of it hard. Eliza bounced upwards.

'Omph! Oh!'

'Sorry. Used to driving this road by myself. I've got the steering wheel to hang on to!' Jacob looked over at her. 'Did you have the broken spring in that seat go up through your bum?' he asked with a wicked grin.

'Something certainly did. Bloody hell!'

'Anyway, you were saying?'

'Oh yeah—I took a steel post up to the top and banged it in while I was up there. It's got a weatherproof photo of a face on it, to indicate it's part of the trail. They'll have to have their photos taken with that to prove they've been there.'

'That's sounds cool. Good job. You've really thrown yourself into this, haven't you?'

'It's a good cause. How are you going with the bra ping-pong?'

A disgruntled look crossed Jacob's face. 'How can I do anything when you haven't given me any of your black lacy bras?'

Eliza threw him a look. 'How do you even know I own black lacy bras?'

'Don't all women?'

She snorted. 'Not this one.'

'Damn.' Jacob looked crestfallen. 'I'll have to figure out another way to get into your bras, then.'

Widening her eyes, Eliza said: 'Don't bother. I've sworn off men.'

'Why?'

'No reason you need to know.'

'Well, that's being told.'

'I hope you've listened,' she answered, looking out of the window. 'Oh, look! What's that? Are they *goats*?'

Jacob slowed down and glanced in the direction she was pointing. Sure enough, there were black and white goats of various ages. Some were sleeping under the bushes next to the road and a few were out grazing on the hills.

'Can you stop?' Eliza asked excitedly. 'I want to take a photo.'

'They'll take off,' Jacob warned, but he came to a stop anyway.

She scrambled to get her camera out of its bag and set up a shot. By the time she had everything organised, the goats had their heads in the air and were moving, confidently, towards the top of the hill.

'Bugger,' she muttered, refocusing with the zoom. 'Nope, missed them.'

'We might see some up a bit further,' Jacob said, putting the ute back into gear and driving on.

The road was winding, with one side bordered by the mountains and the other by a sheer drop. Eliza was amazed they didn't fall off the edge.

Without warning, Jacob pulled off the road and drove on a hidden two-wheel track. A few hundred metres in, there was a windmill and a set of yards, full of sheep, on the bank of a creek. It was all surrounded by green grass and trees, and Eliza thought how wonderful it would be to work in such a gorgeous area.

To the left, there was a shearing shed, and out the front, she counted eight cars. From the road, there would have been no indication this place even existed.

'We're crutching,' Jacob said, as if by way of an introduction.

Without thinking, she threw a sly smile his way. 'I'm assuming that isn't something rude.'

A funny smile crossed Jacob's lips. 'Are you sure you aren't flirting with me?'

'In your dreams.'

He let out a loud sigh. 'One can but dream.' Opening the door, he got out and walked towards the yards. Eliza followed.

'You have to crutch every year to keep their rear ends clean,' he explained. 'The wool, when it's hot and wet, creates perfect conditions for flies to lay their eggs and hatch maggots. They love eating into the flesh of the sheep.'

'Oh my God, that is totally gross!' exclaimed Eliza.

'It's reality,' Jacob answered. 'Although mostly it's too hot for flies here, it only takes a thunderstorm dumping an inch of rain for the weather to heat up the next day and the green backs are right there.'

'Green backs?'

'They're a type of fly that lays eggs to produce maggots.'

They walked into the shed and Eliza's fingers itched to take photos.

There were four men, wearing singlets, lined up across the back of the shed, each bent over a sheep. They were holding some type of mechanical tool that was cutting the wool away from the rump.

Jacob took her elbow and moved her closer to the men, then talked over the noise. 'The blokes use what is called a handpiece and they shave—or "shear" is the right terminology—the wool around the rear end. It helps keep it clean. It doesn't always take rain to cause problems. Sometimes, when the season is good, the digestive system isn't quite used to the feed. Things can get a bit, um, green, to say the least. Flies are attracted by the smell, warmth and moisture.'

'I get what you're saying,' Eliza interjected.

Jacob nodded, then indicated a couple of women using what looked like brooms.

'The paddle sweeps the wool away, then they pick it up and put it into the bale. That's all there is to it.'

'Can I take photos?'

'If you like.'

Eliza set up her camera, thinking only about the humming of the engines and the sounds of the shed. Occasionally, a sheep would bleat, then thump its hind legs on the floor, and a shearer would mutter an explitive. She could feel the vibration of the engine coming up through the floor, making her feet tingle.

She took close-ups and wide-angle lens shots, macro shots of the wool and eyes. She wished she could capture the smell, of lanolin and sweat. Shit and ammonia. It was a beautiful odour.

As she lined up to take another photo, Jacob walked into the shot, bending down to scoop the wool away. His arm muscles were thrown into definition, and his grin was beautiful. Startled by what she saw, Eliza looked up from the camera screen and saw him gazing at her. Arranging her face into a neutral expression, she indicated she'd finished and he pointed to the door.

Out in the sunlight and fresh air, Eliza watched as a couple of men worked the sheep in the yards, using dogs.

'What are they doing?' she asked.

'Drafting. Pulling the lambs off their mums, so the mums can get crutched. There's a few straggler lambs that have missed being marked, so these guys will make sure the ones who haven't been are marked while they're in the yards this time.'

'What's "marked"?'

'When the lambs have their tails cut off, and tags put in their ears to say who owns them.'

'Why are you cutting their tails off? Does it hurt?'

The ewes ran up and down the side of the fence, trying to get through to their lambs, while the lambs jumped over each other, baaing loudly.

'The tail's another place that can get hot and humid and have shit hang off it. It's a flytrap too. When we mark, we take off a bit of the skin around the tail, which tightens the area up. The whole reason we do all of this is flies. It hurts the lamb for a moment or two, although they all get some type of pain relief, and then they're set for life. Bit like if you've got a tag of skin on somewhere that rubs, like your shorts line, you go to the doctor to have it taken off.'

'Right.' Eliza thought she understood.

The workmen shouted instructions at the dogs. One man was down the end of the race, working what looked like a small gate to divide the sheep from one another. The dogs were forcing the ewes down the race and circling to make sure none got away. To Eliza, it looked like poetry in motion.

'This is so beautiful,' she said, taking more photos.

'Beautiful?' Jacob looked at her as if she were from another planet. 'Those buggers aren't running. See how they're baulking at the end of the race? It's making it hard for Jamie, who's drafting. They're being pains in the arses.'

'Why don't you help, then?'

'I will, once I've shown you something. Come on, let me take you to Forget-me-not Well.' He pushed her in the direction of the ute and yelled over his shoulder, 'I'll be back before smoko!' One of the men gave him a thumbs up before yelling at a dog.

'What's so special about Forget-me-not Well? Chris told me a bit about it,' Eliza said once she was settled in the ute.

'There are quite a few stories about this place,' Jacob answered, 'Some are beautiful and others are quite tragic. But that's why I think it'd be great for the project—not many people know about it. Raising awareness of mental health issues, as you know, is really important to me.

'So, I'll tell you one of the stories. Clara was a local, good friends with Mary. She'd lived here for many years with her husband, Richard, working on stations around here. I don't

165

know too much about the whole history, more about what happened after Richard was killed.'

'Bloody hell, how many people have died in this area?' Eliza exclaimed. 'That's all I seem to keep hearing about—tragic stories of untimely deaths. I'm surprised there's anyone left up here.'

'That's a very good point,' Jacob answered seriously. 'It's to do with the tenacity of people who live up here. They've refused to quit or become downtrodden by events.

'And it's certainly not as bad as it was in previous generations. You've got to remember, they didn't have what we do now. We've got air conditioners that help stop the elderly or very young from dying from the temperature; we've got CB radios and other types of communication in place if someone goes out and doesn't return when they should. We're in a much better time than we were thirty years or more ago.'

He pulled the steering wheel to the left and followed a track along the edge of a hill.

Eliza looked down. 'Are you sure this is safe?' she asked in a high, tight voice.

'Perfectly. I've done it so many times, I could do it with my eyes shut.'

'Do me a favour and don't do that with me in the car!' She looked down and took a breath as an old man emu and five chicks ran down the hill.

This place was so raw. Maybe that was what had drawn her here. It wasn't the people or the land itself, but the fact it was untouched. It was pure and genuine, the things she had been looking for. There was nothing fake about it.

Jacob continued with his story. 'To cut a long story short, Richard was killed outside the pub in Blinman. No one is really sure what happened, but he was beaten to death. There was talk of a gambling debt, and the collectors going too far, but that was just gossip.

'Anyway, Clara never recovered from his death. Most of the older couples up here are joined at the hip. Take Mary and John, for instance. They've been married over fifty years and they couldn't imagine life without each other. Back then marriages rarely broke up, even if couples weren't happy; they didn't throw things away the way we do today. So Clara and Richard were very close. That's what Mary told me anyway.

'After Richard died, all Clara did was work too hard and make herself sick. She ended up a shell of her former self. Mary showed me photos of her—she was gaunt and her eyes had lost their spark. I think Richard's death killed her too; it sucked her life away.

'Forget-me-not Well was where she and Richard got married, and it was where she was found. Dead.'

Eliza put her hand over her mouth and shut her eyes. 'Did she die of a broken heart?'

'I suppose no one will ever know how she died. Suicide was suspected—I mean, a lady doesn't just sit down next to a well and die, does she?' He glanced over at her. 'But it was a few days before she was found and the middle of summer . . . if you get my meaning. Dessie buried her, and he was so cut up that he hadn't been able to be there for Clara.' He looked thoughtful. 'I always wondered if it was a little bit like the Aborigines when they point the bone at someone. Could she have wished herself dead?'

They looked at each other for a moment, Eliza trying to understand loving someone so much that death seemed preferable to life without them.

She wasn't sure she could.

'That's just horrible.' Eliza frowned. 'Well, why the bloody hell are we including it on the list? It's a sacred site of sorts.' She looked at Jacob as if he'd lost his mind.

'But don't you see?' He turned to her. 'She was grieving for her husband and didn't get over it. There weren't many services out here then. Dessie was it and he might only get here once a year. Roads weren't as good, and he had places further away to travel to. We're raising money for Frontier Services and this is the perfect place, with the perfect story behind it, to make people understand.'

Jacob pulled the ute to a halt and got out.

Eliza remained in her seat for a moment, looking around. The country was different from anything she'd seen. The plain was open. She could imagine the barrenness of the place in dry summers. An image of shimmering heat rising from the earth, and nothing but blue skies, with crows cawing overhead, flashed into her mind.

What Eliza saw now, however, was patchy green grass and bushes. Underneath it was red earth and stones. When she looked across the land, she could see a fence stretching out into the distance, and just in front of her was a structure she couldn't make sense of: cut logs of wood forming a square, as if they were bordering something. To one side of it was a grove of trees, which looked like they'd been planted, because they were in a semicircle. Chris had told her about them.

Slowly, she got out of the car and moved towards the structure. She was aware of Jacob speaking, but couldn't make out his words. All she could take in was the square of logs in front of her.

Swallowing hard, she turned to Jacob.

'What's this place?' she asked, her voice hoarse.

He answered, looking at her strangely. 'It's Forget-me-not Well.'

Chapter 22

Dave pulled up in front of the general store, hoping that only Reen was there. He was pretty sure he would get short shrift if Eliza was.

As he got out of the car and looked around, he was pleased to see a group waiting to tour the mine. Everything in the town depended on tourism, apart from the farmers patronising the pub every weekend and buying meals from the store as they were passing through.

He waved to Gillian, who was the mine tour guide as well as the Cornish pasties chef, before heading up the steps into the shop. He paused briefly, trying to get his thoughts in order, then pushed open the door, a large smile on his face.

Behind the counter, Reen looked up, smiling in return.

'Well. Aren't you a sight for sore eyes,' she said. 'Got Kim with you?'

'G'day, Reen. Not this time. How are you?'

'Going along just fine.' She went over to the coffee machine and started to make a long black, knowing that was how Dave liked his coffee.

'Better make one for yourself,' he said in a serious tone.

Reen glanced up, and got out a second cup and saucer.

They sat on the verandah, looking out across the empty road. The mine tour had left, and now the town was settled and quiet, with a few four-wheel drives and camper trucks parked in the street, awaiting their owners.

'Been busy?' Dave asked as he took a sip of coffee.

'Just starting to pick up. In the next couple of weeks, things'll get much busier. We're only three weeks out from the cook-off. You know how crazy things get around here then.'

'Madhouse,' Dave agreed. 'Eliza much help?'

'Absolutely. I don't know how I managed without her.' Reen paused. 'I know I always managed, but she seems to know when my body aches and just takes over without me asking. I love having her around.'

'That's really good,' Dave said.

A magpie flew down and started to strut around like it owned the town. A gentle breeze touched their faces and the leaves of the cypress pines swished together.

'Got some problems up this way?' Reen finally asked. 'Unusual for you to be up here so much.'

Dave took a while to answer, finally saying: 'Got some intel that doesn't make any sense. Well, there's not enough to make sense of it yet. I'll have to investigate further.'

'Oh yeah?'

'Seen anything odd around here at night?'

'At night? No. Lord, what do you think I am? I'm in bed by eight, if I can be!'

Dave gave a small smile. 'I know. It's a long shot, but I thought I'd ask. You know, anything different, people acting out of character, cars where they shouldn't be. That sort of stuff.'

'Nothing ever goes on around here, Dave,' Reen scoffed, but then her eyes widened. 'Oh yeah! Eliza came in last week and said she'd seen a vehicle—a four-wheel drive type car—with antennas all over it. She was out walking, taking photos in the dark, and it passed her. Whoever was driving couldn't have seen her because they just drove right on by. But it was enough to prick her interest. The way she described it, it sounded like one of those cars they use to track animals.'

'Where was this?'

'I'm not sure she actually said, but I'm assuming it was on the Blinman and Parachilna roads.'

'Why would she have been out there at night?' Dave asked, looking across the street.

'Because it was a nice night for taking photographs and that's what she likes to do.'

'Hmm,' Dave responded, before putting the cup to his lips again. He turned his head as a vehicle entered the town limits and pulled up at the store. 'I'll be waiting here when you've finished,' he said.

Reen raised her eyebrows at him, but didn't say anything. As people got out of the car, she shot Dave an inquisitive look before heading into the shop to serve the new customers.

Half an hour later, she was able to sit back down with him. Two coffees in hand, she headed out the front and placed one in front of him.

'Thanks.'

'You're welcome.' She leaned back in the chair and crossed her legs. 'Want to tell me what's going on?'

'Yes and no.' He sat still, knowing Reen wouldn't ask anything more until he started to talk. He reached into his back pocket and pulled out a piece of paper. He unfolded it before handing it to her. It was a photo of Ashleigh Alberto.

She took it, looked at it and handed it back, her face set.

'So you agree it's her?' he asked.

Reen raised her chin defiantly. 'I know Eliza ran away from a very unhappy marriage. If that makes her a criminal, so be it, but I don't think you should make any judgement until you've spoken to her.'

Dave nodded. 'I won't. And I sort of figured that was the case. She's got that scar on her cheek, which isn't in any of her missing persons photos. That, along with her weight loss, and hair change, made me think there was a lot more to the story than we were being told.'

'You're right. And as for that claim of mental instability, that should be put back onto the ex,' Reen snapped.

Dave nodded slightly. 'Okay, so let me put this to you. Eliza turns up, without any good reason.'

Reen opened her mouth to say something but Dave kept talking. 'Okay, other than an unhappy marriage. She gets involved in the community, starts to do good things to help everyone out, and then I get some intel that there's wildlife smuggling going on in the area. You've just told me she's been out and about, walking at night.' He took another sip of his coffee.

'Wildlife smuggling,' Reen said softly. 'Are you joking?'

'Unfortunately not.'

'And you're wanting to implicate Eliza?'

'Not necessarily. Only if she's involved. I just found it very coincidental that she appeared and then suddenly I started getting these reports. And think about this, Reen. The reports are coming from New South Wales, which is where you've just confirmed she's come from. In my line of work, coincidences are rarely just coincidences.'

'I can't see her involved in that, Dave. Yes, she's on the run from her ex—who beat her black and blue, I might add—certainly. Wildlife poaching? I think you're stretching it a bit.'

'How do you know she's not lying? After all, she's lied the whole time she's been here.'

Reen slammed her hands down on the wooden table and glared at him, her eyes steely. 'That's a bit of a stretch and you know it. She's hiding. She doesn't want to be found. If she said her name was Eliza instead of Ashleigh, so be it. If that makes her a liar, fine, but it doesn't change her personality.'

Dave glanced down at his hands and a silence stretched between them.

'Okay then,' he said finally. 'So, other than this car that, once again, Eliza told you about, you haven't seen anything out of the ordinary?'

Reen, visibly calmer, took a breath and shook her head. 'It's really been pretty boring around here for a while.'

Dave pursed his lips. 'Okay.' He paused again, thinking. 'Okay,' he said again.

'Can you tell me anything else?' Reen asked.

'Only that the animals or reptiles, eggs, or whatever they're poaching, are coming from the Flinders. There's no indication of whether it's from the park—which would be obvious because there are tracks and people coming and going all the time there—or if it's the surrounds. No one mentioned anything about having strange visitors?'

'Not that I've heard of,' said Reen, shifting in her seat as she tried to think. 'But . . .' She looked at Dave. 'I'll tell you what Eliza and I did see when we were on our way to Port Augusta a couple of days ago. There was a caravan parked on the side of the road, with all sorts of boxes and foam eskies around it. I thought it was weird at the time, but not enough to stop or give you a call.'

'How many boxes and eskies?' Dave asked as he got out his notebook.

'I couldn't be sure, but enough for me to know that they wouldn't have easily fitted into a caravan.'

'Make and model?'

'Ah, shit.' Reen thought for a moment. 'I know it was a white four-wheel drive and what I'm seeing in my mind is like an old-style Toyota Landcruiser, square front, not like the new Prados. Do you know what I mean?'

Dave nodded. 'Caravan?'

'White and big with stripes. That's as much as I can tell you. I was looking more at the boxes surrounding it, wondering what on earth had gone wrong to have to haul so much stuff out of the van.'

'That's great, thanks.' Dave looked as if he were about to get up, but Reen put her hand on his arm.

'Are you going to call Eliza in?'

Dave leaned back in his chair and exhaled. 'I should. And I should do it right away. But, like I said, I think there's more to this story than is coming across the airwaves from the New

South Wales police. There's a bit of info filtering through that the copper in Jindabyne is bent. He's on the inside circle of the ex and that in itself is concerning when I go back and read all the reports.'

Reen nodded, relief crossing her face.

'But, Reen, if I talk to her and something else—like the smuggling—comes to light, then, yeah, I'll have to turn her in. I'm sorry.'

'But you don't really think she's got anything to do with this, um, poaching?'

Dave gave her a sympathetic smile. 'I just answered that question, Reen.'

She looked out across the street. Laughter came from a young couple leaving the pub and getting into their car. They reversed out and drove past the store, flicking them both a wave as they went.

Dave knew that Reen couldn't smile back. For the first time in their friendship, he'd broken her heart.

Chapter 23

Dominic looked at the people stretched out along the lake's edge. There were hundreds, all holding candles. There were placards with 'Come home, Ashleigh!' and 'We love you, Ashleigh!' written on them.

He spotted a TV camera to one side and hid a smile. Okay, this was going better than he'd hoped. When all the money in the world couldn't get him an interview with a women's magazine, a few old church ladies could pull off a spectacle like this.

He felt a presence at his shoulder and turned slightly. Simon was standing there.

Neither man said anything, just stood shoulder to shoulder. If it had been a week ago, Dominic would have thought it was in a show of solidarity, but he sensed a change in Simon and wondered if it was a show of defiance.

'Dominic, it's good to see you,' said a soft voice from behind him.

He recognised the voice and rearranged his features before he turned around.

'Pastor Hunter,' he said in a gravelly voice. 'Thank you. For doing this . . .' He made his voice crack and looked down at the ground.

'You're welcome.' The pastor put a gentle hand on his shoulder. 'Would you like to follow me to the front?'

Dominic obeyed, feeling like he was going to a funeral. They weaved their way through the crowd and people stopped talking as they walked by. He could feel their eyes on him.

'Do you think he murdered her?'

Fighting the urge to look over to see who had whispered the question, he kept his head down and walked on.

'Mr Alberto! Mr Alberto!'

A man with a microphone rushed over to him, pushing his way through the crowd.

'Mr Alberto, do you know where your wife is?'

'Not now, sir,' Pastor Hunter held up his hand and lightly pushed the man away.

'Mr Alberto, do you know why your wife ran away? Did you do something to her?'

Anger knotted Dominic's stomach. Why was it assumed that he'd done something to her? Didn't they see he was the victim here? He'd given her a life, a family, a history. She was the one who had chosen to run away. She was the one who had made a statement by leaving her wedding rings behind and taking his most precious possession.

He ignored the small voice that reminded him he was the one who had hit her. *After all, that's what happened to people*

who don't behave the way they should. Whether it was young
children or adults, a good lashing never hurt anyone.

His grandfather had told him that after he'd finished whipping him with a leather belt.

Pastor Hunter indicated Dominic should sit in the front row, surrounded by people from community groups he'd supported in the past. He sat down next to the principal of the school. The man looked uncomfortable, as if he didn't know what to say, but he shook hands and muttered something that was meant to be comforting.

Dominic fought the urge to look around. Instead, he looked at his feet and waited, wondering if there were any police about. Would they mention Crime Stoppers tonight? He hoped so.

'Do you know which TV stations are here?' Dominic muttered to the principal. He felt the man next to him shift as he looked around.

'I can see Channel Seven and Channel Nine, but that's all.'

Dominic nodded. Hopefully, they would be enough.

'Friends,' Pastor Hunter started to speak and the crowd hushed. 'We are here to remind everyone about our dear friend and wife of Dominic, Ashleigh Alberto.'

Dominic listened as the pastor gave a rundown of Ashleigh's life. He continued: 'On the night that Ashleigh disappeared, we have no idea what went on in her mind. What she was thinking to make her do something so drastic. We wish you knew, Ashleigh, that as a community you could have come to any of us and we would have helped you. Whatever the problem was. We want you to know that, as your friends, your husband, your community, all you need to do is contact any of us and we'll help you return to your life here. Help you overcome whatever was troubling you.

'Perhaps you are wondering why I am speaking to her as if she were alive,' Pastor Hunter addressed the crowd now. 'That's because I feel sure she is. People don't take drastic steps like these and not want to live. She has done this because she couldn't think of another way. Ashleigh is out there somewhere and Dominic Alberto, her husband, the one who has borne the brunt of this horrific pain, needs to know where. We, the people of Jindabyne, need to know where she is.

'So, we plead to the rest of Australia, do you know where our Ashleigh is? Do you think you've seen a fleeting glimpse of her, or is she living quietly next door to you? Is there a person you've seen recently who looks familiar and you're not sure why? Find her, have another look. Imagine Ashleigh with shorter or different coloured hair.

'We understand she may not want to be found. Whatever has happened to her might make her reluctant to return to her life here at Jindabyne and we will try to understand that. Ashleigh, you must realise, as much as we may not like it, we will try to understand. Dominic will try to understand.'

No, I fucking won't, Dominic thought as he wiped his palms down the length of his thigh.

Pastor Hunter droned on. 'But you, Ashleigh, *you* need to help us by letting us know you are all right.'

Silence hung in the still night air as Pastor Hunter's voice faded.

Dominic looked up. The sun had slipped just below the hills and the evening star had appeared. Shadows were slipping into the calm, grey waters of Lake Jindabyne.

180

People shuffled behind him. He let a tear slip down his cheek, making no attempt to wipe it away. *Let the cameras get a close-up.*

'Thank you for coming,' Pastor Hunter concluded his impassioned speech. 'Now let us pray for the safe return of Ashleigh, or at least for information that lets us know she's safe.'

He led them in prayer, but Dominic didn't bow his head. He stared straight ahead, giving the cameras every opportunity to film him. At the end of the prayer, he pulled out a hankie and blew his nose.

A reporter sat down and put a microphone in front of him.

'If you could say something to Ashleigh, what would it be?' she asked.

Dominic cleared his throat and opened his mouth, but nothing came out. He cleared his throat again and said: 'It's something I keep repeating over and over. Anytime anyone asks me. Ashleigh, I love you. Please come home. Whatever has made you do this, I'll make it go away. I'll get you the best doctors, anything you need. Just please come home.'

The reporter put the microphone to her mouth and stared straight into the camera. 'And if anyone knows the where-abouts of Ashleigh Alberto, please call Crime Stoppers.' She recited the number then added, 'Jessica Flint reporting from Jindabyne.'

Dominic reached out and grabbed her arm. 'Thank you for coming here. For trying to get the word out about Ashleigh. Any tiny bit of publicity will help. Time goes on and people forget. But I never do.'

'You're welcome, Mr Alberto,' she said. Her face was compassionate. 'I wish there was something more we could do.'

'Will this go interstate?'

'I hope so. I'm trying to get my boss to use it as a news grab.'

'If you could, I'd be so grateful.'

'I'll do my best.' She got up to leave. 'And for what it's worth, I hope she's found safely. Mental illnesses are awful things to live with. You're a very strong man to be able to deal with it.' She walked away with her cameraman in tow.

'There you go, Dominic.' Lilian appeared at his shoulder. 'I told you we could get it organised. Let's hope it does the trick!'

'I hope so, Lilian. I'm very grateful for the work you put in. Now, I really must go home. I feel very worn out.'

'Of course you do, you poor thing. Don't be a stranger, Dominic. We're all happy to help and support you in any way we can. Night night, then.'

Dominic said his goodbyes and walked away, back towards his house. The street lights were on now on but the road was empty. He could smell wood-fire smoke and still hear conversations coming from the edge of the lake. Pushing his hands deep into his coat pockets, he walked with purpose. Somehow, somewhere, someone knew something.

'Mr Alberto?'

Dominic slowed his pace and eyed the stranger standing in front of him at the edge of the light.

'Yes?'

'I have a message for you. It came from interstate, yesterday.'

'Who are you?' he asked.

'No one you need to remember, but I have information you'll be interested in.'

Dominic narrowed his eyes, while the man spoke quickly. So quickly, Dominic didn't understand the first few words.

'. . . from Port Augusta.'

'Wait. Pause for a moment. Slow down,' said Dominic, holding up his hand as he gathered his thoughts. 'Now start.'

'A pocket watch matching the description of your stolen one was pawned three days ago. The report has come from the Port Augusta pawn shop and was picked up by police when they did their weekly check.'

Dominic tried to control his breathing. The first lead and the TV shots hadn't even gone to air yet. 'Do you know who pawned it?'

'Mrs Ashleigh Alberto.'

He drew in a quick breath.

'Address?'

'Fake. It's already been checked out.'

Suddenly, he no longer felt in control. To be so close, then lose her, was something he couldn't let happen.

'We need to make more enquiries,' he snapped.

'It's in progress.'

'Have you talked to the guy who owns the shop?'

'All he said was she haggled with him. He asked her about the watch and she said she was selling it because she needs the money.'

Dominic slammed his fist into his hands, while the stranger stood by impassively. 'We'll smoke her out,' he said. 'She'll run out of money and she'll come crawling back.' He jerked around to look at the man. 'How much did she get for it?'

'Just over three grand.'

'Won't take long, then.' He smiled without humour. 'Anything else?'

'Not at this stage.'

'Who sent you?' Dominic asked.

'Just let's say, someone who owed your father a favour. We'll be keeping an eye on things.' The man nodded to him, then melted into the darkness. Dominic stood there, and a few moments later heard a car start up and drive away.

He was furious. As much as he appreciated the information, he should have been able to get it from Simon. Now, at the end of all this, he was going to owe someone a favour and he didn't know who it was. It was how these things worked.

If Simon hadn't fucked up, he could have had the information without owing anyone anything.

He walked quickly towards his house, his coat flapping out behind him. There were plans to be put in place.

Chapter 24

Dave used the phone in Reen's shop to check in at the station, as he was out of mobile range. He could have accessed the secure police radio station but preferred to use the phone. Plus, he wanted to talk to Kim.

'Boss, you won't believe what's come through on the loop this morning,' said Jack, one of the younger officers at Barker police station, as soon as Dave identified himself.

'What's that?'

'The pawn shop in Port Augusta has bought an item from that missing girl, Ashleigh Alberto. You know, the one from New South Wales? The one who seems to have—'

'Yeah, I know the one you mean,' Dave interrupted, glancing around to see if he could see Eliza. 'What did she pawn?'

He listened as the officer gave him the details. He knew why Jack was excited. Nothing big happened in small country towns. Well, that's what he thought. Dave could have told him with authority that anything and everything could happen in the country. And Jack had been part of the investigation of the rodeo money last year. 'When did she pawn it?'

'Only a couple of days ago.'

'That's interesting. I guess she could be anywhere by now, though, couldn't she? Port Augusta is the gateway to the west and north.'

'But it proves she's still alive.'

'It proves that someone with her identification and access to the pocket watch is alive. Remember, nothing is ever as clear as it seems until it's proven without doubt.'

Jack was silent and Dave knew he'd taken the gentle reprimand on board. 'I guess you'd better get on and ask a few questions then, Jack,' he continued.

'In Port Augusta?'

'No, just around the town and surrounding areas. See if anyone has seen anyone who resembles her.'

'I'll get onto it right away.'

'Good lad. Now, is there anything else I need to know?'

'There's a phone message from someone called Simon McCullen, who wants you to give him a call. Get a pen and I'll give you the number.'

Dave wrote it down in his notebook. 'Did he say what he wanted?'

'Nope, just that he wanted to talk to you.'

'Okay, anything else? Nothing on the smuggling?' Dave looked up as the bell tinkled in the shop. He heard Eliza call out to Reen and shut his notebook with a thump.

'No, not that's come through recently.'

'Righto, I'll call in tomorrow.'

'When are you back?'

'Might be another couple of days yet. Got a few things I want to follow up.'

'All good. Catch you later.'

Dave hung up just as Eliza stuck her head through the door.

'Oh, hi,' she said and started to back out of the kitchen. 'I was just looking for Reen. Sorry, didn't mean to interrupt.'

'You're not interrupting. Come in. Reen just took off to Gillian's to grab some more pasties out of her freezer.'

'No, that's fine. I need to go and freshen up. I've been out with Jacob, looking at crutching, today.'

Dave started to walk to the door on his way out. 'What did you think?'

Eliza smiled, which made the scar on her cheek more obvious. 'I'd never seen anything like it before. The little bit I've had to do with animals was the wildlife back where I was from. Used to see wombats and koalas, brumbies, all sorts of things, but nothing to do with farming.'

'Where are you from?' Dave asked.

'Oh, here and there. I was in New South Wales before I ended up here.'

Dave nodded and studied her closely. 'Reen mentioned that you saw a strange vehicle on one of your nightly walks the other day. Can you tell me about it?'

He noted that Eliza froze as he asked the question and a look of uncertainty crossed her face.

'Nothing much to tell. Just that a four-wheel drive drove past me late one night last week and it looked unusual.' She shrugged and moved back into the shop area to let Dave out.

'In what way?' He kept watching her face, his eyes flicking over her scar.

She reached up and gave it a tentative rub before quickly pulling her hand away.

She told him about the aerials and when she had seen the vehicle driving around. 'It just seemed weird. I haven't lived here that long, but I know it's strange to see cars driving around at that time of night, covered in all sorts of tracking equipment.'

'Why do you think it was tracking equipment?'

Eliza paused. 'I guess I can't say for sure. It's just what it seemed like. I only saw it for a moment or two in the moon-light.' She sounded annoyed now.

Dave knew it was time to leave it alone, so he gave her a smile and thanked her. 'I'll be off then. Got to head back to the national park.'

'See you around,' she answered.

'Yep, I'll be back later tonight. I might have to catch up with you again to ask a couple more questions.'

'I don't think I've got any more to tell you, but whatever.' Eliza gave a hoist of her shoulders and turned away, heading to the kitchen.

Dave got into his car, trying to work out the best plan of attack with Eliza. He wasn't sure he wanted to let her know he knew who she really was yet. First, there was the chance she might run again; second, if she'd come here on purpose, it might hinder his investigation into the wildlife poaching. He really was in a quandary.

∽

Eliza watched Dave leave the shop, her stomach churning. She felt like everything was beginning to unravel. Her confession to Reen had left her with an uneasy feeling. One part of her was pleased to have been able to tell someone everything and know they understood, and the other part felt she had undone all her hard work to get where she was now.

Dave seemed to have been around a lot in the last couple of weeks and she knew that wasn't normal. Something was bringing him up to Blinman and she could only hope like hell it wasn't her.

❦

'Dave!' Chris strode over from the camping ground as the detective pulled up.

'Looks like you've got it fixed and the grounds have emptied out a bit.' Dave nodded at the post that had been hit the previous evening.

'Got it all fixed this morning.'

'Where are the girls today?'

Chris glanced around. 'Oh, who knows? It's not a school day, so they could be anywhere! Climbing hills, trees; causing mischief somewhere.' He smiled contentedly. 'I love they have this type of lifestyle. So much better than staring at computer screens all day, don't you reckon?'

'You've got that right,' Dave agreed. 'Have you got time for a chat now, do you think?'

'Absolutely. You've got me intrigued with what you were saying before. Come and have a coffee over at the house.'

They walked over, exchanging pleasantries. 'Are you going to play cricket again this year?' Chris asked Dave.

'I might be getting a bit long in the tooth for that,' he answered.

'Oh, come on! You guys smashed us last season.' Chris gave a loud laugh. 'You beat us by forty runs and three wickets!'

Dave nodded. 'Yeah, but I also pulled up pretty sore after taking that catch that got you out! Pulled a hammy 'cause I landed wrongly.'

'I reckon the few beers you had afterwards would have helped with the pain.'

'Yeah, yeah, and I didn't see you being a saint either!'

'It was a good night,' Chris said. They went into the kitchen and he put the kettle on. 'So, want to fill me in on what's happening? Coffee?'

'Thanks.' Dave collected his thoughts. 'At this stage, it's just a bit of prelim investigating. There's certainly something happening up here, but I haven't got enough information to know where to start. That's why I need to talk to you.' He repeated what he'd already told Chris and then said: 'I've had a report of an unspecified car, driving at odd times at night. It seems to have tracking devices on it. It's only been seen once, but with the info I have, it's enough to get me curious.

'I've also been given a bit of hearsay-type evidence about a caravan stopped in a parking bay with foam eskies and boxes laid out on the side of the road. I pricked my ears up because that's how the transportation of wildlife is supposed to be happening. Caravaners are collecting from up here somewhere and taking it across the border.

'There was a signed statement from a couple who'd camped here, saying they'd overheard a conversation that indicated this is going on.'

Chris handed over the coffee and shook his head. 'It all sounds pretty bloody out there, if you ask me.'

'I guess that's how these things stay under the radar for so long,' Dave answered, taking a sip. 'So, you haven't seen anything odd that you can remember?'

Chris wrinkled his brow as he stirred sugar into his coffee.

'You've thrown a different light on some of the things I've seen, certainly, but I'm not sure there's enough to give you any information.'

'The smallest pieces of info finish off the puzzle, as my old boss used to say.'

Chris sighed. 'The girls reported that a goanna's nest didn't have any eggs left in it a while ago. I didn't think anything of it because the foxes can come in and take them.'

Dave jotted that down on his notepad and looked up.

'Um,' Chris scratched his head. 'What else, what else?' he muttered. 'A while back now, I found a wedge-tailed eagle nest smashed on the ground.' He stopped and his face brightened. 'Now, that was interesting. There should have been eggs in that nest. I'd watched the birds come and go from there for a while. Wedge-tailed eagle nests just don't fall out of trees. They're built real strong. Some of the sticks they use are thicker than your finger, you know?

'When I found it, I remember thinking how strange it was. I went over to have a look, thinking there should have been eggs, or at least shells, where they'd hit the ground. But there weren't. And I tell you what else. I never saw those particular eagles again.' He stopped again, thinking. 'Yeah, that's exactly right. I haven't seen them.'

191

'How would you know it was them?' Dave asked, looking up from his notebook.

'They had identification tags on their legs,' Chris explained. 'We did a count up of birds a few years ago— they're endangered. You probably know that. Farmers love to kill them because they take lambs.'

Dave nodded. He knew there was always a fight between farmers and rangers when it came to wedge-tails.

'So, we counted them up to see what type of numbers we had around here. See, now you mention it, I would have just assumed that they'd been shot by farmers, or died, or something. Now you're throwing a completely different light on this.' He shook his head.

The sound of running feet and little voices was suddenly heard, and the door was flung open.

'Dad! Dad!' Heidi puffed. 'There's car tracks up onto Halley's Bluff. There shouldn't be, should there? Isn't that where those Aboriginal carvings were found last year and—'

Chris held up his hand. 'Hold on, girls, hold on. Settle down. Take it from the top and tell me slowly!'

Heidi and Tilly looked at each other, then Heidi started to talk. 'You know that emu nest that's out on the flat, in the bushes, halfway up the hill?'

Chris nodded.

'We went up to have a look.'

He frowned. 'I've told you not to go up there without someone with you. Old man emus are nasty creatures.'

'Anyway,' Heidi continued, ignoring her father's reprimand, 'I saw all the grasses squashed down, so I went to look and it's a track, like a ute track, going through the bush. They shouldn't be doing that. There isn't a track there and they could hurt an animal. This is a national park! They've got to stay on the tracks. It was the first thing we were taught.'

Dave glanced over at Chris, then looked back at the girls. 'Could you show me?' he asked quietly.

Chapter 25

Dave was frustrated. It was times like these that he realised how much he depended on the internet to do his job properly.

Although he was a technophobe, he had come to acknowledge that machines could make his job much easier, so he had undergone the training the police department offered, as well as mastered Siri. This time last year, he hadn't even known who Siri was. Through the Tardis in his four-wheel drive, he could access information on people and vehicles.

But here he was, out the back of beyond, and there was limited to no internet. Certainly there wasn't any mobile phone signal.

The investigation of Halley's Bluff had instantly raised a red flag with him. He wanted forensics out in the field as soon as possible, but it would take them at least three hours to get there.

Sighing, Dave noticed Heidi and Tilly hovering quietly in the background and wondered if he should ask them to leave.

But they were staying clear of the scene and they were the ones who had raised the alarm that something was wrong. He would have to talk to them too.

Something else occurred to him, and he looked over to where Chris was on his knees, hands behind his back, peering at the ground. 'Mate, have you emptied the drop box lately?' Dave asked. He was referring to the locked honesty box in which visitors to the park had to leave their details and the entry fee.

Chris looked up and nodded. 'Took everything out yesterday.'

'Have you still got those records or do you have to send them to head office?'

'I've still got them.' Chris swished at the flies and looked down again. 'I can't believe this.'

Other than crushed grass and wheel tracks, there was little evidence of poaching visible to the naked eye, but Dave's gut told him otherwise. And it was his gut he listened to the most.

'Look, I think I'm going to cordon off this area. I really want the blokes in forensics to come and have a look, but I'm not sure they'll be able to. These smaller jobs are usually left to me. It's a bugger that the ground is too hard for the wheels to have left an impression on it. Plus, a lot of the driving has been done on the vegetation. But we can see where the vehicle's been. Any evidence is good evidence at the moment.'

'You can do that?' Chris asked. 'Collect what's needed?'

Dave glanced over at him. The man looked shaken. He supposed this was only natural, considering the park was under his care.

'I sure can. I've been doing it for twenty-nine years!' Dave hiked back to the car and got out his camera. Flicking the flap

195

door open, he checked to see that the SD card was in there before walking back up the hill.

Halfway up, he stopped, shut his eyes and listened.

The sun was out today and it warmed his back, even though the breeze was cool. Absent-mindedly, he brushed away the small black flies that bombarded his eyes and nose. Other than their buzz, he could hear birdsong, and the leaves brushing together. Occasionally, he heard a tourist's voice floating up from the walking track, which was about five hundred metres away, along the edge of the creek, but other than that, the park was serene.

He opened his eyes and looked around carefully, picking out the direction of the camping ground and Chris's house. He could see the tip of the tall aerial that was bolted to the roof of the homestead, but in between was a deep creek and another line of smaller hills. He was pretty sure that Chris wouldn't have been able to hear anything and he certainly wouldn't have been able to see lights, unless he was outside at the right time.

Glancing around, he took in the brightly coloured wild flowers that were dotted in and around the dull green scrubby bushes. Someone would have to have known that the nest was there, or spent a lot of time staking out the area during the day, to get in and out quickly and without anyone noticing them.

'Cameras,' Dave muttered. He pulled his notebook out of his top pocket and made a note. Then he scribbled: *long-term visitors—average visit time?*

He continued back up the hill, thinking hard.

'Have you got motion cameras rigged up anywhere in the park, Chris?' Dave asked as he focused the camera on the crushed wild flowers, bush and grass, and started to take photos of the scene.

'Nah, never had any of that sort of shit around here,' the ranger answered. He turned to the girls, who were hovering in the background. 'Listen, you two, how about you shoot back home? I'll be back there soon. I'll just finish helping Dave, okay?'

'But, Dad,' Heidi began.

'No,' Chris answered in a tone Dave had never heard him use before. 'This is grown-up work. Off you go. I'll be back soon.'

Complaining, the girls headed back down the hill, their voices floating up as they went.

Dave straightened up and went back to his car to get out some tape. 'There's not much more I can do here,' he said. 'Let's tape it off and go and see what names you've got in your drop box, and plan from there.' He fastened the crime-scene tape to a tree and started to walk towards a bush, the tape unrolling as he went.

'Is there anything else you know about that could be poached easily? More eggs, or chicks, or something?' Dave finished what he was doing and put the roll back into his ute.

'I don't often know where there are any nests or babies, or the like, unless the girls tell me. I'm usually so busy cleaning up after tourists, or policing them, I don't get around the park as much as you'd think I would.' He stood with his hands in his pockets, rocking back and forth on his heels.

'Righto, drop box it is, then.' Dave took one final look over his shoulder and jumped into his car. Chris followed in his ranger vehicle.

᠅

Back at the house, Chris handed over the drop box and Dave started sifting through the pieces of paper.

'Can I also have your records of people who've stayed or have national parks passes?' he asked without looking up from the cards spread in front of him.

Chris wordlessly passed over a logbook.

'What did you find?'

Dave looked up to see Heidi peeking through the door, her eyes wide with curiosity. He smiled at her.

'It's not going to be that easy to find out what's going on here, Heidi,' he answered. 'I'm going to have to do a bit of detective work.'

'Why would someone take eggs and animals?' she asked. 'They'd be hard to look after, out of their natural habitat.'

'People make money from it, by selling the product,' Dave answered, then, seeing the puzzled look on her face, explained: 'Okay—say someone has taken these emu eggs. They're worth a lot of money on the black market. So, they steal the eggs, then sell them on to another person. It's how some people make their money. It's wrong, but it happens. Sometimes the animals are sold overseas, sometimes to private collectors. There's lots of markets for them. Australian wildlife can be prized possessions for overseas collectors. The lizard and bird trades are huge.'

Heidi stood there silently, and Dave could tell she still didn't understand. Why would you take an animal out of its natural habitat, why would you put it through the stress of travel, why would you risk it dying? Its life was worth so much more here, where the animal or reptile belonged.

Both girls had been raised to love and respect every animal in the park. He looked over at Chris, whose face was glowing red. Maybe it was a good time to leave and let him explain it to the girls, better than he, Dave, could. Anyway, he had a heap of things to get on with. He gathered up all the paperwork and tucked it under his arm.

'I might head off with these,' he said. 'I'm going to go back to the station, and start to do some background checks on the names and regos I've got here.'

Chris finally opened his mouth. 'Am I allowed to let you just take these?' he asked. 'Isn't there a privacy law or something?'

'It'll be okay. I'm just going to start the investigation with these and see where it leads. There may not be anything that jumps out at me, but I do want to run these names through the computer. I might hit something, you never know.'

'Okay. I guess you'll let me know if you find anything?'

'Sure will. And you'll let me know if you see or hear anything?'

'Shit, yeah.'

Dave nodded. 'All right, I'll be in touch. Catch you later.' He turned to Heidi. 'Thanks for your help on this, Heidi. Can I come and talk to you about it soon?'

Heidi puffed her chest out. 'Yes,' she answered.

'Great. I'll be back tomorrow.'

෫෨

It was a long drive back and Dave was exhausted by the time he drove into the main street and pulled up at the police station. Darkness had fallen and the town was quiet as he arrived. There were lights coming from the houses along the street and, as he got out and stretched his legs, the smell of wood smoke hit him. He breathed it in and raised his face to the stars, glad the air was cold. It would wake him up.

The notes and files under his arm, he unlocked the station door and flicked on the light switch. Sitting at his desk, he held down a button on his iPhone and said, 'Send text to Kim' when Siri asked what he wanted.

'I'm at the station, working,' he said to the phone and watched as it created his text message for him. 'Will be home later. Working on a case. Love you.' The words flashed onto the screen as quickly as he could say them.

Turning to the computer, he switched it on and opened his email account. With two fingers he typed out a request for forensics to head up to the park, thinking it would probably be denied because he had the skills to do it himself. He grabbed a fresh notepad from his drawer and, starting with the top card from the drop box, he typed the name on it into the IMS—instant management system.

No hit, no flags, no nothing. Not even a parking fine.

He nodded. That was what he had expected. It would be a long night, but if there was someone whose name raised a flag, he would find it before he headed back to Blinman.

Chapter 26

'Okay, it's only two weeks until the cook-off,' Reen said to the group gathered around the table in the pub. 'We've got to up the ante here or we're not going to be organised in time.'

There was a general murmur of agreement, then Mary spoke up.

'I've ordered all the meat, potatoes, carrots, onions and flour from Port Augusta. We're lucky the grocer offered to donate all the produce again. Do we have an up-to-date number of entries?'

All heads turned to Mark Patterson, who was in charge of the entries. He opened his notebook. 'Okay—as of yesterday, there were twenty-two. I'm expecting another five or ten, at least.'

Jacob spoke up. 'I've got the firewood organised and will start bringing that in over the next few days. There's a few other blokes who'll start to bring in loads too. Has anyone done anything about booking the Portaloos and showers?'

Reen nodded. 'Yep, I did that a few weeks ago. They'll be delivered next week.' She leaned back in her chair. 'What about the selfie trail, Eliza?'

Eliza looked down at her notes. 'Well, I've got five different sites they have to visit. Two in the national park, one on the way here, then they'll need to go to the mine and to Forget-me-not Well.' She took a shaky breath as she remembered her reaction when Jacob had taken her there.

She still didn't understand why she had felt the way she had. Jacob had been stunned by her response and taken her away as quickly as he could.

To stand where someone had died was a haunting and eerie experience. And knowing that Clara and Richard had been married at the beautiful, isolated spot made it worse. How could happiness be so tangled with sadness?

After being told one of the stories about the well, Eliza had asked Jacob not to tell her any more. The crazy emotions she was experiencing couldn't be explained, although she wondered if it was all her pent-up feelings about leaving Dominic that were affecting her so much.

When Jacob had driven her home, she'd tried to laugh her reaction off, saying she was just tired, but she was sure Jacob didn't believe her. How could he? She didn't believe herself.

Eliza just wished she could understand what the hell was going on with her, especially when, a couple of days later, she had driven herself back there and experienced different emotions. She had felt peaceful and at ease. She'd walked around and soaked in the quiet atmosphere. She had sat on the edge of the well, looking in. She'd begun to wonder if she'd got upset about nothing.

'Eliza?'

She blinked at the sound of Jacob's voice and the pressure of his hand on her arm. 'Sorry,' she said and looked back down at her notes. 'I've been out to all the spots and taken photos of them, and drawn up the entry form and map, so I think I'm as organised as I can be.'

'Did we decide on an entry fee?' Julie asked.

'Yep, one hundred dollars per car.'

'And prizes?' she asked, as she scribbled down notes to be typed up at a later date.

'A carton of white wine or two cartons of beer, donated by the pub, as first prize,' Eliza answered, referring back to her notepad. 'A voucher to tour the mine as second prize, and a meal voucher for Cornish pasties and quangdong pies as third prize.'

'Right,' Julie answered. 'That sounds really good. But we're going to have to promote this a bit more. It's something new and different, so let's plug it as hard as we can. I've got an interview with local ABC radio on Wednesday, so I'll mention it then.' She paused and turned to Reen. 'Were you liaising with the newspaper?'

Reen nodded. 'Yeah, I've got that all sorted. Eliza, can I get a copy of the map and entry form, so I can forward them to the journo who's writing the article and she can put them in the paper?'

'Sure.'

'Drinks anyone?' Jacob asked as he got up from the table. He took a couple of orders, then asked, 'Eliza?'

'Just a lemonade, please.'

'Can I interest you in a wine?'

She shook her head. 'No, thanks.'

'Ah! You're no fun!' He smiled and went over to the bar.

The door opened and Eliza heard Jacob say: 'Well, well, well, look at what you see when you don't have a gun! Dessie, how are you, old mate?'

She looked around and saw a hunched-over man with snowy white hair grinning at Jacob. They shook hands.

'We're just talking about a fundraising idea for Frontier Services,' Jacob said. 'Come on over—you might have some suggestions.' He steered Dessie to the table and grabbed him a chair.

Eliza watched as Dessie was greeted with genuine pleasure and affection. She could feel how his presence lifted everyone there. He radiated calmness and gentleness. His grey eyes rested on her, and in them she saw kindness and compassion. Then she saw them briefly widen, before he very quickly slid his gaze over to Mary and back to her.

'Well now, lass, I don't think I've had the pleasure.' Dessie held out his hand. 'I'm Dessie, and who might you be?'

'I'm Eliza,' she answered, suddenly feeling shy in the presence of a man who was obviously such a local legend.

'Eliza, it's lovely to meet you.' He turned back to the rest of the table and smiled. 'So, are you all dreaming up mad things?' he asked.

Reen laughed. 'A selfie trail is the new thing at the camp cook-off and all that money is going to you. Along with all the normal things to do with the cook-off.'

'That sounds very interesting, Reen. And it's very kind of you all to think of doing something like this.' He smiled kindly at them.

'So, how long are you here for?' Jacob asked.

'As long as I'm needed, Jacob,' he answered.

'I'll make up a room for you,' Reen said, struggling to get up. 'Have we finished here, do you think?'

Julie went back through her notes. 'I think we've covered everything.'

'I'd better head off too,' said Mark. 'I'm putting down another bore and the contractor's coming tomorrow to start. I should get an early night. It's bloody good to see you, Dessie.' He shook his hand and headed off into the darkness.

Jacob stood up and touched Eliza's shoulder. 'Come on, I'll walk you back to your room, and let everyone else catch up. Dessie, Mary can tell you what we're up to, and I'll see you at Manalinga tomorrow?'

'I'll be there, Jacob,' Dessie answered in his soft voice. 'Eliza, it was lovely to meet you. I'm sure we'll see each other again soon.'

Pushing back her chair, Eliza got to her feet. 'I'll look forward to that.'

Once she and Jacob were out of earshot of everyone, she said, 'He's just like I imagined he would be after you told me that story.'

'He's a good bloke.'

'He's so engaging—have you noticed he always uses people's names when he talks to them? That's a sign of someone who wants to make you feel like you're the only person in the world. I bet that's why he makes such a good pastor.'

Jacob paused. 'I've never really noticed that before, but you're right. That's how he talks. Dessie always uses your name when he speaks to you.'

They came to a standstill in front of Eliza's room. The moonlight cast a ghostly shadow over Jacob's face as he turned to her.

'Guess I'll catch up with you sometime,' he said.

'Guess you will,' she agreed as she pushed open her door and felt for the light switch. Before she could turn it on, Jacob leaned down and kissed her cheek.

Eliza felt his lips linger there for a moment. All it would take would be for her to turn her head and she'd be able to touch her lips to his.

But she didn't. She gently pulled back.

'Good night, Jacob.'

❦

Dessie came back from the bar and put two glasses of port down on the table.

'How have you been, Mary?' he asked as he carefully sat back down. 'And John, how's he?'

'We've been fine,' she answered slowly, 'although we've had some old memories dragged up recently.'

Dessie nodded and sat there quietly before picking up his glass. 'Here's to good health,' he said. 'And to the future.'

Mary raised her glass too and took a sip before asking, 'You see it too, don't you?' She stared at the glass of ruby-coloured liquid she held. Her arthritically gnarled hands looked like claws to her.

How had she got so old, she wondered. She didn't feel old on the inside, and every time she stared in the mirror, she wondered who the stranger was staring back at her. When she looked at John, she saw the young, handsome man he had been, not the grey-haired, lined man he was now. Getting old could seem cruel. This was even more so when a ghost from her past entered her life. A ghost she'd had no idea even existed.

'There certainly is a resemblance,' Dessie agreed. 'I'm pleased you rang and asked me to come up.'

'What do we do? Do we say something? We've got no idea if we're right. What if we're so wrong that we make a big mistake? John's sure they're related, but we don't know how. '

Dessie steepled his fingers and held them against his lips, thinking. 'Is she asking questions? Does she have any idea?'

Mary shrugged. 'I'm not sure,' she answered hesitantly. 'All she's said to me is that she was drawn to this area, and to a photo of John and me. She did make it clear she wasn't sure if it was the area or us that had attracted her. I don't know how to ask any more questions without arousing her curiosity.'

'Has she said where's she's from?'

Mary went on to relay the conversation she'd had with Eliza when she had visited with Heidi and Tilly.

'Hmm, so it's really all hearsay, isn't it? Her reactions could have been for any reason—something deep-seated in her that we know nothing of.'

They sat silently, the two old friends, staring into the fire.

Mary would never forget the day she and John and Clara and Richard had walked up the plank and onto the ship that was sailing to Australia. They were full of excitement about the future.

Getting away from London and its grimy, dirty streets seemed a blessing. Stories had filtered back from people who'd gone to Australia about large skies, so blue it felt like you were staring into an abyss.

As the boat sailed and Australia went from being a dream to being reality, opportunities stretched out in front of them. When they had first arrived on Australian soil, John had wondered if all the good news stories had been made up. The heat and flies were oppressive, and the pastures weren't green, as they'd heard, but dry and brown. It never seemed to rain.

It had taken time, but Mary had fallen in love with the Flinders Ranges and knew she would live there until the day she died. The red dust had not only got under her fingernails and into her hair, it had got into her blood. Clara and Richard had joked that it had literally got into all of them as they breathed in the dust storms.

It had taken a couple of years for them all to become accustomed to the climate, but they had been good times. They had been hard, for sure, but good times. Fun times were the social occasions, the tennis and cricket. Good times were all about seeing the land develop under their care, and having new experiences, like their first flood, or dust storm, and the way their dreams were turning into reality, strengthening their friendships. Clara and Richard had loved the land the way that Mary and John did, and Mary remembered the two men having many lively discussions about animal husbandry practices and other issues.

Richard and Clara were perfect for each other. It had only been in the years before his death that things had started to change.

Richard had been laid-back and charming, quick with a smile. Mary had loved his jokes, and even when things looked dire, he could always make them laugh. He enjoyed cards more than he did sport but happily played tennis, just so long as there was a drink afterwards.

Clara, Mary remembered fondly, was graceful but also tough. She would drive a hard bargain with the travelling salesmen and fiercely protected those she loved. The trouble was that she could only be tough and strong for so long, and then she would fall into bouts of deep depression. It did take its toll on Richard, but he never once waivered in his love for her.

The death of their two closest friends had almost been the undoing of Mary and John. They'd tried to turn back time by asking all the 'what if?' questions. Would things have been different if they hadn't left England? What if Richard hadn't died?

'Sometimes I wonder if we would have boarded that ship if we'd known what was in front of us,' Mary said sadly.

'Come now, Mary,' Dessie said, getting up from his chair. 'We can't dwell on the past. You know that. Whatever will be, will be.'

'Of course you're right,' Mary answered, looking up at him. To change the subject, she added, 'John will be pleased to know you're here. Will you come out tomorrow?'

'Your place will be my first call, with Jacob my second.'

Mary smiled at him. 'Dessie, I don't know how this community would have survived if you hadn't been here. You're a godsend.'

'That was who sent me,' Dessie said. He patted her arm and walked out.

Chapter 27

Dave stared at the computer, deep in thought.

He wasn't sure what he had just found—but it was intriguing.

He'd typed in Eliza Norwood's name and found nothing. That hadn't surprised him. Then he'd typed in Ashleigh's name.

The IMS flashed up the missing persons report.

Dave carefully reread all the information and looked at the photo again.

Eliza had certainly made a good job of changing her appearance. It was off-putting unless you'd spent a bit of time with her. The scar would help throw your average Joe off the scent too. But Dave wasn't your average Joe, and after Reen's confirmation, there wasn't any doubt. It was the animal trafficking that bothered Dave now. Could there be a connection?

He clicked on the tab that said 'persons'. The computer would connect every person it could to Ashleigh.

Only one name came up. The person who had reported her missing: Dominic Alberto.

As he looked at the screen, Dave saw that Dominic had an alert against his name.

'Believed to be involved in organised crime.'

He dragged his hand across his face and heard the scratching of skin on stubble. He got up and went through to the little kitchen to make himself a cup of coffee and rest his tired eyes.

As he stirred in sugar, his mind whirled, trying to link the dots.

Eliza appears.

Reports of animal poaching.

Hearsay statements from two people.

Emu eggs missing.

Dominic Alberto believed to be involved with organised crime.

Organised criminals trafficked anything from guns and drugs, to humans, to wildlife.

Was it too big a leap to think that Dominic could be involved in the animal trafficking, which was why Eliza had turned up in Blinman? Maybe Eliza's story about being an abused wife was just that—a story. The scar on her cheek could be the result of an accident. He had certainly thought before that Eliza could be involved, but this threw a whole different light on things.

Glancing at his watch, he saw it was three in the morning. He returned to his desk, then clicked on the *'persons'* tab for Dominic.

A name jumped out at him.

Simon McCullen.

He'd heard that name before, but where? Damn, that's

right, there had been a message. He'd forgotten. Why hadn't he made the connection between the name on the report and the phone message he'd received when he'd read it last time? He remembered telling Reen about the bent copper in Jindabyne and swore in frustration. How the hell had he forgotten that as well? God, he must be tired. Flicking through the piles of paper on his desk, he found his phone messages and read through them. There it was, written in Jack's scrawly hand-writing, Simon's name and phone number. He tapped at the piece of paper and returned his attention to the screen.

After a few more clicks, he realised that *Simon* was the policeman who had been stood down, pending an internal investigation.

There's something off here. Really off.

Why was Simon ringing to talk to him? How did he even know who Dave was?

Eliza was the only connection he could see. *But how . . .?*

He groaned and let his head fall back on the chair. In a matter of moments, he was asleep.

౿

It was after lunch the next day by the time Dave had finished running the rest of the names from the national parks records through the computer and, not surprisingly, he hadn't come across anything as interesting as his discovery the night before.

He'd only found a couple of DUIs, someone having had their licence suspended, and another having been charged with public disturbance. There was nothing that indicated an involvement with poaching or organised crime. There were three or four people who stayed at the park several times a year, but they didn't raise any alarm bells with Dave. He guessed that if someone loved the area as much as the locals did, they would visit often.

Jack had woken him up when he'd arrived at work in the morning. After he had got Dave a coffee, they had talked about what he had found the night before.

'That's a pretty big leap to make,' Jack said. 'I mean, what's the likelihood really of Dominic being behind the poaching?'

'Stranger things have happened,' Dave answered. 'That coffee's good. I guess you only got me the one?'

Jack grinned. 'Yeah. You need to go home and have a shower and freshen up. Have another one there.'

Dave nodded. Kim was the best reason to go home, but a decent coffee was a good one.

'New South Wales is a long way to get wildlife to,' Jack continued. 'If they were driving, which they'd have to be—'

'Gotta be driving,' Dave interjected. 'The airport screening would have picked it up if they were flying.'

Jack nodded. 'So, yep, it's such a long way to drive with live animals. It would be high risk.'

'Absolutely. Eggs wouldn't be a problem if they had an incubator in the caravan, but any live animals—it would be a hell of a job to keep them healthy.'

'I just think it's a stretch,' Jack finished.

'You're probably right. But it's certainly worth keeping it in the back of our minds.' Dave yawned and stretched. 'Anyway, I'm going home to sleep, but I'll be heading back up to Blinman tomorrow.'

એ

Dave waited for Eliza at the shop. Eventually, he heard a diesel vehicle approaching, and turned his head to see the battered dual cab she drove come around the back of the building to where her room was. He waited until she went inside, then went over and knocked on the door.

She opened the door with a smile, which, he assumed, was because she was expecting Reen. It faltered the second she saw him.

'Can I come in, Ashleigh?'

He saw her freeze and different emotions cross her face. He tried to read them: panic and trepidation were certainly there, but perhaps also a small amount of defiance.

Finally she pulled the door open a little wider and let him inside.

They stood facing each other, Eliza with her arms crossed, as if warding off whatever might be coming her way.

Finally, Dave sat at the little table and started to speak.

'Obviously, I know who you are,' he began.

She took a sharp breath. 'I'm not going back,' she said quickly. 'I'm not.'

'You don't have to,' he answered. 'But I have a responsibility to let your loved ones know you're alive and well. I can then just say you don't want to be found and I can leave it at that.'

'Don't be ridiculous. He doesn't love me. No one at Jindabyne loves me. You don't need to tell them anything.' She stopped and took a breath. When she spoke again, there was panic in her voice. 'And Dominic won't leave it at that.

'Can't you see, I've had to run from him so he won't hurt me anymore? The minute he finds out where I am, he'll come and make me go back with him. Even if you don't tell him where I am, he'll find me.'

Tears began to slide down her cheeks and she hugged her arms around herself.

'Can I just confirm you are Ashleigh Alberto?'

She nodded.

'Okay. Did you pawn a pocket watch in Port Augusta?'

Eliza nodded again.

'Do you want to tell me what led to you leaving Jindabyne?'

Slowly and haltingly, Eliza began Ashleigh's story. Half an hour later, Dave had filled eight notepad pages and knew she was telling the truth.

'What happens now?' she asked in a small voice.

'I have to file an information report. I'm not going to get to that for a few days, because I'm going to be up here investigating a couple of other matters, so you have time to work out what you want to do.

'There are options. You can file a complaint against Dominic for assault or take out a restraining order against him.'

'He's not going to take any notice of that, Dave. He's evil and violent.' She looked down at her hands and spoke in a low voice. 'I left a fairly obvious "fuck you" and he'll make me pay for that.'

'You'd better tell me about it.'

Dave kept his face neutral as she explained about her wedding rings and the pocket watch. He admired her spunk and determination. They would explain the defiance in her face he thought he'd seen earlier.

He made some more notes, then told her: 'Look, as I said, I'm not in any hurry to file this report and that'll give you a few days to work out what you want to do. In time, I'll have to let the Jindabyne police know that you've been found safe and well and won't be returning there. My advice would be to hire a lawyer and have any paperwork mailed to you through them.'

'What sort of paperwork?'

'Divorce papers, settlement papers, that sort of thing.' He stopped and looked at her. 'You won't be able to stay as Eliza unless you change your name by deed poll and, of course, you tie up all these loose ends: like getting a divorce, getting a new tax file number. Until you do, you won't be able to live a normal life and move on.'

'I hadn't thought about that. I've just been living off cash I've got one way and another.'

'Just one more question, Ashleigh.'

'My name is Eliza,' she broke in. 'I'll never go back to Ashleigh.'

Dave nodded. 'Eliza.' He stopped for a moment, choosing his words very carefully. 'Why did you chose Blinman as a place to hide?'

Eliza pushed her lips together and closed her eyes. Slowly, she went over to the cupboard and pulled out a cardboard box. She fished around in it until she found what she was looking for and handed it to Dave.

'I saw this picture in *OUTBACK* magazine and I felt like I was connected to this place.'

'So, you just decided to drive here?' Dave asked.

'I had nowhere else to go.' She paused. 'I'd like to find out about my real parents. I thought that if I felt so connected to this place, or to Mary and John Caulder, through this photo, I might find the answer here. Sounds crazy, I know.'

Dave nodded. He'd heard wilder ideas in his time, and no one could explain how another person's mind worked. He'd learned a long time ago not to judge.

'Have you had any luck?'

Eliza shook her head. 'I haven't really done too much about it yet. It's not long since I met Mary and John, but I'm certain they felt something when they saw me. I'm not sure what, but they were looking at me intently. Almost like they recognised me, but couldn't work out where they knew me from.'

'I hope you find out,' Dave said, getting up. He paused at the door. 'You know, it worries me that you think Dominic will threaten you. I'll be putting that in my report and also mentioning it to the police at Jindabyne.'

Eliza screwed up her nose. 'Won't make any difference,' she said. 'They're all in his pocket. They're his mates—the policeman, the doctor, whoever else you'd like to mention. I just have to make sure I'm not found, and I'll be fine.' She gave a watery smile. 'Anyway, who's going to think to look for me deep in the Flinders Ranges?'

Dave said his goodbyes and left, feeling apprehensive. He'd heard people say things like that before.

Sometimes, those people had ended up dead.

⁊

The door clicked behind Dave and Eliza was left alone, staring into space.

Well, that was it. He knew now and soon Dominic would too.

She had tried so hard to forget her old life. As with 'Fight Song', often Eliza looked to affirmation quotes to help her get through the hard times. She had a few Blu-Tacked to the wall.

One, from *Outlander* by Diana Gabaldon, read: '*You forget the life you had before, after a while. Things you cherish and hold dear are like pearls on a string. Cut the knot and they scatter across the floor, rolling into dark corners never to be found again. So you move on and eventually you forget what the pearls even looked like. At least you try.*'

It wasn't the things she cherished that she wanted to roll into the darkest corners; it had been the abuse she'd suffered at the hands of a man who declared he loved her. She had been succeeding too. The sadder thoughts and experiences, even though they still emerged occasionally, were the pearls resting in dark corners. But there were others still spinning across the floor or under chairs, ones that could be seen.

Now, the pearls from dark corners were reappearing. The lump of anxiety in her throat sat like a stone. The need to run, to hide, to lash out and scream, or hit something, was at the surface.

She didn't want to feel like this again, dammit! She wanted to feel free, and cared for and safe. Here, in this little town, with these people around her, she did.

Or, at least, she had.

Chapter 28

Dessie woke and stared at the ceiling, gently testing his body as he did every day. There seemed to be ever more aches and pains but, at eighty, he wasn't surprised. Still, whatever his physical shape, and after all these years, he still loved giving pastoral care to people in northern South Australia.

Blinman, in particular, had seen its fair share of tragedies since its establishment in the eighteen-fifties, when copper had been found in the area. He'd first arrived in 1955, as a fresh-faced twenty-year-old, and he'd had one steep learning curve. Over the years Dessie had discovered how best to talk to these people, and it was straight down the line. There was no time for anything else out here.

The men were tough, strong and resourceful. Resilient. They had to be, and the women were too. Now, two generations on, Dessie could see the children had been raised to be the same way. It gladdened his heart to see the younger generation standing strong, like their fathers before them.

Jacob Maynard was one of them; as was Stuart, who had just married Stacey; and Mark Patterson. They were community focused, as he'd seen last night.

He reflected now on how the townsfolk and surrounding station owners had reinvented themselves more than once. He'd watched the pastoralists struggle in the nineteen-sixties, as wool prices started to drop and drought had begun to bite hard.

That was the problem with this area, Dessie thought as he stared at the ceiling, his hands behind his head. *It was boom or bust. It was either drought or the best season they'd ever had.*

Many had thought the closing of the police station in 1970 would be the end of Blinman. They had feared that other essential services, like the post office, would be taken away too and suddenly there wouldn't be a town at all.

It hadn't been the end. The community had once again banded together, by building a golf course and cricket pitch. Sport was such a big thing in country towns and Blinman was no different. Saturdays had been spent on the golf course, with a few beers at the end of the day. This had given the pastoralists an opportunity to talk to each other about how they were going and how the season was coming along. Cricket provided light relief—if also fierce competition—as had tennis.

And the women in the area found companionship through the Country Women's Association meetings, and then the party line phone system had been installed, making a world of difference. Of course, you'd have to talk in code on the phone or avoid discussing private business, given the temptation everyone had to pick up the receiver and listen to someone else's conversation. Dessie smiled to himself, still hearing all the women chattering on the phone line, organising dances and dinners.

He smiled again as he remembered the old black phone with one handle. Every house had a different ring, which was how you knew if the call was for you. Or you could dial the exchange and ask for an extension. 28H had been Mary and John Caulder's number. He'd rung it often. Dessie hoisted himself up and looked at his watch. It was time to get a move on.

༄

The countryside looked in good shape, he acknowledged, as he drove to John and Mary Caulder's station.

The native grasses were six inches tall and stood waving gently in the breeze. He thought to himself that the colours in this part of the country were different. The grass wasn't the rich, deep green that was found in the south of the state—it was more of a lighter khaki. Some of the bushes were blue— hence the name bluebush—and the acacia trees were olive.

As he neared the homestead, he looked across the flood plain and saw sheep sitting contentedly under the trees along the edge of the creek. He was pleased to note they had full stomachs.

He could remember when the same area was nothing but dry and barren ground. There wasn't a blade of grass, and the bushes and trees had barely any leaves, as the sheep had eaten them. Skinny ewes, with hip and rib bones protruding from under their freshly shorn skin, would walk the paddocks endlessly, looking for even a skerrick of grass to eat. Carcasses would litter the watering points, and the sun shone endlessly from a cloudless blue sky, day after day.

He pulled up in front of the Caulders' house, where roses and geraniums were flowering. The lawn was a lush green, and Dessie knew that around the back, there would be a flourishing vegie patch.

John opened the front door immediately; it was obvious that he had been watching for his friend. They shook hands and slapped each other on the shoulder.

'Come in, come in. It's good to see you.'

'I was just thinking how beautiful the paddocks are looking at the moment,' Dessie said once they were sitting in the sunroom and he had accepted a cup of tea from Mary.

'It's a wonderful season,' John agreed. 'I can't remember when it looked so good.'

'Do you remember the times when the only patch of green would be where you threw the washing water onto the lawn?' Dessie asked Mary.

Mary looked over at John with a sad smile. 'Oh, yes,' she answered. 'And the dust storms that would blow up. You couldn't see your hand in front of your face sometimes. I was always scared I'd get caught out in one and suffocate.' She shuddered. 'Ugh, the grit! Cleaning up afterwards with a shovel and a broom.'

'I can remember shooting sheep,' John said. 'It was kinder than letting them starve.' He closed his eyes and Dessie knew he was trying to shut out the memories.

'But then the rains come,' he said softly.

John grinned as he raised his cup of tea, his sadness gone. 'Always rains after a dry spell.'

'Yes, dear,' Mary said. They laughed. It wasn't the first time she'd heard that!

Then she banged her cup down and laughed again. 'Do you remember when the party line was first installed? Mrs Green couldn't help herself. She picked up the phone whenever it rang, and always listened to everyone else's conversations.'

John's face darkened. 'That was how everything got out after . . .' his voice trailed off. He looked down and picked at a thread on his overalls.

They all knew what he was talking about.

The three of them never talked about the tragedy if they could avoid it. Dessie had always told them they should, and they had made themselves at first. But, as time went on, the memories had become more painful, rather than time lessening them, and now it was easier never to mention it.

But Eliza coming to Blinman had changed all that.

'Come on.' John stood up.

Dessie could see he was keen to escape the conversation, so he gulped at his hot tea.

'I'll take you for a drive and show you a bit of the country,' John said. 'Might as well see it when it's looking as good as it is now.'

೮౩

After the men had gone, Mary sat lost in thought. She missed her friend every day, but tried only to think of her when she was by herself.

On a whim, she dragged out some old photo albums and started flicking through the pages. There they were, the four of them. Young and happy. With unlined faces, and unaware of what was going to befall them.

She traced the young John's face. He was sitting on a horse, behind a mob of cattle. Mary could remember the day clearly. They were taking the mob into some makeshift yards to brand the calves.

She'd loved sitting behind a mob, moving them gently across the countryside. The air had been beautiful that day: smelling clean and moist after some drizzle the night before. Mary wished she could bottle the smell of rain on dry earth.

Once the cattle were safely in the yards and drafted up, Mary lit the fire for branding. When it was hot enough, John and Richard put the branding irons into the fire. They had then worked methodically through all the calves, cutting the bulls' ballsacks open, extracting the balls, then putting a hot iron onto the rump and leaving a burn mark with their brand on it.

After they had branded the heifers, they opened the gate, and let the cows and calves mother up and graze across the paddock. The branding fire was turned into a barbecue fire, and the four of them sat around on logs, swishing away flies, and eating damper and salted beef. They boiled the billy on the coals and drank black tea with lashings of sugar. Nearby, the horses grazed, hobbled by chains around their pasterns.

On the ride home, they'd raced each other and John had won—he was the best rider of them all. They'd arrived back at the homestead just as the sun was going down. Sharing a bottle of rum, they sat and watched the colours of the ranges change from pink, to purple, to red, to gold, and finally to a deep blue.

It had been a perfect day.

Mary jolted her mind back from her memories, and swallowed hard before shaking herself.

'Come on now, Mary-May,' she said to herself, using her mother's pet name for her. 'You can't get to your age without a few regrets and a bit of sadness.'

She flicked quickly through the rest of the photo album. Two pages from the end, she stopped at a portrait. Leaning in close, she adjusted her glasses and stared at the face for a long time.

They had the same shaped eyes. She looked harder. *Perhaps their noses were similar? And the shapes of their faces?*

Mary closed the album. She wished she understood.

Chapter 29

It had taken him a while to decide, but now he was convinced it was the only way to go. Dominic would go to Port Augusta and see if he could find Ashleigh himself. Simon was obviously going to be no use to him.

Simon. He'd turned out to be more of a hindrance than a help. Dominic thought he had enough of a hold over the other man that he wouldn't turn on him, but he had to be sure.

Dominic knocked on Simon's door and waited, his hands in his pockets. When the door opened, Simon just waited, not inviting him in.

'You're not going to let your old friend in?' Dominic asked in a jovial tone, his breath white in the cold night air.

'What do you want, Dominic?'

Dominic looked around.

'You should probably ask me in.'

Wordlessly, Simon stepped out of the doorway and let him through.

He'd just closed the door and was turning back to face him when Dominic shoved him violently. Simon staggered backwards, smashing against the door.

'What the—' Simon groaned and stood leaning against the door.

'That's just a little reminder,' Dominic said, standing tall and imposingly over Simon's hunched frame, 'not to cross me. You'll regret it if you do.'

'I'm not going to turn on you!' Simon snapped, gently feeling his cheek.

'Really? That's good,' Dominic said quietly. 'I'd hate to have to silence you, you know?' There was a pause while Simon took in the insinuation. 'So, how about you prove it?'

Simon looked down. 'I won't grass on you, but get the fuck out of my house now and don't come back. I'm done with you, Dominic.'

'No, you're not. You're done when I tell you you're done. I've got one more job for you. How about we go into the lounge and talk about it? After you.' Dominic indicated for Simon to go before him.

When they were sitting on the couch, Dominic leaned forward and spoke in a low voice. 'After that vigil, there's got to be information coming in from the Crime Stoppers hotline.'

'Not necessarily,' Simon answered. 'If no one's seen her, they won't be ringing up, because there's nothing to report.'

'Someone knows something. I was given information that she pawned the pocket watch in Port Augusta.'

Simon snorted. 'She won't be there now. She could be north, west or south of there.'

'That may be the case, but I'm going to try. I need any

information you can get. I'm flying out tomorrow morning and hiring a car. I'll stay away until I find something.'

Dominic watched Simon swallow nervously, his Adam's apple bobbing up and down. There were beads of sweat on his face.

Good, Dominic thought. *Be very afraid*. Then he told him, 'And you'll be coming with me.'

Simon said nothing.

'Good, there's no argument, then. I'll see you at seven in the morning. You'd better pack a bag.'

Dominic turned and left the room.

☙

Simon sat on his couch, Dominic's words echoing in his mind, and shook his head. Half of him wanted to cry, he was so frightened, and the other half of him wanted to hurt Dominic very, very badly.

If only he'd realised that Dominic would own him forever, he would have taken his chances with Internal Affairs nine years before.

Simon had been an up-and-coming star at the Police Academy. He'd blitzed all his courses and everyone knew he would climb the ranks quickly. Jindabyne was his first posting and he had tackled it enthusiastically. Five weeks after he'd started in the job, though, it had all turned to shit and never got better.

He'd been on night patrol and, after a busy night of breath-testing drivers, he'd gone to the pub for a quiet drink with his partner. The next day, when he woke up, he found a woman he didn't know in his bed. She had fresh bruises on her face and handprints on her upper arms.

He remembered staring at her, wondering what the hell had happened. Dread and panic had crept over him like an oil slick over water. Looking at her more closely, he realised that she was unconscious. His police officer instincts kicked in and he started to check her vitals, but she came to and started to scream.

'Get away from me! I'm going to have you charged with rape.'

Simon had tried to calm her down, to tell her that he didn't remember anything and—although he couldn't explain the bruising—he was sure nothing had happened.

It didn't make any difference. She held out her hands to ward him off while picking up her clothes, then fled from the house.

He'd wandered around in a daze until, two hours later, Dominic had arrived on his doorstep, with photos of the woman propositioning him—or, at least, someone who looked like him—and of the two of them in bed. He promised that if Simon got information for him when he needed it, he would make this little problem go away.

Being so young and green, Simon had immediately agreed. He'd regretted it ever since. Now he knew there had been no evidence of him hitting the woman and that someone else had done it. He'd often wondered why Dominic had chosen him, and the only reason he had been able to come up with was that he, Simon, was new in the job and would be easy to manipulate.

Leaning forward, he rubbed his hand over his face and closed his eyes. *What to do now?* Stabbing the digits of the number he had committed to memory, he then listened to it ring and ring.

Fuck.

He could send an email but that would leave a paper trail. The phone would leave a trace too, but it would take longer to find—Dominic wouldn't be able to pull his phone records quickly.

He knew he should just go straight to the New South Wales police and tell them what Dominic was planning.

But he couldn't. He was in too deep. He had to go along with his plan.

He hoped that, wherever Ashleigh was, that she was well hidden. Maybe he could save her life and his own. He would pack his bag and hope like hell that things would turn out okay. There was nothing else for it.

'Damn.' He ground his teeth together, feeling the panic in his stomach rise. He tried the number again but there was still no answer. Of course there wouldn't be. Those tiny police stations in tiny towns were never open at night. But there was usually an answering machine at least. He wondered why his previous call hadn't been returned.

And then there was the man who had come to him on the night of the vigil.

'Now, Simon, I know you're not a bad man and you'll do the right thing,' he'd said. 'You've just been caught in a trap with Dominic. I know that you wouldn't want anything to happen to Ashleigh—can you imagine the guilt you'd feel?'

Simon had rubbed his hands together and kept glancing over his shoulder. He didn't know who this man was or why he was speaking to him. Or how he knew Simon was involved with Dominic.

The man's message was clear, though—a contact and a number to call if there were any threat to Ashleigh.

The name was that of Detective Dave Burrows.

Sighing deeply, Simon went to his desk, took out a piece of paper and a pen and began to write. He described how he had been roped into Dominic's gang and what they had done since he had been involved with them. He wrote as much as he knew of Dominic's business dealings and, lastly, about the assault on Ashleigh and why she had left.

When he'd finished, he put it in an envelope and wrote on the front: 'In the event of my death, please post,' giving the address of the organised crime unit. He left it leaning against the phone on his desk. He could only hope that if something happened to him while he was away, the police, not Dominic, would find the letter.

He began to pack his bag slowly. Every time he placed an article of clothing in the suitcase, he felt like he was taking a step closer to death.

ↄ

The next morning when Dominic pulled up outside his house, Simon walked out to the car with a feeling of dread. He'd tried all night to get through to Dave, without success.

After a silent drive to Canberra airport, Dominic handed Simon his ticket and they both checked in their bags.

'I'm going to get more coffee,' Dominic said.

Simon nodded.

As soon as Dominic was out of sight, Simon raised his phone to his ear and dialled.

This time, an answering machine picked up.

His heart rate sped up as he listened to a woman's voice telling him he'd called the Barker police station and to leave a message. He cleared his throat, keeping a close lookout for Dominic, then started to speak.

'This message is for Detective David Burrows. My name is Simon McCullen and I was with the New South Wales police force. I have been stood down, pending an internal investigation regarding my dealings with one Dominic Alberto. I was given you as a point of contact regarding the missing person case of Ashleigh Alberto. Mr Alberto is travelling to South Australia to search for his missing wife. I believe that Mrs Alberto may be in danger.

'I am not contactable.' He was about to say more when he saw Dominic walking back towards him. Hoping that he hadn't seen what he was doing, Simon very slowly turned away from him and slid the mobile phone into his pocket.

It didn't matter that he hadn't said everything he'd wanted to. He'd got his main message across.

Chapter 30

Eliza walked slowly down the main street of Blinman, with a weeding tool in her hand. Everyone was out and about, making sure the town was tidy and presentable.

So far today, she'd pulled out two bagfuls of weeds and cleaned the windows of Maureen's store, and she'd just about had enough. The flies were crawling all over her and it was the first really hot day she'd experienced since she'd arrived. Up here the sun certainly had a different feel than in Jindabyne. Its fierce heat was unrelenting and made the air feel like it was crackling.

'It's a bit unseasonal,' Reen had agreed, when Eliza had asked if it usually went from being cool in the morning and bearable in the afternoon one day, to baking the next. 'Might get a thunderstorm if the heat keeps up.'

Eliza had glanced disbelievingly up at the sky. It was a clear blue and she couldn't see a cloud anywhere.

Reen saw what she was doing and laughed. 'Oh, you won't

see anything yet,' she said. 'It'll be later on this afternoon, when you least expect it. You might look up and one moment there's nothing there, and, five minutes later, when you look again, you'll see just a wisp of cloud. Then, before you know it, the clouds have formed. Then they join up and, the next minute, you hear the rumbles.' She sighed wistfully. 'I *love* thunderstorms.'

'I can't wait to see one,' Eliza said. 'I've been reading up on how to take photos of lightning.'

Reen laughed. 'You should be able to get plenty of practice. Trouble is, if it's been a good season and the dry storms come through, they can start fires.'

'Where's the closest fire brigade?' Eliza asked.

'Honey, there ain't no such thing up here. It's all of us doing the best we can. Some of the places are inaccessible and they just have to burn. All the pastoralists have fire units, and there's a small one in town here that we all take turns jumping on.' She paused for a moment. 'Well, the blokes do. Us women, we tend to just feed everyone.'

Eliza shook her head. *Still*, she thought, *there's no hospital or police station; why would there be a fire brigade?*

A ute drove in with a pile of wood on the back, and Eliza recognised the vehicle as Jacob's. She smiled and waved as he slowed down.

'Come and give me a hand?' he asked, leaning over to the passenger's side window and smiling back at her.

'What are you doing?'

'Gotta get all this wood unloaded. We light a huge fire the morning of the cook-off and, as you can see, there's not a lot of wood around here, so we bring it in from the stations.'

Eliza turned to Reen. 'Can you do without me for a little while?'

Reen waved her away. 'Go on, you two, I'll be fine.'

Eliza climbed into the ute and Jacob drove the short distance to the creek. There were plenty of other utes with piles of wood on them. They climbed onto the back of Jacob's ute and started throwing the wood into the pile.

'Have you been out to the park recently?' Jacob asked.

'No,' she answered as she hoisted another large branch onto the pile. 'It's school holidays, so I don't really need to go. I'm sure I'll see the girls here and they'll have a heap of stories to tell me when I do.' She reached back for another one, and her hands connected with Jacob's as he also reached for another.

'Sorry,' she said and immediately pulled her hand back.

'I don't bite, despite what you may have heard,' he answered, his eyes twinkling.

Eliza turned away before he could see her smile. 'Tell me a bit more about the cook-off,' she asked, stretching her back. Looking across the creek bed, she could see Mark and Stu shovelling ash out of fire pits. John Caulder had made a rare appearance in town and was standing next to Dessie's four-wheel drive, deep in conversation with the minister.

'It would be easier for you to experience it than for me to tell you! But I'll try. All the tourists start to roll up a day or so out, and set up their caravans and camper trailers.'

'Where do they all park?'

Jacob spread his arm to indicate the whole area. 'Anywhere they like. If they end up out at the golf course, there's a long drop they can use out there, but, honestly, just as long as they're here, we don't care where they park.' He threw off the last piece and then jumped onto the ground, his hat falling off. He offered his hand to Eliza and helped her jump down before he picked it up. 'The morning of the cook-off, we stoke the red steer.'

'The what?' Eliza crinkled her brow as she looked at him.

'Sorry, the fire. We get the fire going and make sure we've got coals. You need coals to cook with, not flames.'

Eliza nodded and swiped at flies, wishing she'd brought her fly net with her.

'When it's ready, me and a few others cart all the coals around to the entrants, put them in the fire pits and let them loose!' He turned and grinned at her. 'We're called the fire boys,' he said in a suggestive tone while wiggling his eyebrows at her.

Without thinking, she quipped: 'Tell me you wear a uniform? I like men in uniform.'

He snapped his fingers at her. 'See? You're flirting with me! Good girl. Nice to know you haven't totally sworn off men.'

Eliza blushed and turned away, then felt a hand on her shoulder.

'Hey,' Jacob said quietly, gently turning her back to face him. 'I'm only joking. Don't panic. Whatever you've been through, I know you're not ready yet. But when you are, I'm first in line, okay?'

Eliza realised she had no damn idea what to say to that.

What she did know, through Dave's kindness after he had confronted her about her true identity, was she didn't need to be as frightened of men as she had thought. And it wasn't just Dave who had proved this. It was Chris, Jacob, John and Dessie.

Not all men were bad.

It was Dominic who was.

She glanced up at Jacob and realised he was still looking at her. She blushed.

'Eliza! Hey, Eliza? Uncle Jacob!'

Grateful for the distraction, she turned, and saw Heidi and Tilly running towards her.

'Hello, you two,' she said, trying to act like nothing of note had been happening. 'What are you doing all the way up here?'

Heidi gave her a strange look. 'It's not that far.'

'No,' Eliza agreed. 'It's not really.' *What a thing to say*, she thought, embarrassed. Jacob's words had really thrown her.

'How are you, squirts?' Jacob asked, reaching down to ruffle both the girls' hair. 'Been a while since I've seen so much mischief in one place.'

Tilly had a serious expression on her face. 'We're not as much mischief as *someone* is.' She scuffed the ground with the toe of her boot and looked up, her head on one side.

Eliza could see she wanted to spill the beans about something. 'That sounds mysterious.'

Heidi elbowed her sister. 'Shh. You're not supposed to say anything.'

Jacob squatted down, and looked from one girl to the other. 'You can always tell your Uncle Jacob anything and he'll never say a word to anyone, you know that!' He winked at each girl.

Eliza swallowed hard and wondered if he had any faults. He had to. Everyone did.

Tilly fixed her sister with a stare. 'I know,' she said in a stern tone, 'but Eliza's been out there a lot and she might have seen something. That's the only reason I'm telling her. And Uncle Jacob is her boyfriend, so he won't say anything.'

237

'What?' Eliza said before she could stop herself. 'No.' She paused. 'Where did that come from, huh?' She didn't dare look at Jacob. She knew he'd be grinning at her. 'What cheeky rabbits you are!'

'You just looked like it, that's all,' Heidi said before turning to her sister. 'I told you not to say stuff like that.'

'It's okay, girls,' Jacob broke in. 'Rest assured, we're just mates.' He slid a sideways glance at Eliza and winked. 'For the time being,' he finished in a lower voice.

She glared at him, then turned her attention back to the two pairs of brown eyes staring up at her. 'So, what's your news, then?' She sat down on the ground, crossed her legs and patted the dirt beside her. 'It sounds like it's a big story, so we might need to sit down.'

'So big it needs milkshakes?' Jacob asked.

Tilly frowned at him. 'Uncle Jacob! This is important.'

'Sorry, Tilly. I just thought you might need a chocolate milkshake for strength.'

'Someone's been stealing animals and eggs in the park,' Tilly blurted out before anyone could interrupt her again.

There was a silence and Eliza blinked a couple of times, trying to take in what she had said.

Beside her, Jacob let his breath out in a *'whoosh'* and slid to the ground too. 'That's pretty serious, little dude,' he commented. 'Where have you heard this?'

Heidi launched into the story of how they found the emu eggs missing and what Dave had done when he'd gone out there.

'Hey, you lot!' Mark Patterson called as he started shovelling out another fire pit. 'Not slacking off, are you?'

'Looks like you've got everything under control, Mark,' Jacob called back, giving him the thumbs up. 'You don't need us!' He turned his attention back to Tilly. 'Sounds like Detective Dave is managing it, though.'

'I guess,' Heidi said, her head cocked. 'Have you seen anything funny, Eliza?'

'Not really, Heidi. I'm not sure what I'd be looking for, though. I think you two would know more about it than I would.'

'But I think we should go out and see if we can catch them. These people are really naughty, Uncle Jacob.'

'I totally agree with you,' he said, pushing his hat back further on his head. 'But this is not a job for little people. You're too precious to be wandering around the bush at night when there's bad people out there.'

Heidi and Tilly glared at him. 'We weren't going to go by ourselves,' Tilly said. 'We wanted you to come with us.'

Eliza quickly held up her hands and shook her head. 'That's a very big no-no, Tilly. It's dangerous. I'm pretty sure these people don't want to be caught, so they wouldn't be nice to you if they found you watching them.'

The girls looked disappointed. 'But we've got to help,' Heidi whined.

'This is a lesson in patience,' Jacob started. 'Something I know a lot about.'

Eliza avoided looking at him.

'Detective Dave is going to know how to catch these people and he's going to need time to do it. So, the best thing you girls can do is watch and listen, but nothing more. No nightly jaunts out into the bush, no questions for tourists—just watch

239

and listen, and tell Dad, or me or Eliza or Dave, if you see or hear anything.'

Tilly crossed her arms.

Eliza leaned forward and touched her knee. 'We're very serious about this, Tilly. It's not something you can get involved in. Promise me you won't.'

Both girls looked down at the ground. Tilly picked up a handful of creek sand and let it drift through her fingers.

'We need an answer, girls,' Jacob insisted. 'Heidi?' He poked her with his boot.

'Suppose,' she said sullenly.

'Tilly?'

'I want to help.'

'I know, sweetheart, but staking out somewhere at night isn't the way. Now, promise me and I'll go and get those milkshakes.'

She had a very cranky look on her face when she finally looked up at him. 'Okay.'

Chapter 31

Chris wiped the cobwebs from his hair, dusted down his shorts and stood for a moment, his eyes adjusting from the dimness of the shed to the bright sunlight.

He'd counted fourteen marquees stacked in the shed and knew there were three that needed new frames. On his last trip to Port Augusta, he'd had them made up and they were in the back of the ute. Now all he had to do was find which bag held the buggered ones, and he'd be able to check that the loos in the tennis clubrooms were all in working order. After that, he'd head over to Reen and see what other jobs she had for him.

He was trying to keep busy. When Dave had come to talk to him about the poaching, he hadn't known how to respond or what to do. After a while, he'd decided he just needed to keep on doing what he had always done—run and look after the park. But he would be keeping his eyes a little more open and his wits about him.

The cook-off was a great distraction for him. As much as he liked keeping to himself, he enjoyed helping out with getting ready for the big event.

The main street was a hive of activity. A couple of kids ran across the road, shouting and laughing. Another group, of station kids, was kicking a footy down the dusty street. There were five four-wheel drives belonging to tourists parked in front of the general store—they were covered in mud and the swags on the roof racks looked like they'd been well used. Further on, near the pub, more vehicles were parked and they had obviously been driving on dirt roads too. Laughter rang out from the beer garden of the pub, where people were eating lunch. He found it amazing that a town of eighteen people could swell to as many as seven hundred in the space of a few days.

'Dad!'

He turned, and saw Heidi and Tilly crossing the street from the shop.

'Look what Uncle Jacob bought us!' They held up their milkshakes.

'Aren't you the lucky ones,' he said, smiling at them. He looked around to see if he could see Jacob. He wanted to talk to him.

He inhaled deeply as he saw Eliza and Jacob walking down the steps of the store, laughing together. He pursed his lips, then turned back to the girls.

'Did Eliza make them for you?'

Tilly spoke around the straw. 'Nope, Reen did.'

'Hey, look, there's Nicki!' Heidi cried excitedly, seeing one of her friends from the School of the Air. 'I'll be back later, Dad.'

'No worries, take your sister with you,' he called after her, and watched with pride as she stopped and waited for Tilly to catch up. Chris thought to himself that he was glad he'd made the sacrifices he had to make sure his girls stayed with him.

'Hi, Chris,' said Eliza, coming to stand next to him.

'Chris.' Jacob acknowledged his brother while taking a long swig on a cool drink. 'Reckon we've got everything nearly organised.'

'I'm just trying to find those three marquees from last year that had buggered frames.'

'Oh yeah, that's right,' Jacob nodded. 'I'd forgotten. One day, we'll get organised and make a list at the end of the cook-off, so we don't have to try and remember what needed fixing from the year before.'

'Nah, wouldn't be as much fun!' Chris answered wryly.

Jacob looked around. 'I really hope this is going to be a good one.'

Eliza smiled at him. 'Well, I can't wait to see what it's like,' she said, her eyes shining.

'Everything all right out at Manalinga?' Chris asked, turning to Jacob.

He nodded. 'Things are looking a picture. I bet the park is too?'

'Incredible,' he answered. 'It's been a hell of a long time since it's looked as good. And the amount of tourists we've had through,' he shook his head with a grin, 'bloody truckloads of them.'

'It's so great for Blinman, when we've got to rely so much on the tourist dollar.'

'Dead right there.'

'Guess I'd better be off,' Jacob said. 'I've gotta shift a mob of sheep before dark tonight. I'll be back in with another load of wood tomorrow morning.'

'Yeah, I'd better get back and help Reen,' Eliza said. 'See you later, Jacob.'

'Catch you, mate,' Chris answered, relieved to see his brother go. 'Eliza, are you coming to the park tomorrow?'

'Oh, Chris, I wasn't going to. It's school holidays, Reen needs me to help out as much as I can at the moment. Do you mind?'

'Nah, not at all, just thought I'd check.'

Eliza started to move away, but abruptly stopped and looked back.

Chris quickly averted his gaze, hoping she hadn't seen him staring at her. By the look on her face, he hadn't been quick enough.

'I just need to talk to you quickly about the girls.'

He sighed. 'What have those little ferals been up to now?'

'Nothing yet,' Eliza laughed. Her expression was soft as she talked about them. 'You've done such a great job of raising those kids, Chris. They're lovely, and independent and self-sufficient. Smart too.'

A one-sided grin played around Chris's mouth. 'There's a huge great big bloody "but" coming here.'

'No,' Eliza said, then paused. 'Well, sort of.'

'Come on,' Chris said in a resigned tone as he put his arm on her elbow and turned her towards the shop. 'Let's get a coffee and you can tell me all about it.'

❧

So they would have privacy, Chris and Eliza took their mugs of coffee back to the tennis clubrooms. As they sat in the cool darkness, Chris could see she didn't want to blurt anything out, so he started talking about the cook-off last year and how many people had come.

'This selfie trail you've got going is a great drawcard too. I don't know why we hadn't thought of something like that before.' He hesitated. 'Actually, I don't really have a lot to do in the twelve months leading up to it. Reen and Mary are the ones who chase the sponsorship and pull it all together. Many of us just turn up in the two weeks beforehand and help out. I'm one of them.'

Eliza took a sip of her coffee. 'So, what's your job on the day?' she asked. 'Are you a fire boy too?'

Chris looked at her for a long time and then a wicked expression crossed his face.

'Whaaaat?' she asked.

'I'd rather put the fire out than start it,' he said in a suggestive tone.

Eliza's eyes widened and she started to laugh. 'Well, I probably walked into that one!' She put her coffee cup down and looked at him, still smiling. 'I didn't know you had a depraved sense of humour!'

'There's a few things you don't know about me,' Chris agreed. He tried to hold eye contact with her, but a now-familiar uncomfortable expression crossed her face and he knew to stop. He wondered if it happened when she was with Jacob or if it was just when she was with him.

'So, about these kids,' he prompted.

'Again, Chris, they really are such great kids,' she said.

'But, listen, they both came to me today and told me what was going on at the park.'

Chris looked down, his stomach dropping. 'They weren't supposed to say anything.'

'No, but they wanted to tell me, in case I'd seen anything. Which I haven't,' she added quickly. 'But what worries me is that they're going to sneak out at night to try and see something.'

Chris felt shock travel through him. 'Surely they wouldn't do that.' He stopped. 'Actually, you know what, I can see them doing *exactly* that.'

A little laugh escaped Eliza. 'Yeah, I could too. And as much as I think it's funny, it's pretty serious too. I'd hate for them to accidentally get in the middle of something they shouldn't. Because you know what?'

'What?'

'They are the type of kids who'll find something. They're too clever for their own good. And they'll get into trouble.'

Chris tried to quell his anxiety. He'd never thought about the possibility of the girls getting involved but he should have. Of course they weren't going to stand back and let fauna be taken from their home. He'd brought them up to love this place. God, what an idiot he was. He shouldn't have let them hear as much as they had when Dave had come by.

Eliza laid a hand on his arm. 'I'm sorry I've upset you. I just thought you should know.'

He covered her hand with his. 'I should have seen it coming. Thank you.'

They sat like that for a moment, and then Eliza gently extracted her hand and walked over to the honour boards on the wall.

'Recognise any names?' Chris asked.

'Only Mary and John Caulder,' she answered. Her voice echoed in the gloomy room. 'Oh, there's Jacob. I didn't know he played.'

'He's pretty good. Mary and John would always drag us to the tennis. Wasn't something I got into. I much preferred the cricket.'

'And Stacey and Mark.'

There were photos on the other wall as well, and Eliza moved over to look at them. 'Mary was so beautiful when she was younger,' she said softly.

Chris came up behind her and stood so close he could smell her shampoo.

'See this picture here?' he asked, pointing to a black-and-white photo next to Mary's portrait. 'I reckon you look so much like her, it's not funny.'

Chris watched as Eliza turned to look. An emotion he couldn't put a name to crossed her face and she reached up to trace the image of the woman in the picture.

'You guys related or what?' he asked.

Eliza shook her head. 'I wouldn't have thought so,' she answered softly.

'What do you mean you wouldn't have thought so?' he asked, puzzled. 'Don't you know?'

'No,' she answered softly. 'No. I wouldn't have any idea.'

Chapter 32

Dessie stopped to speak to a few people as he walked slowly down the main street of Blinman. There was always someone calling out to him and wanting his attention. Even though he was usually happy to give it, today he had other things on his mind. He was in turmoil and wasn't sure what to do.

He noticed Eliza and Chris standing out the front of the tennis club, deep in conversation. He stopped and watched them for a moment and, as if she knew he was watching her, Eliza looked over at him. She gave him a small smile before turning her attention back to Chris.

A mob of galahs swooped down and flew through the main street, squawking loudly, before coming in to land in some gum trees on the outskirts of town. They'd come so close to Dessie that he had felt the air move above his head.

He smiled contentedly. He loved this place.

'G'day, Dessie.' The voice behind him made him turn. 'Long time, no see.'

'Dave! Good to see you.' Dessie offered his hand.

'Here for long?'

'I'll stay until the cook-off is finished, but then I need to head over Coober Pedy way. You been busy?'

'Hasn't been too bad until recently. There seems to be a bit of action in the national park that needs looking at, but the last big case I had was that rodeo money being stolen last year.'

They leaned companionably against the railing at the front of the shop and chatted for a while. Presently, Dave said, 'I'm in a bit of a quandary, Dessie.'

'Are you now, Dave? What seems to be the problem?' *You and me both*, he thought.

'I've got a report I need to put in but I'm sure it's going to put someone at risk of retaliation. I'm an above-board cop, I always have been, but for some reason this particular investigation has made me feel something I've never felt before. It doesn't seem right to put someone in danger. Of course, we as a police force can look out for this person—put him or her in protective custody, but that doesn't sit well with me.'

Dessie didn't say anything, picking off some flaking paint from the rails.

'I feel like this person has done a lot to change their life, and they should be given the opportunity to go ahead without fear or having to go into something as severe as witness protection.'

'Sounds pretty serious.' Dessie looked across the road. He never rushed speaking to people about their problems. He was content to let them talk and, while they did so, let his mind run over the scriptures. Usually the answer was in them; he just had to find the right one.

'I think you have to do what you swore to do, Dave,' he

finally said. 'And then keep an eye and ear to the ground and help protect whoever it is. I don't see any other way. If you don't put in the report, you're breaking your contract with the police force, but when you do put it in, then within the limits of your job, you'll be able to protect this person. But,' he held up a finger as he looked at Dave. 'You might need to call in reinforcements. You have to remember, you're not a one-man band. You're part of a group of people who work together to protect the community.'

Dave nodded slowly. 'Yeah, you're right. I knew you'd say that. I don't even know why I'm questioning what I should do. Something just feels different about this case.'

'Well, maybe you can delay putting the report in for a few more days? But is it really going to change the outcome?'

'No. I need to put it in when I head back today. And probably not. Might as well just bite the bullet and get it over with.'

'Good man,' Dessie answered. He noticed that Eliza and Chris were now walking away from the tennis club, towards the fire pits in the creek. He had a thought.

The tennis clubrooms! Of course! Why hadn't he thought of it earlier?

'Would you excuse me, Dave?'

'Yeah, no worries, mate. I've got to get on the road, so I can turn around and come back here again!'

'Drive carefully, my friend.'

'See you in a few days.'

Dessie crossed the road as quickly as his ageing body would let him and pulled open the door to the tennis clubrooms.

When his eyes had adjusted to the dimness, he gazed around, remembering the times he, Mary and John and Richard and Clara had sat here, watching others play, or playing themselves.

There had been so much camaraderie within the community. Everyone was on a level playing field, experiencing the same thing at the same time.

Of course, there had been sad times. As he sat there, he recalled the time a local girl had started to complain of leg pains and how, shortly afterward, they had found a lump on her hip. He remembered how he had sat with her father day after day, while they waited for news from his wife and the specialist in Adelaide. In the end, the man hadn't been able to stand it any longer and left late one night to drive down to the city. Dessie thought about how he had tried to talk him into waiting until morning, but had no success. So, as the next best thing, he offered to drive him.

At the hospital, they sat by her bed until early the next morning, when the specialist arrived to tell them the lump wasn't malignant.

Together, they had wept at the good news.

When Dessie visited the stations and the owners were too busy to stop work, he'd jump in and give them a hand. He'd spent countless days in dusty yards, walking behind mobs of sheep and helping herd cattle. He found it a little harder now, but he still enjoyed stock work if there was something for him to do.

After receiving a call via the UHF radio that someone needed him, he would drive through the night to offer comfort and help. He'd buried the community's loved ones, married them and christened their babies. He'd even been invited to a birthday party or two.

He loved his job, and there was no better place to do it than the Flinders Ranges.

He looked at the photograph of Clara for a long time, before the sound of the door opening and a beam of sunlight streaming in made him turn around.

Eliza was silhouetted in the doorway.

'Oh, sorry,' she said. 'I didn't realise you were in here, Dessie. I was just coming to . . .' she trailed off.

'No worries, Eliza. I was just resting my legs in the cool. It's begun to get a bit warm outside.'

'You're not kidding!' She stepped into the room and walked over to sit alongside him. 'I knew it'd get hot, but the change has been huge, and so quick!'

'It's a changeable landscape,' Dessie agreed. 'And that includes the weather.' He turned to look at her. 'So, Eliza . . .' He left the words hanging, to see if she would start to talk. When she didn't, he asked, 'Are you looking forward to the cook-off?'

'Yeah, I am. It's so lovely to be in a community where everyone works together and wants to help each other out.'

'You're liking it here in Blinman, then?'

'I really am. The people are great, and the countryside . . .' she shrugged. 'How do you even begin to describe the beauty of it?'

'Where were you before this, Eliza?'

'Oh, here and there.'

With his years of experience, Dessie could tell she wanted to talk but wasn't sure how to open up to him. 'You like photography, so I'm told,' he commented, leaning back in his chair and giving her his full attention.

'It's a new interest,' Eliza said brightly. 'How could you come here and not take photos? I've started selling them in

Reen's shop. Some are framed, some not. It's pretty hard to carry around photos in frames when you're camping.'

'Have you got a favourite spot to go and take photos?'

She shook her head. 'No. Just anywhere. I've got to admit, I love a good sunset and sunrise. The colours—well, I'm sure you've seen plenty!'

'That I have,' he said with a smile. 'And, let me tell you, there are none better than anywhere in the Flinders Ranges. Except, perhaps, parts of the Northern Territory. But I think it's the ranges that make the ones here so beautiful.' He paused. 'I think I like sunrises just slightly more than sunsets.'

'Why's that?'

'Well,' he crossed his arms over his stomach and closed his eyes as he thought about what to say. 'I think it's because it's the dawn of a new day. Every day is a new start and it's a gift. "*A new day will dawn on us because our God is loving and merciful.*"'

'Luke 1:78,' she said softly.

He looked at her in gentle surprise. 'You know the scriptures, Eliza?'

She said quietly, looking down at her hands, 'I thought I'd forgotten a lot of them, but I guess once they're ingrained, they're hard to forget. I was made to go to Sunday school, where we repeated heaps of verses, much to the joy of our teacher. Not so much the students.'

Dessie nodded. 'Yes, they would be hard to forget.' He looked at her for a long moment, trying to work out what he was feeling. Relief? Sadness? Joy? A mixture of all three? 'You don't have any family then, Eliza?' he asked softly.

She sat there for a long while. He had begun to think she wasn't going to answer, when she looked up at him, a strange look on her face. 'No,' she answered in a high, thin voice. 'No, I don't have any family. I was left at a church when I was a baby, only a few days old. There was no information on who my birth mother or father was. For a long time, I didn't really care who my mother was.' She took a shuddering breath. 'Actually, to be honest, I always cared, but as she'd abandoned me, I thought she'd made her feelings pretty clear, so I didn't think there'd be any point in looking. I never let myself think about her.' Eliza looked down. 'I thought I'd made a home with a man who loved me. Not having had a family didn't matter. But it turned out I didn't really know him and, suddenly, all that mattered to me was having a family.'

She stared at him intently. 'I want to know who my mother was, but I can't see any way of finding out. So, I'll stay where I feel like I have a mother, and that's here. In Blinman. Reen is like a sister and a mother rolled into one. Mary and John are very kind, like grandparents, and everyone else is like my aunts and uncles. They're interested in me and I'm interested in them.' She took another breath. 'Does that make sense?'

'It makes more sense than you realise,' Dessie answered from the bottom of his heart.

Chapter 33

Dominic sat in a darkened corner of the pub, nursing a whisky. It was his third day in Port Augusta and he hadn't made any progress.

Simon slipped into the seat opposite him and shook his head. 'No go.'

Pressing his lips tightly together, Dominic knew he had to control his anger in public, though what he really wanted to do was slam his fist into the table. He also knew he had to be patient. She would slip up, and when she did, he would be waiting. Ready to pounce.

'Damn.'

'I've got one more pawn shop to try.'

Dominic frowned. 'Why haven't you been there already?'

'Everything takes time, Dom. When you're in the police force, you realise that as much as you want to hurry things, you can't. Then there are other times that it all falls into place so quickly, you'd think a bushfire is chasing it. This isn't one of those times.'

They sat in silence, both staring out into the street. Dominic was sure he'd recognise her. No matter how dramatically she could change her appearance, she wouldn't be able to alter her movements, her mannerisms or her voice.

That would be the real giveaway: her voice.

He ran his hands over his face and rubbed at his stubble. The five-day growth was a bit of a ploy too. If she could change her appearance, then he could change his. Dominic figured she would have no idea he had an inkling of where she was. He assumed Ashleigh had begun to relax, to feel safe, wherever she was.

Simon got up from the table. 'Right, well, I guess I'll go and have a chat to the bloke in this next pawn shop.'

Dominic threw down the last of his whisky. 'I'll come too. I might be a little more persuasive than you.'

ை

Looking around the pawn shop, Simon marvelled at how much was crammed into one small area. A man sat on a stool, a newspaper spread across the glass-topped cabinet that acted as a counter. He looked at them over his glasses, which were perched on the end of his nose.

Simon hoped that by now Dave had received his message and communicated it to Ashleigh. He still didn't know for sure if this Dave Burrows knew where Ashleigh was or how he fitted into the picture. The last he'd heard, there hadn't been an information report on her.

All Simon could do was hope that she would stay hidden and safe.

'Can I help you?' the man asked, sounding bored.

'I hope so,' Dominic answered in his most pleasant tone. 'I'm wondering if you've had any pocket watches pawned here recently?'

Simon watched as the man froze and looked closely at both of them. He pushed his glasses back onto the bridge of his nose. 'And why would you be asking that?'

'Because we want to know,' Dominic sneered.

Simon stood back, still watching the man. It was clear he had bought the pocket watch. Maybe it was even on display. Dominic was so stupid, he hadn't even thought to look for it before asking the question.

Quietly, Simon moved over to a jewellery cabinet and peered in. Rings, necklaces and bracelets covered the top shelf. On the second shelf, there were watches, coins and a few other trinkets.

The watch wasn't there.

'I have a privacy policy that I have to adhere to, I'm sorry.' The man looked back down at the paper, as if he were dismissing them. 'If you had the ticket—well, that would be a different story.'

Simon walked over to the counter, hoping to stop Dominic from doing anything stupid. 'We're just wanting a little information on the person who might have pawned it,' he said, as he tried to make eye contact with the man.

'Sorry, can't help you with that.'

'We'd be very grateful if you did.'

The man shook his head again. 'Sorry, no can do.'

Dominic elbowed Simon out of the way and slammed his hand down on the counter, before leaning forward and grabbing the man's collar and pulling his face towards his own. 'Who. Pawned. The. Watch?' he spat.

The man screwed his face up as Dominic's spit landed on it.

'Let go of me or I'll call the police,' he said in a frightened voice.

'I'd like to see you try while I've got hold of you.'

'It was a girl,' he gasped.

Simon put his hand on Dominic's and tried to get him to loosen his grip. 'He'll talk more if you let him go,' he said. There was no way that he could be party to Dominic hurting anyone else.

Six months ago, it wouldn't have bothered him. Back then, Dominic still had a hold over him. Now, he didn't care a toss what Dominic thought and he, Simon, would protect the people he wanted to hurt.

He'd worked it out on the plane to Adelaide. It was the way Dominic kept people living in fear that had made Simon start to despise him; it was the way he had dominated Ashleigh and then physically abused her. But the truth was, as each year went by, he was more disgusted with himself for his weakness. He had to stand up and be strong at some point in his life, and that was now.

Simon ignored the glare Dominic shot at him and kept pulling Dominic's hand away, until he finally released his grip and the man sank back onto the stool.

He raised a hand to his face and wiped away the saliva that was gleaming on his top lip. 'It was a girl,' the man repeated, looking over at Simon. 'She haggled on the price a little bit, but I didn't shift much.'

'Did she have anyone with her? What did she look like?' Dominic rasped.

Simon glanced over at him, and saw his chest heaving and the veins in his neck pulsating. He feared that if Dominic didn't get the information he wanted, he wouldn't be able to control himself and all hell would break loose.

'She was by herself. And she didn't look much like the photo on her licence, I can tell you that much,' the man said. 'Her face was skinnier and not as round as in the photo. She mentioned that she'd lost weight since it was taken.'

'What did her hair look like?'

The man didn't answer.

'Answer me!'

'I'm thinking,' he said, his voice raised in panic. 'I can't rightly tell you. It was sort of shaggy. About to her shoulders, but all raggedy. And the colour . . . I think it was dark. I can't tell you anything more.'

Simon stepped in between Dominic and the counter. 'Did she say where she was living?'

'No! I just photocopied her licence, took the pocket watch and gave her the money. If I'd known it was going to bring you two to my door, I'd have told her to go somewhere else.'

'Can you tell us anything more? What she was wearing? Anything!'

The man shook his head. 'Nothing. I remember the weight loss and hair colour change. And she seemed nervous.'

'I want the pocket watch,' Dominic said.

'I don't have it.'

Dominic let fly with an expletive and made a sudden move towards the man.

Simon caught hold of him just before he reached the counter. The man cowered against the wall.

'I don't have it, I promise you. The police have already taken it.' He was almost sobbing and Simon assumed nothing like this had ever happened in his little shop.

'Thanks for your help,' he said, keeping a firm grip on Dominic. 'We'd really appreciate it if you didn't mention our visit.' He gave the man a small smile and pushed Dominic towards the door. 'You're not going to get anything else out of him,' he said quietly in his ear. 'You've probably made a big enough impression, so let's get the fuck out of here.'

Dominic shrugged his shoulders, rearranged his clothes and turned back to the man. 'If you mention this to anyone, I will come back and kill you.'

'I won't say a thing. You have my word. I'll take it to the grave.' The words tumbled out of the man's mouth in his speed to reassure them.

Out on the street, Simon turned angrily to Dominic. 'Well, that was fucking memorable. That bloke in there is never going to forget either of us now. He'd probably even be able to pick us out in a line-up. Did you have to throw your fucking weight around?'

'He was being smart. Not answering the questions.'

'Better to be a little less pushy than draw any more attention to ourselves by getting angry. You're a fuckwit.' Simon turned and walked down the street.

Once again, all he could do was hope that Burrows had got his message and knew how to contact Ashleigh. Dominic was becoming more of a loose cannon by the hour.

☙

Dominic went back to his darkened corner in the pub. The place was grotty and the carpet was stained. The few men who were sitting at the bar looked like they had been there for years without moving. They smelled like that too. He wished there were somewhere cleaner and nicer he could be. Somewhere that overlooked the water, maybe. It would calm his nerves. He signalled to the barman to bring him another two whiskies.

Simon was sitting with his back to him. That worried Dominic. There was something unpredictable about his copper mate these days and he wasn't sure he trusted him fully. But he still needed him.

Dominic raised a fresh glass of whisky to Simon.

Deep in thought, he didn't notice when two new people arrived in the pub. By the time he realised they were standing at the bar, talking to the bartender; he couldn't know how long they had been there. Their voices filtered through the mist of his anger and pierced his brain.

Could that woman be her?

He glanced across at Simon, who had swivelled around to face him, his eyebrows cocked in the same question. Dominic tried to make himself unnoticeable, all the while listening and watching intently.

She had black hair that reached her shoulders, with purple streaks running through it. Her skin was very brown, and she was wearing shorts and a singlet.

He couldn't see her face.

The woman spoke: 'We really appreciate your donation, Martin. It's very generous of you.'

It was her.

'No trouble at all. Good cause and all that,' the bartender replied.

From what he could see of the man standing next to her, he had a red neck and weathered hands. He wore a broad-brimmed hat. *A farmer? A fisherman?*

'Can we come round the back to pick it up?' the man asked Martin.

'Yeah, if you drive to the storage shed right at the back of the block, you can get it from there.' He fished around under the bar and handed them a key. As Ashleigh reached out to take it, her hair fell forward. Dominic watched as she tucked it back behind her ears. It was a gesture he'd seen thousands of times before.

'Beautiful, thanks muchly. Eliza will bring the key back as soon as we're finished. Are you heading up to Blinman for the cook-off? You came so close to taking out the grand prize last year!'

Dominic kept watching the three of them chatting, his fingers covering his face.

'I'll be up there for sure,' Martin said.

'Excellent,' Ashleigh—or Eliza—said. 'Righto, we'd better get on. We've got a heap more donations to pick up.'

'Drive safe. I'll see you in a couple of weeks, Jacob.'

They shook hands, and the two of them walked out of the pub without noticing anyone around them.

Dominic let out a breath, unable to contain his glee. 'We got her.'

'Are you sure it's her?'

'Positive. The voice . . .'

Simon nodded. 'Yeah, that's what I thought too.'

Dominic went to the window and stared out. *Ashleigh and this man . . . Jacob? Was that his name?* They were walking to a dusty dual cab. Ashleigh looked up at him and laughed at something he said.

Dominic watched the way she walked; the gentle sway of her hips and her rapid steps were all-too-familiar.

Anger welled so brutally in his chest, it almost took his breath away. He watched as they drove behind the pub and out of sight.

Returning to his seat, he made sure he sat with his back to the door and waited for her to come back inside.

Simon did the same, his heart thumping.

Minutes later, the door pushed open and Simon felt Dominic stiffen beside him. He tensed too, in case he had to tackle Dominic. He wouldn't let Ashleigh get hurt.

'Thanks, Martin. Thanks again for donating. All of the Blinman community really appreciates it. See you soon.' Her voice rang out clearly through the quiet pub.

'See you, Eliza. I'll be up there next week.'

Seconds later, the door had closed.

Chapter 34

Dave had pondered Dessie's words on the long drive back to the police station. The chaplain was right, he finally decided. *I have to put the report in.*

As he walked into the Barker police station he was greeted by Joan, who worked on the front desk. Her face was flooded with relief. 'I'm mighty pleased to see you,' she said.

'I like that type of greeting,' Dave grinned, then looked serious again. 'Unless you've got bad news for me,' he went on, watching her carefully.

'Not bad news. Just odd, and a bit scary.'

He gave her his full attention. 'Sounds interesting.'

'Listen to this.' She hit play on the answering machine.

Dave listened to the message in full and asked her to play it again.

'There's that name again,' he muttered. 'How the hell does he know me? And how the hell does he know I know where Eliza is?' He thought for a moment before focusing on Joan.

'Did you play this to Jack and Andy?'

'They haven't been in since we got it. I called Kim to ask when you were going to be back, as I knew this would be categorised as urgent, but she didn't know. I was just hoping it was today. And, well, here you are.'

'Right, leave it with me. Don't delete it.' He strode off to his office, shutting the door behind him. Running his fingers through his hair, he quickly made a decision.

'Reen?' he said into the phone. 'Is Eliza around?'

'No, she and Jacob have gone to Port Augusta, to pick up some of the donations. Do you want me to get her to give you a call when she gets back?'

'Yeah, please. Don't frighten her, but let her know it's very important.'

There was a silence. 'Anything you can tell me?'

Dave hesitated. 'I think her ex might have a bead on her.' He heard a sharp intake of breath.

'As in, knows where she is?'

'It's highly unlikely that he knows that she's in Blinman. More likely, he knows she's been in Port Augusta and is using that as a starting point.'

'But that's where she is today!' Reen's voice rose in panic.

'I realise that. I can't be sure if he's even there yet, so don't worry too much. Just get her to give me a call when she gets back.' He looked up at a soft knock on the door. Kim popped her head in and smiled, but backed out again when she saw he was on the phone.

Dave covered the mouthpiece with his hand. 'It's all right, I'm nearly finished—come in,' he said to Kim. Turning his attention back to Reen, he asked, 'Okay?'

265

'Okay,' she answered, sounding unconvinced.

'Any problems or anything weird, just let me know.'

'When are you back up here?'

'In the next couple of days. I'll be coming to stay until the cook-off.'

'Right. I think I'll be pleased to see you.'

'You usually are,' he said with a smile in his voice. 'Okay, I'll catch you later, but ring if you need to.'

'Sure.'

He hung up the phone and held his arms out to Kim. 'I've missed you,' he said before kissing her.

'Mmm, nice,' she muttered against his lips. 'I've missed you.'

He held her close, breathing in her perfume, then kissed the top of her head.

'You have to go back up there again?' she asked.

'Yep, and you can come next time, if you like. There's always plenty of helpers needed to get ready for the cook-off.'

'Anything to spend more time with you.'

He kissed her again, then tightened his arms around her. 'I really have missed you.'

'What's going on, sweetheart?' she asked into his chest.

He began to tell her about Eliza and the phone call. About his uncertainty regarding filing the report and about Dessie's advice.

'You know Dessie is right,' Kim said.

He nodded.

'Why aren't you ringing Adelaide and getting other officers involved?'

'I'm about to. This has gone beyond what I can deal with

myself.' He sighed. 'I really believe that he'll hurt her, if not kill her, if he finds her.'

'What about shifting her to somewhere different? Adelaide or Sydney?'

'I've got to go through the right channels to do that and we have to prove there's an actual threat against her.'

Kim crinkled her forehead. 'There *is* an active threat against her. You've got that message saying so.'

'From a cop who's under investigation by Internal Affairs.'

Kim walked to the window and looked out. Dave knew by her stance she was about to argue with him. That was all right. He knew what she would say and he agreed with her.

'It's Eliza's life you have in your hands.'

'I know,' Dave answered. 'It's okay—I'll call in STAR, as soon as I need to,' he went on, referring to the Special Tasks and Rescue Group, 'but I need to report to Steve first.'

Kim turned back to him with a lovely smile. 'I'll leave you to it, then,' she said.

જી

Everything was organised. Dave had filed his report and spoken to Steve, his boss, and organised to have Simon's message emailed to him.

Steve and Dave had worked together on the rodeo money theft and they respected each other. However, Dave knew that what Steve would like to do and what he was able to do were often two different things. He had to work within budgets that didn't always enable him to provide the equipment or back-up that Dave wanted.

In this case, Steve was assigning Adelaide detectives

to try to find out more about Dominic Alberto and Simon McCullen. Unexpectedly, Steve had also offered to put surveillance cameras in the national park to assist with the poaching investigation, which Dave had requested earlier, but said that Dave was more than capable of doing forensic work out in the field. He also said he would get a warrant to put a tap on Dominic's and Simon's phones. Whether he would be able to do so would depend on the amount of incriminating evidence the Adelaide detectives could find on both men.

↭

Three days later, Dave and Kim pulled into Blinman.

'I've made Eliza go and stay with Jacob for a while,' Reen said by way of greeting.

'Not a bad idea,' Dave answered as they all made their way to the verandah.

'I thought she could go and stay at the park with Chris, but there's too many people coming and going through there. He might be one of them.'

'Honestly, Reen, why would he target Blinman? He probably doesn't even know the town exists,' Kim interjected.

'I know, but I'd rather be safe than sorry.'

'We all would be.'

They stood silently together. It was still warm even though the sun was sinking over the hills. Voices drifted over from the pub and a swarm of flies buzzed under the tin verandah.

'Well, I'd better get going,' Dave said, soberly.

Kim turned to him, her face set. 'You'll be careful, won't you?'

'I always am, Kimmy,' he answered.

As she tried to smile at him, he continued, 'You know this is important.'

She swallowed and nodded.

He bent to kiss her, then quickly walked down the stairs without looking back. As he did, he heard Reen say: 'Come on, let's go and sit in the beer garden and have a drink. God knows we both need it.'

With that, Dave knew that Kim would be just fine. Reen would look after her.

Turning his mind to the job at hand, he drove out of town.

❦

Dave killed the lights on his vehicle just before he reached the park, and was thankful for the full moon, which would guide him from now on.

Parking behind a cluster of thick acacia bushes, he turned off the engine and got out. He pushed his door shut, the click loud in the quiet of the bush. It was still so warm that he broke into a sweat as he hoisted his pack onto his back, adjusted his night vision goggles and started through the bushland.

He walked five kilometres straight, stopping only to take a swallow of water. Dave loved night vision goggles for this type of work. He could avoid tripping over stones or bushes; he could quickly do what needed to be done and get straight out again.

Shortly after becoming a detective, he had investigated cannabis plantations, staking out plots with night vision goggles. He'd spent many nights hiding in bushes, documenting the comings and goings into and from plantations. Then motion detection cameras had changed the game.

He stopped, breathing heavily, and took a look around. There was a grove of trees growing on the edge of a sheer, rocky cliff, which was where he wanted to rig the surveillance cameras. With the Eliza problem, the poaching investigation had taken a back seat, but now it was time to get back into it.

A fox barked nearby and his heart rate sped up. He looked around. Dave wasn't sure if the government had baited for foxes this year, but there seemed to be fewer around and he was surprised to hear one.

Wiping an arm over his brow, he kept on going.

Half an hour later, he reached the grove of trees he was aiming for. He stood still and watched silently. The moon was lighting the landscape so brightly, the magpies had begun to sing, even though it was night-time.

Dave dropped his backpack on the ground and looked up into the trees. He needed a clear, but hidden, spot.

The rustling of a bush behind him made him freeze. Slowly, he turned and looked over his shoulder. A pair of eyes was looking at him. From beneath the brush, a rabbit crawled out and hopped off into the darkness.

'I don't think you're too welcome in a national park, buddy,' he muttered.

Turning back to the task at hand, he opened his backpack, and got out a drill and one of the cameras. Shimmying up the gum tree, he placed the camera inside a hole in the tree's trunk. He assessed the camera's view and screwed it into place. He repeated the process with another three cameras in another three trees.

There was nothing left to do now but wait.

And hope like hell something was captured on those SD cards.

Chapter 35

Eliza walked along the gum-lined creek, taking deep breaths of the morning air. It was difficult walking in some spots; the stones twisted under her feet and made her stumble. It didn't matter, though. Around her neck was her camera, and every so often she stopped and took a photo.

There were so many things to photograph: the galahs sitting in the trees, preening each other. Ragged fence lines and rusted barbwire. Rocks covered with moss, and gum trees that would be hundreds, if not thousands, of years old.

She chose a rocky outcrop and sat down, her face turned towards the horizon, where the sun was rising. The contentment she'd experienced since being on Manalinga had been wonderful. Dominic had been relegated to the past. She rarely thought of him anymore, and even though she knew he was a threat, it didn't seem to matter. Here there was nothing but tranquillity and it seemed to be seeping into her.

She heard rocks scatter and turned. Jacob was walking

towards her, holding a travel mug and something wrapped in alfoil.

'You took off early,' he said.

'Much too nice a morning to stay in bed,' she replied, reaching up to take the mug. 'What's this?' There was a very appealing smell coming from the alfoil.

'Bacon and egg sandwich, complete with barbecue sauce.'

'Yum! Thank you. Where's yours?' Eliza started to unwrap it and her stomach rumbled. She laughed self-consciously and put a hand on her belly. 'Looks like you turned up just in time.'

'I've eaten mine,' Jacob answered, sitting down next to her. 'I have to take off in about twenty minutes and check a couple of tanks. I'll come back and pick you up before I head into Blinman with another load of firewood.'

'Okay. I'll be ready.'

They both looked at the creek, drinking in the view.

'This place is so serene,' Eliza murmured. 'I love it here.'

'Do you feel safe?'

'More than.'

'Doesn't bother you going into Blinman?'

Eliza glanced over at him. 'No. Should it?'

Jacob shrugged. 'I don't know—I just thought being around people might make you a bit jumpy. If he's around . . .'

'Out here, it's like he doesn't exist. If I was in a city, I would feel less safe, even with more places to hide.' She nudged his shoulder. 'I think you're more worried than me!'

'I'm sure that's the case,' he answered seriously.

'All I know is, I feel at ease and it's the first time I've ever felt like this. I can't explain it. I think it has a lot to do with the country and the people. I don't want to be anywhere else.'

Jacob was silent for a moment.

'Well, my friend,' he finally said. 'You might change your mind when it's forty-eight degrees in the shade and you can't see your hand in front of your face for the dust. Enjoy loving it! I'd better get going. See you in a couple of hours.' He got up and stretched, then touched her shoulder and left.

Eliza watched him go, a warm feeling spreading through her. She was so blessed to have friends like Jacob.

∾

'Thanks again for your help,' Dessie said into the phone. 'It's much appreciated.' He hung up and took a deep breath in, then exhaled slowly.

Well, that was it. That was the last lead he'd had on the foster parents and it had turned out to be a dead end. There didn't seem to be anywhere else he could get information. All he could do was make a call according to what his gut was telling him.

He sat for a long time in the quiet of the Parachilna Gorge that morning. The wide open land, and expansive blue sky, was a better church than any building could ever be. As he did whenever he needed to think something through, he sat on a rock and closed his eyes, listening to the sound of nature. After opening them, he sat a little longer and soaked in the beauty of the area.

It was all about emptying his head of excess noise and concentrating on what really needed attention, so that he could hear what God was trying to tell him. 'Be still and know that I am God' was in the scriptures for a reason.

Dessie had kept this secret for many years and had never

273

thought he would have to reveal it. If he did, so many people would be affected, so many lives would be turned upside down.

He'd always been Clara's confidant and she had loved to talk. She was one of the few up here who did. Most were the strong, silent type—they used words sparingly. *Until they'd had one drink too many, that is!* he thought. Clara had usually been a pleasure to be around. But, while she liked to laugh and spread joy, without warning she would spiral into a deep pit of despair and anxiety.

If she was feeling well and a dust storm came through, she'd write messages for Richard in the dust. When sheep were dying, she would find something of beauty in nature and show it to everyone. When bushfires raged around them, Clara would get on with helping everyone. But when the black dog sat next to her, it was difficult for anyone to get even a word out of her. She would lie in her room, the curtains drawn, and not get out of bed for days.

Richard, on the other hand, while he'd loved a good time and was also quick to make a joke, kept things to himself. He had been a risk taker, and not in a positive way. He had ended up betting and losing much more than he could repay. He paid with his life.

Clara had never recovered from Richard's death. The black dog took hold and for months she couldn't function. It was all guesswork, but Dessie was pretty sure he knew what her final days were like. No one really knew how long Clara had been missing, but then one day Mary took a meal over and found the house empty. Roseanna had said she hadn't seen her mother for a few hours.

Two days later, she was found at Forget-me-not Well, among the grove of trees. It was where she and Richard had been married, and where Roseanna had been christened. Dessie would never forget Mary's reaction to the bloated body being found. He was sure Clara had died of a broken heart.

After that, Mary and John informally adopted their daughter, Roseanna, and she had been raised alongside their own daughter, Karen. Child welfare laws were much less stringent back then, especially in the isolated areas, and it seemed easier for Roseanna to be raised by people she knew, in the land she had been born in, than to upend her young life and take her to an orphanage in Adelaide. It gave him a start to realise she would be sixty now.

Pondering Mary and John's probable reaction to what he was about to tell them, he clasped his hands together, as if in prayer, stared up at the hills and asked for peace for everyone who would be affected.

❧

'I have something I need to talk to you about,' Dessie said as he sat next to John in the sunroom.

'That sounds very serious,' Mary answered as she set out a tray with biscuits, a teapot, a jug of milk and a sugar bowl.

'It is,' Dessie said haltingly. 'Before I start, you have to remember I took an oath of confidentiality.' He saw the way Mary's eyes suddenly narrowed. He continued, 'You both know how devastated Clara was when Richard died.'

He looked at his friends, who were sitting upright, staring at him.

'He had such a tragic, pointless death. It affected all of us

275

so deeply—it wasn't something anyone could have got over easily. And, as we all know, Clara never did.' He sighed and kept going with his story.

'As you both remember, of course, she became so unhappy that she lapsed into a deep depression. That was understandable. Roseanna was there too, but alone she wasn't enough for Clara, and Roseanna always knew that.

'When Clara died, it changed everything for Roseanna. She was young and impressionable. She remembered the dark days when Clara didn't get out of bed. The times she would forget to put tea on the table or when there weren't any clean clothes. Roseanna remembered having to ride out to paddocks and check the water tanks then call on you, John, if there was something wrong. So much responsibility fell on her young shoulders. And then she fell into the same trap as Clara.

'When I took her to Adelaide, to try to help her, and she stayed at Mannah Church Homes, it took her so long even to be able to get out of bed, let alone eat a meal with other people.' He took a deep breath. 'That's why we didn't notice.'

'Notice what?' John asked, his voice barely audible.

'John. Mary.' Dessie looked from one to the other. 'Roseanna was pregnant when she left here.'

'No!' Mary's pale face wore a look of complete shock. 'But when she came back, there wasn't a baby.'

'She didn't know she was with child when I took her away,' Dessie said. 'I certainly didn't know, and I feel a deep amount of guilt. Maybe if I'd left her here, with you, she would have got better of her own accord. I just couldn't see it. That's why I was so insistent that she come with me to get professional help. I thought I'd done all I could to help her here.'

'The baby?' John asked.

'Let me finish the story first.'

'No!' John was shouting. 'No. You tell us right now where that baby is. We have a right to know. We could have raised it, helped Roseanna. Bloody hell, we raised that girl as if she were our own. I can't believe you haven't told us any of this. Tell us now.'

Dessie held up his hands in a calming gesture. 'The child was born in Adelaide on the first of March 1988.'

Mary smothered a cry by putting her hands over her mouth.

'I wasn't able to get back to Adelaide to see Roseanna and the baby for a while. Then, when I arrived, Roseanna told me she hadn't been able to cope and had left her at a church.'

'Oh, the poor little mite,' said Mary.

'I was deeply shocked, of course. I desperately wanted to find out and keep tabs on how the child was getting on in life, but Roseanna wouldn't allow me to, as she was desperate not to be identified as the mother. We had more than one argument about that.' Dessie raised a shaking hand to his mouth and took a sip of tea. 'Despite all she'd been through, I really did believe Roseanna would be okay. She seemed amazingly strong and positive. She was really keen to come back here and get on with her life. With you two.

'You must believe me when I tell you that I watched her very closely before bringing her back up here.' He shook his head sadly. 'I spent a lot of time talking to her. But she certainly had her mother's tendency to fall into a deep, dark depression.'

Mary, with tears rolling down her wrinkled cheeks, reached out to grab John's hand. 'Who was the father? It must have been someone from up here.'

'She would never tell me, but she swore it wasn't someone you knew.'

There was a long silence.

'Why did she jump into the well, if she was pleased to be back here?' Mary finally asked.

'It was ten months to the day after the baby was born. I wonder if she had undiagnosed post-natal depression. And then there was the guilt she must have felt over abandoning her baby.' He leaned forward and spoke intently. 'I was frightened it would happen. I was watching, I promise you, but I never saw any sign of her wanting to take her own life.'

Mary said softly, 'She did seem happy when she came back here. I thought she talked to me about everything.'

'As I say, I think she put up a very good front,' Dessie said gently.

'She never mentioned a baby. How could she have a child and not tell us? Not give us the opportunity to help her? We were her *family*. I'm sorry, I don't understand any of this,' John said. He looked Dessie in the eye. 'I can't believe you're only telling us this now. What kind of friend are you?'

'I'm a friend who has to keep people's confidences,' Dessie answered, with a sinking feeling in his chest.

'Even if it affects their families?'

'Even if it affects their families.'

Mary went on, 'So, this child . . .'

Dessie swallowed and started to speak. 'Yes, this little girl. I saw her once. Just after she was born. I didn't see her face, just a mop of hair. Roseanna was my main concern at that stage.

'When I was able to return, and Roseanna confessed she'd left the baby at a church, she wouldn't tell me anything about it. Over the years after Roseanna died, I tried to find her child, to find out if her life was going okay. That she was happy. I never could, though. She seemed to have disappeared off the face of the earth, and it's also pretty hard to find someone who doesn't have her parents' names on their birth certificate.'

'Until now?' Mary asked.

Dessie sighed again. 'All I have to go on is my gut instinct. Eliza's story fits. She was left at a church,' he ticked the first fact off on his gnarly finger. 'She has a birth certificate without her parents' names on it. She doesn't have any family she knows about. For whatever reason, she's drawn to this place and, finally, she is the spitting image of Clara. Roseanna resembled Clara, but she had a lot of Richard in her features too.

'Eliza is a young Clara all over again.'

Chapter 36

Jacob opened the door of his homestead and stared in surprise.

'Hello. You've all come for a visit?' he asked.

Dessie indicated Mary and John. 'We'd all like to talk to Eliza, if we can, Jacob. Reen said she was here?'

Jacob nodded. 'Her ex is in South Australia, so we thought it would be a good idea if she was kept out of sight for a while.'

'What do you mean?' John asked, pushing himself forward.

Dessie held him back. 'Let her tell you that story.'

Jacob wrinkled his brow, and looked from one to the other. 'Anyone want to tell me what's going on here?'

Mary said. 'Can we come in, dear?'

Jacob held the door open for them and they all trooped in.

On the back verandah, Eliza was sitting in a swinging chair, her feet tucked under her, reading a book.

As Dessie caught a glance of her through the kitchen window, his heart started to race. He put a hand to his chest and stopped briefly, before starting to walk towards her again.

It was too late to turn back now. He'd thrown the cards in the air and now they had to fall where they would.

'Got some visitors, Eliza,' Jacob said. 'Anyone want a beer? Mary, do you want a wine?'

'No, thank you. Maybe later,' Mary answered, sounding distracted.

'Hello, all of you!' Eliza said with a smile, coming into the house. 'What are you doing here?'

'We thought we'd come and visit and see how you were holding up,' Dessie said as he pulled up a chair and sat down. Mary and John did the same.

Eliza's expression sobered. 'He won't find me here,' she said softly to Dessie. 'It's a long way away from Port Augusta. And, like Dave said, there are too many roads leading in too many different directions. It would be amazing if he thought to come here.'

'And he'll have to get through me,' Jacob said from the doorway. He focused on Eliza. 'I'm just going to shut a wind-mill off. I'll be back in about half an hour.'

Dessie noticed her smile held a particular sparkle when she answered that she would see him soon.

The door slammed and Jacob was gone.

'What do you mean "'he won't find me here"?' John asked.

Eliza cocked her head to one side and looked at him. 'I have a violent ex, John,' she admitted.

Dessie watched her intently. Despite what she was telling them, she seemed freer, as if a weight had been lifted from her shoulders. With that one admission, her life had changed. She wasn't hiding anymore.

He leaned forward and fixed his gaze on Eliza. 'You've probably guessed we're here for a reason,' he said.

She gave a half-smile. 'I was wondering!'

'Can you tell Mary and John about your childhood?' he asked.

Eliza gave him a questioning glance.

'I know it sounds strange, but could you?'

Mary and John leaned towards her as she looked at them. 'What's this about?' she asked slowly.

'Eliza, we believe we know who your mother was.' He said it as gently as possible, but even he wasn't prepared for the level of shock that appeared on her face.

'Wh . . . What? No, no, you can't! No one does. Why would you say that?'

'Eliza, you've seen the photos of Clara. You must agree that you resemble her?' Mary said, taking Eliza's hand in hers.

'She's too old to have been my mother. I'm only twenty-seven. She can't be my mother!'

'We don't think she is,' Dessie said, as soothingly as he could. 'We believe she might be your grandmother.'

Silence hung in the air as Eliza clearly tried to process what he had said.

'Grandmother? I don't understand,' she whimpered.

'We don't either, dear,' Mary said. 'We've only just found out about it ourselves. It's a lot to take in. But Roseanna, Clara's daughter, left here and went to Adelaide, and it turns out she was pregnant when she left. We didn't know, otherwise we never would have let her leave. We would have helped her raise you.'

Eliza stood up and walked to the window, banging her fists into her side. She stared outside.

'Love, you need to know that you are part of our family if you want to be,' John began.

Dessie watched Eliza, unmoving, reflected in the window. He could see she was crying.

'Clara's daughter?' Eliza finally asked in a low, shaky voice. 'You said she was yours. The one time you talked about Karen and Roseanna, you said, "That's our daughters." You've only got a couple of photos of her up on your walls. I know, because I've looked. I tried to match who I looked like with you, Mary, but couldn't see any resemblance. I thought it was you two I was drawn to. What the hell is going on here?'

Mary started to explain, in a faltering voice, about their friends' daughter. How they had raised her after her parents' deaths. How their daughter, Karen, and Roseanna had been best friends. How they had learned to ride horses together, done School of the Air lessons together.

'They were inseparable. We used to call them the terrible twins.' She took a shaky breath. 'We sent Karen to boarding school. She's very clever—now she's a lawyer in England. We saw how bright she was and wanted her to have the best. Clara and Richard couldn't afford to send Roseanna away, so she stayed and Clara helped her with the secondary-school School of the Air lessons.

'Then Richard was killed and, not long afterwards, Clara died. Suddenly, Roseanna had no one, except John and me.

'She struggled, and went off the rails a bit, but we hauled her back on and thought she was going along okay. Unfortunately, though, she took after her mother and suffered very badly from depression.'

Dessie interrupted Mary's tale. 'I thought if I could take

her to Adelaide and get her some help, she might get better. Find the skills to help her deal with her depression and be able to live a normal life.

'After a couple of months of her being down there, it became clear she was pregnant.' He looked down. 'I offered her support. I wanted to take her back to John and Mary, who I knew would help look after her and the baby. She wouldn't accept any of it.

'As soon as Roseanna's child was born . . .'

Eliza swung around. 'You were there?'

Dessie nodded. 'I was there.'

'Did you see the baby?'

'I saw a mop of blond hair, but that was all,' he answered.

Eliza swallowed hard and looked at the three of them.

'You really think I'm that child?' she asked in a small voice.

'I'm not sure there's any way to be certain,' Dessie said calmly. 'But you do have a similar story to what this child's would have been.

'When's your birthday?'

Eliza blinked. 'Um—first of March 1988.'

Mary and John exchanged glances, and Dessie nodded.

'You see, to me, that's too much of a coincidence,' he said. 'Especially since you look so much like Clara.'

Mary reached into her bag and drew out a photo album. 'Would you like to see some pictures?'

Eliza froze and Dessie could see it was almost too much for her.

'I'm back!' called Jacob, the door slamming. 'I reckon we might get a thunderstorm—I can smell moisture in the air.'

He stopped as he took in the atmosphere of the room. 'So, it appears I've missed something. I'll just grab a beer, and then I'll be in my room if you need me.'

Eliza shook her head and reached out her hand to him. 'No,' she said. 'I need you to stay with me.'

❦

Dessie knew that if Mary and John had been hoping for a loving family reunion, they were disappointed.

It was clear to him that Eliza had basically been by herself for so long, with no one to rely on, that having an instant family, even though that was what she badly wanted, wouldn't be possible.

Soon after Jacob had returned, Eliza had excused herself, barely saying goodbye to any of them. Mary, John and Dessie had been silent on the car trip home. There really was nothing to say.

Once they'd arrived home, Mary and John had gone straight to their bedroom, leaving Dessie in the sunroom, staring out into the gathering darkness.

He got up and went outside. The air was starting to develop a slight chill and he pulled his jacket a little tighter. The moon threw long shadows from trees and bushes, and covered the countryside in a ghostly light.

He looked towards the hills and heard voices.

It was two young girls on horseback, racing towards the yards. Dust kicked up from beneath the horses' hooves and the crack of a stockwhip rang out. He could hear the girls' laughter as each egged the other on to ride faster.

The horses were running at full stretch, the girls moulded

to their backs as if they and the animals were one. They raced over the flat towards where he was standing. Sheep scattered as they rode through the middle of the mob, and one of the girls let out a whoop and cracked the stockwhip again.

Dessie turned and looked towards the sheep yards, where there was a very old pepper tree. The branches and leaves were so bowed they almost touched the ground. Under the tree was cool and protected from the sun. Dessie stared at it for a long time and saw Richard. He was leaning against the trunk, his legs outstretched and his hat tipped down over his face. Beside him was a small smoking fire with a billy on it, and he was holding a mug of tea. As Dessie watched, he took a sip without needing to move his hat.

A sad smile crossed Dessie's face as Clara materialised from the woolshed and, hoisting up her skirt, sat down next to Richard, putting her hand on his leg. He flicked his hat up, and gave her a grin before offering her a cup of tea.

The horses came to a stop in front of them, covering the foursome in dust.

Dessie waited.

When the dust cleared, no one was there.

He blinked and looked around to get his bearings. The stars were appearing as dim lights in the sky. Everything was silent and still.

These people, who had been such dear friends, were nothing but ghosts from the past now, only memories and feelings—ones that haunted him daily.

The mournful and eerie call of a crow reverberated around and bounced off the hills. Another answered. As Dessie turned to go inside, the frogs started to call and the crickets came to life. The sounds of the bush washed over him and he finally felt untroubled.

He'd done what he'd had to, what God had told him to do, and he was sure that everything would be all right.

Chapter 37

The sound of laughter filled the main street. For the past few days, caravans and campervans had been dribbling into Blinman. The tourists were setting up camp anywhere they could find a space.

Eliza watched contentedly as everything started to come together. She'd had five entries in the selfie trail so far—that meant five hundred dollars already for Dessie and the Frontier Services. She expected many more entries to flood in on the day of the cook-off as people got into the spirit of things.

'Eliza, can you grab this?' Reen called out from underneath a marquee that had collapsed on top of her.

'What the hell are you doing under there?' Eliza scolded as she ran to help. 'That's not going to do you, or your body, any good.'

Reen fixed her with a steely stare. 'And when have I ever let my body stop me?'

'Good point. But you don't need to do this, you know.'

Eliza pushed the top of the marquee up and tried to pull it over the corner of the frame. One of the legs came out and it collapsed again.

She started to giggle as Reen swore.

Reen tried to pick up the leg but couldn't reach it. Frowning at Eliza, she started to say something but her friend's laugh was infectious and she started to giggle too.

Once Eliza had started to laugh, she couldn't stop. So many overwhelming things had happened over the last few days that laughing was a much needed relief.

When she'd told Jacob about the revelation that she was Clara's granddaughter, he'd been as shocked as she was. Neither of them had talked much that night as they both absorbed the information.

The next morning, the only thing that Jacob had said about it was: *'If you're going to have a family, the Caulders are the best one to have.'*

Reen had agreed, when Eliza had confided in her about what had happened. 'Mary and John are the nicest people. They'll love you as if you're their own, not just their friends' grandchild. So, yes, if you're going to get an instant family, they're the best one!'

Eliza agreed, but was still struggling to come to terms with how her gut feeling, that she should come to Blinman, had paid off. It was a lot to process.

'Not much point in getting too stressed, is there?' Reen said now, once she had got herself under control. She put the marquee cover on the ground.

Eliza shook her head. 'Nope! It's all about fun.'

'Good point. Sometimes I forget that. I just want everything to be right.'

'And it will be. It can't not be with all the effort you and everyone have put in.'

'You girls need a hand?'

They turned, and saw Chris and his daughters standing there. He had his hands on his hips and a half-smile on his face. 'Looks like that marquee is trying to wrap you up as Christmas presents!'

'Ha ha,' Reen said as she pushed the marquee towards Eliza.

'Don't worry. I'd unwrap you,' he said, winking at Eliza.

She gave a small smile in return.

'What are you up to, standing there like the cat's got your tongue?' Reen asked, looking at Heidi and Tilly.

'Being polite,' Heidi answered.

Eliza fixed both girls with a stare. 'Really?' she drew the word out in disbelief.

Tilly crossed her arms. 'We can be, you know.'

'Right, here you go,' Reen interrupted and pushed the marquee cover at Chris. 'Eliza and I have other things to do!' She limped back towards the shop. 'Like, get all the food ready!'

Eliza tipped her head to the side and looked at Chris. 'Thanks,' she said. 'I think you'll be much better at this than Reen and me.'

'No problems.' He stared at her for a moment. 'How have you been?' he asked. 'Seems ages since I've caught up with you.'

'Hasn't been that long,' she said, as she bent down to ruffle the girls' hair. She looked back up at him. 'But there's been a fair bit happen since!'

'Sounds interesting! Have you got time to grab a coffee and tell me?'

Eliza wiped away the sweat on her brow. 'It's too bloody hot for coffee. I'll grab some cool drinks from the shop and meet you over at the tennis clubrooms, if you like. Do you girls want anything?'

'No, thanks. I'm going to go and play with my friends,' Heidi said. 'See ya.'

'Back here in two hours,' Chris told her.

'Okay!'

'I saw Uncle Jacob over there. I'm going to see him,' Tilly said.

'Same goes for you, Twinkle Toes. Two hours.'

'Yup!'

'Okay, I'll just get two drinks,' Eliza said. 'Be back in a minute.' She went over to the shop and grabbed two cans out of the fridge. 'I'll be back shortly, Reen,' she called through the open door into the kitchen. 'I'm just going to have a quick chat to Chris.'

'No worries.'

In the clubrooms, she couldn't help looking straight over at the picture of Clara. It was so strange to have been yearning for a family and then suddenly have one.

It's not a real family, one half of her mind kept arguing with her. *It's a pretend one. One by association.*

Doesn't matter, the other half argued. *They'll love you. Everyone keeps telling you that and there's no reason to doubt it. They weren't the ones who gave you up.*

She handed Chris his drink, popped the top and took a long swallow of her own. 'That's so refreshing,' she said, holding the cold can to her cheek.

'You'll acclimatise,' Chris said, nodding. 'It always feels like a pretty fierce heat to begin with but, in time, it just seems normal. Like the flies. You just don't take any notice of them eventually.'

'And the dust. I kept wiping everything down when I first got here, but I don't bother anymore.'

'I've gotta say, though, that when it comes to the heat, you ain't seen nothin' yet. Summer is still a couple of months away.'

Eliza groaned.

Chris leaned back in his chair and put his feet on the table. 'So, what's been going on with you?'

'It seems I've found a family,' she answered, the words out of her mouth before she could stop them.

'Yeah? Is that good? Sometimes I'd do anything not to have one!'

She began to tell him her story—she wanted him to hear it from her. If she was going to keep teaching his kids, it was only fair that he heard everything straight from the source.

When she finished, Chris was quiet, and Eliza could tell he was thinking about what to say. She'd got to know his little habits over the past few months and that when he absent-mindedly rubbed his elbow, he was formulating words. That was one of the things she really liked about him: he didn't speak before he had thought through what he was going to say.

'So,' he said slowly, 'it's all circumstantial, is what you're telling me.'

'Yep.' She took another swallow. 'Part of me so wants it to be true. After all, family is really important. It gives you a sense of identity, all that sort of stuff, but the other half of me is too frightened to let it be true.'

Chris nodded. 'Not a bad family to be a part of, though,' he commented, taking another sip.

'But John and Mary aren't my real family, even if this whole story is true! They're friends of my family. They're people who knew my mum, my grandparents.'

'But, at the end of the day, they'd know something about your family in England. And they're the closest you've got to family out here. Why not embrace it?'

She sighed. 'I know, I know. I said to Jacob last night, it's like a spider web that stretches out, isn't it? They've got all the answers to a lot of the questions I have. They can tell me what Roseanna was like, what Clara and Richard were like. It's a win win all round. I just feel . . .' she searched for words, '. . . that because there isn't any proof, I'm too scared to let myself accept it. I don't want to finally think I've found a family, and then another woman turns up and she's the real daughter.'

Chris reached over to her, grabbed her hand and held it tight. He looked her in the eye. 'Honey, even if that happened, do you really think they'd let you go? That they wouldn't be your family anymore? In my experience, family are people who love you. They don't have to be blood relations. They can be friends. And that's what Mary and John are. They're friends who are offering to love and accept you. Just run with it and see where it leads. I can't imagine there's any pressure from them.'

Eliza looked down and fiddled with the can. Finally, she put it down and looked over at the photo of Clara.

'I do look a lot like her, don't I?'

'I reckon I was the one who told you that in the first place.'

'Yeah,' she said softly. She turned back to Chris and her breath caught in her throat as she saw something in his face she'd never seen before.

He held her eyes as he leaned towards her, hesitating for a split second before he put his lips on hers.

A number of emotions ran through her, but apprehension was the strongest of them. She pulled away and looked down at the floor.

'Think I'd better go,' she said and, before Chris could say anything, she got up and walked quickly to the door, shutting it quietly behind her. The glare from the sun stopped her in her tracks briefly before she headed across to the shop.

She berated herself. How did she get herself in that situation? She had always promised herself she would never let anyone in again. The only reason she'd talked to Chris about all this was that she felt she owned him an explanation.

It seemed that Reen had been right about his feelings all along.

∾

Dominic was camped near the golf course. He had been angry when he discovered there was only a long drop there and no shower facilities.

'I should have bought a bigger van,' he muttered as he stomped across the stony land to line up to use the toilet.

He kept his head down and his hat tipped over his face. He was only leaving the van for essentials, like showering and using the bathroom, but had been doing his best to spy on her.

The more people who arrived for the cook-off, the easier it would be. He'd seen Ashleigh, or Eliza, as she was known now, earlier this morning, running like a startled rabbit from one building to another. As he'd been standing in the shadows, he'd been able to wait until he saw a tall, broad-shouldered man follow her out of the clubrooms.

Dominic was sure this other man wanted her to stop so he could plead his case, whatever the fuck that might be. The anger in his gut sat there day after day, eating away at him. Sometimes he was so livid, he would get spots in front of his eyes and couldn't see properly.

Still, he knew that patience was the key. Dominic realised he *had* to keep a level head, even though what he really wanted to do right now was grab hold of that man walking across the street and bash him within an inch of his life.

His thoughts flicked briefly to Simon. He wondered if his body had been found yet. He was pretty sure it wouldn't have been. There were so many gorges and gullies. And he had chosen one that was well off the road.

He did feel a very small amount of regret at killing him. Realistically, though, he very much felt that Simon had brought his death on himself. After all, he couldn't be trusted anymore.

And he hadn't made him suffer—if knowing you were going to die wasn't suffering, that is. He'd marched him, at gunpoint, to a deep ravine in the heart of the Flinders, and quickly shot him in the head. Simon would have died instantly. Not like some of the people Dominic had killed.

Getting to his final resting place had taken a while and Simon hadn't said anything the whole time. Dominic assumed he knew there wasn't any point in trying to talk him out of it, but Simon's lack of fight disgusted him. He had turned out to be weak and inadequate.

Dominic focused again on the tall man, who had stopped to talk to an exhibitor setting up a brewery stall.

He wondered who he was and what role he played in Ashleigh's life. Was he her new lover? Dominic couldn't stand that thought.

After committing the face to memory, he dragged himself back to the caravan. If he stayed where he was, he might not be responsible for his actions.

Chapter 38

Heidi and Tilly piled into the car, and Chris waved goodbye to a couple of blokes who were still in the street.

'Okay, girls?' he asked as they drove out of town, back to the park.

'I'm okay,' Heidi answered, with a secret smile at Tilly.

'Me too,' Tilly answered.

'Are you getting excited about the cook-off? Only two days to go!'

'It's always fun seeing my friends,' Heidi answered. 'Sometimes I wish I lived closer to them, Dad, but then I think if I saw them every day, I might get bored playing with them.'

'You'll never tire of good friends,' Chris answered.

Heidi watched her dad, who had his eyes on the road. She couldn't quite make sense of all the thoughts in her head. She'd been sure Uncle Jacob and Eliza would be boyfriend and girlfriend really soon.

Then she'd seen how her dad had looked at Eliza today and

she got a funny feeling in her stomach. Maybe he liked Eliza too.

If he liked Eliza and she was going to be her dad's girl-friend, what would happen to her and Tilly? Heidi crinkled her brow as she looked out the window.

The sun was going down and there were dark clouds to the north. She wished she was outside, at the park. She'd be able to work out if there was going to be a thunderstorm by the atmosphere and by which direction the wind was coming from—if there was any wind.

She loved thunderstorms, and the way the lightning forked across the sky and lit up the land. Sometimes there wasn't any rain, but when there was, the drops were large and fat.

Her favourite thing to do when it rained was to run outside and open her mouth. Sometimes the drops fell in and hit her tongue; other times they hit the back of her throat and made her cough. The smell of moisture on dry earth was her favourite smell in the whole world.

'Heidi?'

She blinked and looked at her dad in the rear-vision mirror. 'Uh-huh?'

'Did you hear what I said?'

Heidi shook her head. 'No.'

'I asked what you wanted for tea.'

Heidi glanced over at Tilly, whose eyes were heavy and hooded. She'd be asleep in a few moments.

'Whatever's easiest for you, Dad.' She wanted to ask him about Eliza.

'We can have Dad's chicken surprise, or chops and salad.'

'Chops'll be easier. I can make the salad and you can cook.'

'That sounds like a plan,' Chris said, nodding. 'Much easier than having to cut all the chook up.'

Heidi turned and stared out of the window again. A few seconds later, she looked back at the rear-vision mirror to see that her dad was still watching her.

'Dad, if you got a girlfriend, what would happen to Tilly and me?' she asked quickly before she could chicken out.

There was a long silence, and Heidi wondered if he had heard her above the road and engine noise.

'Why do you ask that?' he finally answered.

Heidi thought his voice sounded all funny. She shrugged. 'Just wondered.' Pretending not to care, she closed her eyes and feigned sleep.

❧

That night, Tilly crept into Heidi's room and shook her awake.

'I'm hot,' she whined.

'Put the air conditioner on,' Heidi mumbled as she fumbled for the light switch next to her bed.

'It's not working.'

'Go and tell Dad. I'm sleeping.'

'He's sleeping too.'

Heidi sighed. She knew that Tilly had actually had a nightmare and wanted company. She sat up.

It was hot. Almost stifling. It would be cooler outside.

'Come on,' she whispered. 'Let's go out. There might be some wind that can cool us off. I wish Dad would put a pool in.'

They crept down the passageway, careful not to wake Chris. They knew he worked hard and often fell into bed exhausted.

He needed to sleep well, so he could run the park and look after them. It made Heidi angry whenever she thought of the way their mother had left.

She had never even said goodbye to them.

Heidi had watched her dad be so sad that he would cry at night when he didn't think they saw him. But she had. She'd sat at his closed door and listened to him sob. She'd seen him sneak a few drinks in the middle of the day, when she knew he shouldn't. Recently, though, she'd seen him start to act more like her old dad again, the way he was before her mum left.

Tilly flipped on the outside light and Heidi turned it straight off.

'Don't,' said Tilly with a frown.

'You can't put that on. All the mozzies and midges'll come to it and just be annoying. It's better when there's no light anyway. I can see the stars.'

She led the way out to the backyard to the trampoline and got onto it. Tilly did the same and Heidi felt the mat sag under their weight.

She stared at the stars and felt the stirring of a breeze brush her skin. A big cloud moved slowly across the sky, blocking out the moon.

'It's too hot,' Heidi complained as Tilly snuggled closer but the older girl put her arm around her anyway.

'Why do people take animals from the park?' Tilly asked.

'To make money. Isn't that what Dad said?'

'Yeah, but I still don't get it. Why would they hurt them by taking them out of their natural environment? They'll just die. I bet the people who are doing it don't know how to look after them properly.'

'They must be able to, 'cause I don't reckon they'd get paid if they handed over dead animals.'

'I s'pose,' Tilly agreed.

They lay there for a little while longer and Heidi felt Tilly start to relax. She'd go to sleep out here if she wasn't careful.

'Tilly,' she said in a low voice. 'Tilly!'

'Hmm?'

'Let's go for a walk. It will be cooler again out on the flood plains 'cause the breeze'll be able to get at us.'

They got off the trampoline and walked silently out through the camping area and onto the flood plains. The moon was visible again and lit the way for them to walk without tripping or falling. Heidi knew she didn't need to but pointed out the Southern Cross and told Tilly that was how the explorers used to navigate their way around the bush.

'I know,' her sister answered in a huffy tone. 'I'm not stupid.'

As they got further away from the camping grounds, Heidi lifted her head and gazed at the sky. The little bit of breeze there had been at the house was stronger out here. She was pleased they'd come outside. As much as she loved her home, there was nothing worse than the heat arriving quickly and without warning, as it had done in the last couple of weeks. She liked it when it got hot gradually.

The wind played with her hair as a wallaby stood up and looked at them curiously. The moon was reflected in its eyes and it had its paws to its mouth, holding some grass.

They both stood very still, then Tilly whispered, 'That's a yellow-footed rock wallaby.'

'I know! How cool is that?'

They kept watching the wallaby until it finished eating and moved slowly away.

Heidi caught hold of Tilly's arm. 'Guess what we should do?'

'What?'

'Let's go up to where the emu eggs were taken and see if we can see anything. We might see someone walking about at night, or anything.'

Tilly's eyes grew wide. 'But Eliza and Uncle Jacob said not to.'

'How are they going to know? They're not here.'

Tilly hesitated for only a few more moments before saying, 'Come on.'

They ran hunched over towards the creek and started to climb up the rocks.

က

The moon slid behind another cloud and Heidi looked up. She'd felt the wind change a few moments ago and, in the distance, there had been the rumble of thunder.

'One elephant, two elephants . . .' They counted the seconds in between the rumbles and worked out the storm was probably about twenty kilometres away.

'Might not even get here,' Heidi said with a shrug. 'Let's walk up to the top of the bluff and watch the lightning.'

With the nimbleness of mountain goats, the girls continued towards the bluff, climbing over rocks and pushing their way through the bushes until they came to a sheltered spot with a cave at the top of the hill.

Heidi liked to pretend that no one except her, her dad and

Tilly knew there were Aboriginal paintings inside it. They didn't come here that often, but it was always lovely and cool, deep within the side of the hill, and had an amazing view over the flood plains. They settled into the cave.

Heidi searched the sky and saw the clouds really beginning to build. When the clouds blew across the moon and blocked it out, they would be left without light and that would make it much harder for them to get home.

For the first time, she felt some apprehension run through her. It was forgotten, though, the minute the sky split with a huge electrical crack and, a few moments later, there was a thunderclap. Heidi felt the force of the thunder through her body and she smiled.

The power of nature was awesome, as was the speed of the storm. The clouds moved quickly to black out the sky, and the rumble of thunder was constant, like a surround sound system repeating the same music. It echoed around them, from every direction.

They watched, their faces alight with pleasure, as the lightning spread across the sky like white veins, showing the deep indigo purple of the clouds.

Inky blackness overtook them whenever the lightning wasn't flashing. Heidi could smell the moisture of the storm on the wind, and almost as soon as her senses knew it was going to rain, it did.

The sort of drops that she had been thinking about in the car on the way home started to fall. Fat and heavy, they splattered hard against the ground. They were warm at first but, as the rain got heavier, they became cold and Heidi nudged Tilly back further into the cave. The loudest clap of thunder of the night so far shot through the air and she reached over to take her sister's hand.

There was no way they could get back to the house now. Fear started to churn inside Heidi, but she knew she couldn't let Tilly realise it. Her sister had relied on Heidi so much, ever since their mother had left, that sometimes she felt like she was her mum.

'It's loud,' Tilly said, still looking in wonder at the storm.

There was another crack of lightning and both girls watched as it struck the dry creek bed just in front of them.

Heidi was now overcome with terror. She knew what could happen. There could be a fire, even with the rain. They could get flooded in.

She couldn't take Tilly out in the weather to try to run home now. They could be hit by lightning or caught in a flash flood.

There was really nothing they could do but sit and wait it out, and hope they would be able to get back home when the rain stopped.

'Let's go further back into the cave,' Heidi instructed Tilly in a calm voice. 'We're going to get wet with the way the wind is blowing the rain in, and we shouldn't get cold.'

Ducking their heads, they wiggled back in a little further. Then Heidi's feet touched something.

She froze.

Heidi prodded it with her feet, trying to work out what it was. As she pushed the object across the floor of the cave, it made a high-pitched squeaking noise.

Chapter 39

Chris woke to the sound of thunder. Like a snake, anxiety was winding through his stomach. It had been there for weeks—ever since Dave had come to see him about the poaching.

He felt like something bad was going to happen.

Getting up, he padded over to the window, to see what the sky looked like. As he had imagined they would be, deep indigo thunderclouds were rolling in from the north, their colours lit up by the lightning.

It was the lightning that might be a problem in these storms, if there wasn't any rain. Strikes that hit the ground would light the dry grass. Fires like that could burn for weeks because it was so difficult to get access to the range country to fight them.

Chris thought about how much the station owners hated dry storms. There had been instances of stock and property being lost despite all the volunteer firefighters' best efforts. The heat in the northern part of South Australia was intense during summer and that, coupled with dry bushland, paved the way for brutal fires that destroyed everything in their path. Even hearing the first plop of rain didn't make him relax. A good five or ten millimetres would need to fall to make sure nothing went up in flames.

Over the next few minutes, the drumming on the roof got louder and heavier. Lightning lit up the sky every few seconds and the thunder didn't stop. Continuous growling, like an angry dog's, filled the sky.

Chris didn't move away from the window. He loved thunderstorms. He always had, even though he was well aware how vulnerable humans were against the power of Mother Nature. So often they came off second best.

A particularly loud clap of thunder sounded, right over the house, and the windows rattled. Chris glanced behind him, expecting to see one, if not both, of the girls coming to watch the storm with him.

He loved it when they did that. They would all sit on the verandah together, snuggled up on the swinging chair, not saying anything, just watching. If things went the way he thought they might, he knew that watching storms with his girls would be one of the things he'd miss the most.

They must be tired not to wake up with all this noise, he thought. He wandered down the hallway and stopped to listen at each of their doors.

No noise.

Chris opened Tilly's door a crack and peered in. Even before he quite processed what he was seeing, panic surged through him.

He threw the door open and switched on the light.

The bed was empty.

He ran down to Heidi's room and hurled himself inside, turning on the light as he went.

A guttural moan came from deep within him as the rain increased in intensity.

He ran outside onto the lawn, screaming his daughters' names. Within seconds he was drenched, but he hardly noticed.

Frantically, Chris got into his ute and sped away. He swung the vehicle from side to side, trying to get the lights to sweep across the landscape.

The rain was so thick that he couldn't see much more than a couple of metres in front of him. He jumped out of the ute and ran to the closest caravan, pounding on the door.

'Have you seen my girls?' he cried when a sleepy-looking man appeared at the door.

'What? No.'

The man had hardly finished speaking when Chris ran to the next caravan, repeating his question.

Within minutes, most of the caravaners were outside, some with torches and headlights, others shrugging into rain jackets, all ready to help him search for his daughters.

'Have you called the police?' someone shouted to Chris as he ran in the direction of the creek.

He yelled that he hadn't, but had no idea if anyone had heard him. The thunder and lightning hadn't abated one bit, and as he reached the edge of the creek, he saw a trickle of water just starting to run.

'Shit!' he swore. If there was enough rain to make the creeks run, who knew what would happen? *They could be washed away. They could drown—anything!*

Part of him realised Heidi and Tilly would have known to take shelter somewhere, but then, they could only do that if there was some decent cover. If they were out on the flood plains, there would be nowhere. They could get struck by lightning.

He was so *stupid*! Even though they had promised him they wouldn't go and look for the poachers, he should have known they would. What on earth had he been *thinking*?

He tried to wipe away the water that was streaming down his face. It was running into his eyes and stinging them, and he couldn't see properly.

'Heidi!' he screamed. 'Tilly!' But his words were drowned out by the sound of rain drumming into the soil. He fell to his knees, sobbing.

'This is my fault. I'm so sorry.'

∽

The sound of thunder and rain on the tin roof woke Reen in the early hours of the morning.

She smiled as she rolled over to look at the ceiling. A storm before the cook-off would be a wonderful thing. The air might get sticky and humid, but the land would be washed clean and look its best.

She put her hands behind her head and shut her eyes, listening to the sweet sound, and, through the open window, breathing in the vapour created by rain falling on the earth.

The phone rang.

Reen froze for a moment—no one should be ringing at this hour.

Something was wrong.

'Hello?' She couldn't recognise the voice of the person on the other end of the line or comprehend what they were saying. 'I'm sorry, but can you calm down? I can't understand you.' She slowly swung her legs over the edge of the bed and got up, switching on the light.

The sobbing continued but now she could make out some of the words.

'Heidi . . . Storm . . . Not in their rooms . . .'

'Chris?' Her voice went up an octave. 'Chris, are you telling me the girls are missing?'

There was a strangled, 'Yes.'

'We're coming,' she answered quickly.

Putting down the phone, she immediately picked it up again and rang Mark Patterson. He was another SES volunteer, and his station was only a fifteen-minute drive from the national park, so he would be able to get there quicker than those to the north of Blinman. 'Heidi and Tilly are missing at the park,' she said without preamble. 'We need to get a search team together.'

'On it,' he said, obviously immediately as wide awake as she was, and they quickly talked through what to do next.

Reen shrugged into her dressing gown and limped across the street to the units at the back of her store, where Dave and Kim were staying.

Dave answered her banging on the door in seconds, instantly on high alert.

'Tilly and Heidi are missing in the park,' she said.

'Okay. Call the ambulances from Hawker and the SES.'

'Already got Mark on it,' she said.

'I'll be right there.'

Reen hated her body so much when it prevented her from helping out as much she wanted. In years gone by, she would have been part of the search team, but there was no way she could be now. It made her feel so damn useless.

'Eliza,' she muttered, and went to wake her. Eliza was back in Blinman to help prepare for the cook-off.

As she gave Eliza the news, Reen saw tears fill her friend's eyes. Eliza immediately headed to the cupboard and pulled out some clothes. 'I'll help look too,' she said.

'Why don't you stay here and help me make sandwiches? We'll have to take them to the park for the volunteers.'

Eliza stopped what she was doing and looked at Reen. 'I can't, I'm sorry. I need to be out there. Kim will help, won't she?'

'Eliza, you can't go. You don't have any experience with this kind of thing. Something could happen to you. The best thing you can do is to help me make these sandwiches and we'll take them to the park as soon as we've finished. You'll be there when they bring the girls home.

'You've got to remember, those kids are resourceful little buggers. I've got no doubt they'll be holed up in a cave, or hiding under a bush or something. They know that park better than anyone. Even Chris.'

Eliza closed her eyes. 'Okay.'

❧

The rain finally began to ease and the thunder sounded like it was moving on.

Heidi was shaking from both fear and the cold. Rain had kept blowing into the cave, and even though they had huddled as far back inside it as they could, they were still getting wet.

'You okay, Tilly?' she asked in a shaky voice.

'Yeah. Can we go home now?'

Heidi crawled to the front of the cave and looked out. It was pitch black now, with no moon to guide them.

'I don't think so,' she answered. 'It's too dark. We'll just have to wait until sunrise.'

While the rain and thunder had abated, the wind had come up and the way it was blowing on her wet clothes made her feel even colder. At least, though, they'd had something they could use for a barrier. The thing she'd found had turned out to be one of several foam boxes, and she'd been able to use them for some shelter.

'Funny how it can be hot one moment and so cold the next, isn't it?' she commented to Tilly, who didn't answer.

Heidi put her arm around her sister and they sat there, staring out into the darkness.

There didn't really seem to be anything else to say, although Heidi's brain was churning with thoughts. Aside from the storm, there was her discovery of the foam boxes. She'd managed to open one by pulling off the sticky tape it was sealed with. Inside, she'd found a wad of cash, just as a lightning strike lit up the cave. Heidi hadn't counted it but it looked like a lot of money.

She heard noises outside the cave and went back to look out.

There were lights outside.

'Help!' she cried. 'Tilly, come and yell! There's people out here.'

Together, they screamed 'Help!' but not a single light turned in their direction. Heidi's throat became raw from shrieking but she still couldn't make herself heard. 'Tilly,' she said, turning to her sister, 'I want you to stay here. I can get down the hill quicker by myself, and get someone to come and help us. You'll be okay here by yourself?'

'I'll be okay,' Tilly said in her bravest voice. 'You've got to be careful too.'

'I will be.'

Heidi scrambled out of the cave and kept sliding down the steepest part of the hill until her foot hit a rock. Carefully, she held her hands out in front of her and took a small step. *Slow and steady*. Heidi knew she couldn't afford to fall over, and maybe break something.

She walked deliberately towards the lights, checking before each step. The lights were a lot further away than they had looked from the cave.

She kept calling out with every step she took, hoping someone would hear her. The rain had made the creek run, and the rush of the water, not the rain or the wind, was drowning out her voice now.

'Heidi?'

She heard the voice quite close to her. 'Help!' she said, but her throat closed over and nothing came out.

'Heidi?'

It was a man's voice, but she didn't know whose it was. Summoning all her courage, she took a deep breath and yelled, 'Over here!'

The man let out a shout: 'Heidi! I can hear you! Keep yelling, sweetie, I'll walk towards your voice.'

Heidi yelled and yelled, until finally a bright beam from a flashlight came into view. Within seconds, she was in her Uncle Jacob's arms.

Chapter 40

Heidi and Tilly sat in the lounge room of their house, blankets wrapped around their shoulders, sipping hot chocolate. Eliza was sitting opposite them, overcome with relief that they hadn't been hurt.

'It wasn't that scary, Dad,' Heidi said, trying to reassure her father.

'It was for me,' he answered, his hand on her shoulder. 'Don't ever do anything like that again. Promise me? I can't lose you two.'

'Sorry, Dad,' Tilly said quietly. 'We were just so hot. Then the thunder started, and we thought we'd watch the lightning from the cave.'

Eliza noticed that Chris seemed to freeze as Tilly mentioned the cave. He squatted down and looked her in the eye. 'Is that where you hid? In the cave at the top of the bluff?'

'Yeah. I thought we wouldn't get wet there.'

'That was a really good idea,' Eliza said, leaning forward

with a gentle smile. 'You guys are so wise about the bush, you did all the right things.'

Now Dave came into the room and dropped onto the floor in front of the sisters. 'Well, you gave everyone a nasty scare, didn't you?'

'We're sorry,' Tilly said.

'Not to worry, all's well that ends well. I've got to put in a bit of a report, though, so I need to ask you both some questions. Are you up to it?'

Heidi looked at him indignantly. 'We're fine!' she answered. 'We didn't really need you all to come looking for us. We would have been all right to get home by ourselves when it had got light. We just couldn't walk anywhere in the dark.'

'And I am so glad you didn't,' Dave answered with a grin. 'It would have caused a whole new lot of headaches if you'd actually got lost.'

'We wouldn't have got lost,' Heidi said scornfully. 'It was just cold. And dark.'

'And wet,' Tilly added.

'It certainly was,' Dave replied. 'And noisy too, with all the thunder and lightning. Why did you go out in the first place?'

'I was hot,' Tilly answered. 'And we thought it would be cooler out on the flats, so we walked there.'

'Then the storm came,' Heidi put in, 'and we were too far from the house to get back in time to miss it, so we went up to the cave, so we could watch the lightning.'

'Did you have a torch?' Dave asked.

Eliza was listening to what the girls were saying, but couldn't take her eyes off Chris. He was pale and clammy, his hands were shaking, and he kept wiping sweat from his forehead, even though it was now quite cool after the rain.

The shock of losing the girls tonight had really taken its toll on him.

'No, we just went by the moonlight,' Heidi answered.

'True bushmen,' Dave said. 'Oh—excuse me—bushwomen.'

Heidi giggled.

'The cave was okay until the rain started to really hammer down,' she continued. 'We got wet because it was coming in the entrance. We used the foam boxes up there as a barrier, but they didn't really stop us from getting cold. The worst of everything was the cold.'

Dave stopped writing and looked up. 'Foam boxes?' he asked. 'Can you tell me a bit about them?'

Heidi screwed up her face as she thought. 'I think there were about eight or nine. I just set them up across the cave, to try and break the wind and rain up a bit.'

'That was really clever,' Dave said.

Heidi looked down at the mug she held in her hand. 'I found something else,' she said. 'In the boxes.'

Everyone was silent, waiting for her to tell them what it was.

'There's a lot of money up there too.'

෮

The sun was rising, bathing the clean countryside in gold and pink. Normally, Dave would stop to absorb such a spectacle, but not today.

'You need to show me how to get to this cave,' he said to Chris when they were out of earshot of the girls. 'I know you don't want to leave them, but it'll only take an hour or so. I can handle everything once you show me how to get there.'

Chris rubbed his hands over his tired eyes. 'I'm not sure if we can get to it, with all the water in the creek.'

'Let's go and have a look. I need to get up there as soon as I can.'

Chris was silent for a long time. 'The girls . . .' he finally said.

'Come on, mate, this won't take long.'

'Sure. Sure. Okay. Just let me tell them where I'm going.'

Chris led the way in his vehicle. Dave knew that all he wanted to do was get back to his girls—hell, if it was him, he'd never let them out of his sight again! But Dave needed to investigate why there were foam boxes and a wad of cash where poaching could be taking place.

Chris stopped, and Dave pulled up next to him and got out, collecting his backpack with the equipment he would need for the investigation.

'It's a bit of a climb,' Chris said, pointing up the stony hill. 'Come on, I'll show you the easiest way.'

He set off at a quick pace. Following in Chris's sure-footed, quick footsteps was difficult. Dave stumbled a few times, rocks tumbling beneath his feet. 'Shit!' he said as it happened again and he went down on one knee.

Chris didn't say anything in response, just kept striding up the hill.

When Dave finally got to the top, he had to stop for a moment to catch his breath. He took out his water bottle and gulped from it and, even though the weather wasn't hot yet, he wiped sweat from his face. In the silence of the landscape, flies buzzed around his face and he swatted them away impatiently. He looked around and caught a glimpse of the cave entrance.

As it was partially hidden by bushes, his immediate impression was that anyone who wanted to utilise this cave would need to have known about it in advance. No one would just stumble across it.

'How did you know about this place, Chris?' Dave asked, looking around him. Not wanting to be distracted by the beauty of the area, he tried to block out the galahs and their morning screeching, as well as the drops of rain glistening on the ends of the branches.

'The bloke who had the job before me told me about it,' he answered. 'Don't come up here very often. No reason to, really.'

'It's an amazing place.'

'It sure is.' Chris kicked at the ground and Dave knew he was impatient to get home.

'Righto, off you go. Go back to your girls. I'll check everything out from here.'

The ranger turned to go, but Dave hadn't finished. 'Chris, hug them extra tight and don't worry. I'll get the bastard who's doing this poaching. Okay?'

'Okay,' he answered. Dave watched as he went down the hill, got into his ute and drove off.

Then he turned back to the job at hand. Walking up to the entrance of the cave, he stood looking in. Bushes brushed against his jeans, instantly soaking them. All the flora was saturated from its overnight drenching.

'So, what do we have in here?' he asked himself, as he got down onto his hands and knees and crawled a little further in.

Being so tall, it was difficult for him to manoeuvre into small spaces.

He could see the foam boxes towards the back and was in a quandary. He wanted to get in there and examine them, but he'd be disturbing a crime scene if he did that. He'd been hoping he could just drag the boxes out and look at them.

'Bugger—I'll have to get in there and take photos,' he muttered to himself, getting out the camera. Pulling on latex gloves, he went about examining the scene and deciding which angles he wanted to take photos from. He took many photos, from as many angles as he could, then got out his fingerprint kit.

Brushing over a foam esky, he picked up a few fingerprints. He guessed some were the girls', but, with any luck, he would find others that were on the police database.

It wouldn't be so easy, though, Dave was sure. It never was.

Pulling the lids off the boxes, he looked inside each one.

In the third one, he found the cash. Carefully, he photographed it in situ before opening the bundle and counting it out. When he finished, he looked out across the landscape, a chill running through him.

There was fifteen thousand dollars here.

To him, this screamed a high-tech and well organised operation. He assumed that this money was the cut for the person who collected the wildlife.

Thinking out loud, he said: 'Okay, one to catch and supply, one to courier, one to sell, and someone running the whole operation. That's a lot of fingers in one pie. Fifteen grand for the supplier is a bloody lot of money.'

Or was the money for the supplier? Was it the takings from a few deliveries that just happened to be stored up here?

Dave didn't think so.

Packaging the money up, he put it back in the box and wrote a memo to get all the notes dusted for fingerprints as well. He didn't have time to do that while he was out in the bush.

The sun had risen fully and he could begin to feel the sting of the heat. Humidity rose from the soil and, once again, he started to perspire. Now, too, the flies had competition, as mosquitoes buzzed around Dave's ears, making things very uncomfortable. He swatted at them, but with no effect. He decided it would be easier to tape off the cave, cart the boxes to his vehicle and look at everything when he was back in Blinman.

The boxes were large and difficult to carry, so he only took one at a time to the car. As he picked up the third one, he noticed something in the corner of the lid.

He put the box down and looked a little closer.

Handwriting.

Grabbing his camera from the ground where he'd left it, he focused on the corner and took a couple of shots.

'"Frill-necked lizards",' he read out loud.

ɔ

On the way back to the camping grounds, Dave detoured to the place where he had hidden the cameras. Flicking open the catch on the camera, he ejected the SD card and replaced it with a new one. Then he did the same with the other cameras he had placed around the area.

He didn't think he'd find anything on them. But now that his boss had okayed the use of them, he wasn't going to let them go to waste.

Back in his vehicle, with the air conditioner running, he flicked the replay switch on his camera, just to have a quick glance at what the first SD card had captured. The cameras only started to record when motion was detected, and he expected to see kangaroos, birds and foxes.

What he did see made him stop and rewind. He watched the shadowy, grainy images on the small screen four times before he was sure of what he'd seen. Lowering the camera, he stared out the window, trying to piece everything together.

He put the car into gear and drove to the camping grounds.

Chapter 41

The morning of the cook-off dawned clear and warm. Eliza wandered down the main street feeling very satisfied with life. She also had a bubble of excitement in her chest. After the stress of the girls disappearing, yesterday evening had ended up being rather wonderful.

She had gone in search of Jacob, who she knew would be over at the large fire pit they had lit the day before. 'We need coals to distribute to everyone first thing in the morning,' Jacob had told her.

She'd watched the firelight dance over his face and thought how beautiful he was. Chris had been trying to get her attention, she knew, but she hadn't been interested. Not really. It had been flattering, of course, but, as she'd told everyone who asked, she wasn't interested in men.

But then Jacob had turned and caught her looking at him, and held her gaze for a long time, while the fire crackled around them. Eliza knew the heat she was feeling wasn't just from the flames.

'So, you ready yet?' he'd asked very quietly.

'Ready for what?' she'd whispered back.

'Me.'

Her fear had given way to a feeling of peace. She had never felt this way before—a mixture of wildness and safeness. The girls going missing, and the joy of finding them, had made her think about what life was really about. If she held back now, the only person she would be hurting would be herself. She hadn't left a bad marriage just to be scared and alone. Life was about grabbing every moment, every opportunity, and making the most of it.

She knew she could do that with Jacob.

Eliza just leaned over and put her lips on his, concentrating only on how he tasted.

⁓

The storm hadn't kept tourists away or wreaked havoc with the setting-up that had been done. The stall holders were getting organised, and the campers were sitting outside their vans, drinking coffee and talking. There was a buzz of expectation in the air. Some people were swapping recipes, while others were holding their cards close to their chest.

When Eliza arrived at Reen's, she was pulling meat out of the fridge. Eliza and Jacob had picked up the thirty legs of lamb that had been donated by a local butcher. Each cook-out team, of five people, would get one leg each and a kilo each of onions, carrots and potatoes, and flour. What they made with those ingredients was up to the cooks.

'Here, weigh out the potatoes,' Reen instructed Eliza.

She did as she was told, and put each portion into the

baskets lined up on the bench. When they were all loaded onto a ute, Eliza and Reen drove down to the creek, where people were lined up, ready to cook. The tents were enclosed, so the flies couldn't get in, and there was a lot of laughter and chatter. For some, it wasn't too early to open a beer.

The ingredients were handed out, and Mark Patterson got to his feet to explain the rules. At the end, he added, 'Bribery is encouraged,' he paused. 'For the RFDS.'

The assembled crowd clapped and many of them then disappeared into their tents to start on their masterpieces. The ones who weren't cooking were wandering up and down the main street, looking at the displays.

Jacob stopped to drop a quick kiss on Eliza's lips as he delivered more coals to the fire pits. The fire was contained inside an old rainwater tank that had been cut in half. Eliza wrapped her arms around herself, unable to keep a silly grin off her face.

She was pushed sideways as Reen came up to her.

'Got something to tell me?' she asked with a cheeky smile.

Eliza turned to her friend with a very wide grin. 'Maybe.'

'So?' Reen opened her eyes wide and gave a 'tell-me-more' signal with her hands.

'Oh, I don't know. Last night, it all just seemed to be right.'

Reen put her hand on Eliza's shoulder. 'I'm really pleased. But I've got to admit, I thought it'd be Chris.'

'Nah, there was never anything there,' she answered. 'Anyway, I'd better get back to my stall. I really want to sell some of my photos.'

'Good luck!'

Eliza wandered back to the main street and sat at her post.

While there was a lull, she relaxed back in her chair and watched the passing parade. People watching was something she'd always liked doing. She watched a family walk down the street, the mum talking non-stop to one of the children, while the father handed out money to another child who wanted to enter the damper throwing. He put his hand on his wife's arm and turned her to look at him. Eliza could make out that he was saying, 'Settle down, they're not going to get lost here.'

She smiled to herself.

It was such a fun atmosphere; there was so much laughing and cheering. Her gaze roamed over the people sitting in the beer garden.

Then she froze. There was a man sitting in the corner. She couldn't see him clearly but he looked familiar.

'Hi, Eliza.'

She dragged her eyes away, and saw Mary and John Caulder standing in front of her.

'Hi, how are you both?' she asked carefully.

'Well, thank you. And you?'

'Really great.' She tried to keep eye contact with them, but couldn't resist turning to look back towards the beer garden.

He was gone.

Terror coursed through her and it took everything she had for her to stay in her seat. She swung back to look at Mary.

'Eliza,' Mary hesitated, then continued: 'We're so happy that you're here, and we hope that somehow you'll get to a point where you'd like to know a little about your mum. She really was a beautiful person. We miss her very much.'

'I'm just trying to get my head around everything, Mary,' Eliza answered honestly. 'I'm not avoiding you, or disregarding you, or anything like that. Even though I'd half-hoped I'd find something here, I knew it was a long shot. In the end, it was about being safe and away from Dominic.' As she said his name, her heart started to pound. She looked around her again.

'We understand, dear. Take as much time as you need. We're not going anywhere!'

Impulsively, Eliza reached over and gave the older woman a hug, then did the same to John. 'Thank you,' she said sincerely.

Once they'd gone, Eliza swung around and studied each section of the main street, looking for the man she'd seen.

'You're being silly,' she told herself. How could he possibly know she was here? Despite what Dave had told her, there was no real reason to think Dominic would know her whereabouts.

'Hello, Ashleigh,' a voice came from behind her.

She felt something push into her back.

'So, I've finally found you,' Dominic said in a low, menacing voice.

Eliza licked her lips, speechless. She wanted to scream, but couldn't get any sound out.

'What's the matter? Cat got your tongue?'

She was still struck dumb with fear.

'Or maybe you weren't expecting me? We might go for a stroll over to my caravan and have a little catch-up. It's been so long since we talked.' He pushed something hard into her back again and motioned for her to walk in front of him.

They threaded their way through the crowds, Eliza desperate to see someone she knew. But they were all busy, either down at the creek, or organising kids' activities. Frantically, she looked around, making eye contact with whoever she could, trying to convey that she was in trouble. No one took any notice.

Finally, they were standing in front of an old caravan. Eliza recognised it. It had been parked here for the last four days.

He pulled the door open and roughly pushed her inside.

'I am going to kill you, bitch,' he snarled as she tripped up the step and landed inside.

&

Jacob wiped his brow. It was his third trip carting coals. His arm was hot inside the long welding glove he was wearing, and the smells that were starting to come from the cooking fires were making his stomach rumble.

'Hey, Reen, you seen Eliza?' he called as she walked towards him.

'Now, why would you be wanting to see her?' she asked mischievously.

'I thought we'd get some lunch together.'

'Oh right, and leave the rest of the work to us? Slacker!'

'Half an hour, that's all I ask!'

'Last I saw her, she was at her stall, talking to Mary and John.'

He gave her a thumbs up and asked the team where they wanted their next lot of coals. He then walked towards the main street and saw a glimpse of Eliza walking towards the golf club. Strange, he thought.

Then he realised there was a man alongside her, holding her arm with one hand, the other pushed in her back.

He started to run towards her, then stopped. The way that bloke had a hold of her, Jacob was sure he had a gun.

'Shit,' he swore out loud, and a couple of people with young children looked over at him and frowned as they walked by.

'Where's Dave?' he said to no one in particular. He changed direction and ran towards the creek. He wanted to scream out for the policeman, but knew he couldn't alert whoever had Eliza.

Jacob guessed the man was Dominic, but Eliza had also told him about a corrupt policeman called Simon. Maybe it was him, doing Dominic's dirty work.

'Where's Dave?' he puffed when he saw Mark Patterson.

'Haven't seen him, mate.' He gave Jacob a strange look. 'What's up?'

'I need Dave, now,' he bit out.

'Dave?' Reen interrupted. 'He's in his unit at the back of the shop. Doing up the report on the girls, I think.'

Jacob turned to jog back, but Reen caught his arm.

'What the hell's going on?'

'Eliza. I saw her with a man. He was taking her somewhere.'

હ૭

Dominic slapped Eliza across the face.

'Did you really think you would get away with it?' he asked. 'I warned you not to try. I thought you would have realised that I'd track you to the end of the earth before I let you get away.'

Eliza's eyes watered from the sting of the slap and she twisted her hands against the rope that bound them.

'I'm going to enjoy hurting you.' He slapped her again, and smiled when she whimpered.

Holding the gun at her head, he pulled back the slide to cock it.

'Why did you throw everything I'd given you back in my face?'

Eliza wouldn't look at him. If he was going to kill her, then let him get on with it. She'd had a few months of freedom and she'd enjoyed them. If it all had to end now, at least she'd had that.

He grabbed her hair and ripped it downwards. A scream escaped her.

'Shut. The. Fuck. Up.'

With an evil grin on his face, he watched as she swallowed hard and raised her eyes to meet him. There were tears of pain in them. She tried to get her breathing under control, but her chest was heaving so hard, it hurt.

'That's better. Wouldn't want to let anyone know you're here, would we? Especially since we have so much to catch up on.

'Now, answer me. I gave you a family, a history, a name. Why would you throw it all back at me? You still don't have anyone!'

Eliza thought of Jacob and the look on his face when he had kissed her last night. She thought of Mary and John, and Heidi and Tilly.

'Not talking?' He backhanded her from the other direction and Eliza tasted blood in her mouth.

'You bastard,' she spat at him.

He stopped still and raised the gun. She glared back at him.

His eyes on her, he slowly squeezed the trigger.

Chapter 42

'It's going to take too long for the STAR team to get here,' Dave said to his boss. 'I'm going to have to go in. Her life is at risk.'

'You're sure you can't wait until your blokes get up there?'

'I don't reckon. He's unstable, and if everything you've told me today is right, then we've got a very volatile situation. Dominic is unravelling quickly. There are so many people around here at the moment. I'm going to have to shift all of them out.'

'That's why I'd rather wait until we get the STAR team there. I can have them there within four hours.'

'I don't think I've got that long. I've got to go. I'll keep in touch.' He ended the call and swung around to address the dozen or so SES volunteers and locals who were gathered.

'Right, we have to shift everyone to the creek,' he instructed. 'Mark, Chris and John, you'll have to handle this carefully, so you don't scare people. Just say there's an unsafe situation and they need to shift away.'

'Right, we're on to it.'

'Reen, get on the phone to the ambos and get them up here. I've rung my guys and hopefully they'll be here very soon. The rest of you, if you can keep everyone busy down at the creek, that would be ideal. Make sure everyone's as calm as you can keep them.'

Dave looked across, saw Kim's white face and glanced away. He couldn't get distracted now—he was a one-man band.

He went to the car and unlocked the safe where he kept his gun. He slipped on a bulletproof vest and started to walk towards the golf club.

Dave crouched down and ran from caravan to caravan, stopping and listening at each. They were all silent.

Then he spotted one he was sure was Dominic's. Right down in the far corner, parked a little way from everyone else, was the older-style van.

Making sure the path was clear, he ran towards it and ducked down as he arrived. Controlling his breathing, he listened.

First, he heard a slap, and then another. There was a stifled cry from Eliza.

'You don't own me anymore, Dominic,' he heard her say. 'And I have got a family. I've got two people who practically brought my mother up and they love me like I'm their own. So I don't need you anymore. I've got them and everyone in this town as my family.

'I've never been happier, and felt more at home anywhere than I do here.

'So, shoot me if you have to. You won't get away with it. There's plenty of people who know that you're here.'

'No, they don't,' Dominic answered and Dave saw the van move as he shifted position.

'Actually, they do. Simon—your mate Simon—turned on you, Dominic.'

There was a crash inside the van and it sounded like crockery was breaking. Dave crept towards the window, in case there was a crack in the curtain he could see through.

'You going to use that gun or just pretend to?' he heard Eliza ask.

'What the fuck are you doing, Eliza?' he said to himself. 'You're gonna inflame the situation.'

'Don't tempt me, you bitch.' The caravan moved again. 'How do you know Simon turned on me?'

'Because he's been contacting the policeman here. We knew you were in Port Augusta. I told you—there's plenty of people who know you're around.'

Through the gap in the curtains, Dave could now see Dominic holding a gun and Eliza tied to a chair. Dominic's back was to the window, and he was facing the door.

Fuck, Dave thought. He knew as soon as he opened the door and went in, Dominic would start shooting.

A distraction, that's what I need. A distraction.

Or a way to negotiate?

He was still thinking when Eliza began to speak again.

'You're the one who's alone, Dominic. Your mother? She's dead. Your father? He's dead too. Your sister? Well, she might be alive but when was the last time you spoke to her? You think she'd be happy with you dragging the Alberto name through the media the way you have since I left?

'No, I didn't think so.

331

'It hurt when your father put her in charge of the family business, didn't it? Is that why you hate women so much? And Gina has made such a success of it.'

Dave shook his head at the way Eliza was taunting him now.

There was an *oomph* sound and a groan.

'Take that, you fucking bitch. You don't know what you're talking about.'

Dave could hear that Eliza was struggling to talk, as though she'd been winded. He assumed Dominic had punched her in the stomach.

'Ah, but I do. You're a sad and lonely individual who tried to keep people close by blackmailing them. Oh, don't worry, I've only worked that out since I left. I'm the strong one now.'

Dave looked back in through the curtains and saw Dominic towering over Eliza, a gun pointed at her head. He watched in horror as he drew back the slide and cocked it, ready to fire.

Then he saw Eliza draw back her legs and kick Dominic's stomach as hard as she could.

In a split second, the gun went off and Dave was at the caravan door.

'Stop!' he yelled. 'Get down, get down, get down! Police!'

He launched himself into the caravan. Unable to locate the gun, he dived on top of Dominic, knocking him onto the ground.

Dominic kicked up and tried to throw Dave off, but he was too strong. After a short scuffle, Dave had Dominic on his back. Struggling for his handcuffs, Dave yanked one of Dominic's arms behind him, then the other, and cuffed him.

Over his shoulder, he yelled, 'Are you all right?'

Eliza didn't answer.

He turned around to see blood oozing from her torso.

ᴄ⁊

After shutting the ambulance door, Dave breathed a sigh of relief. Considering what could have happened today, it was a relief that Eliza had only been shot in the shoulder.

Andy and Jack, the other officers from Barker, were controlling the onlookers, and forensics were inside the caravan. Dave swallowed hard. The next thing he had to do was going to be tough.

First, he went to see Reen and Kim, who were standing on the steps of the store, arms around each other, watching the ambulance leave for Port Augusta.

'Hey,' he said as he approached the women.

'Is she okay?' Reen asked, in a high, panicked voice.

'She's in the best possible hands,' Dave answered. He wasn't a doctor, he couldn't be sure what the prognosis would be, but he did know she would live.

'Now, I need you to do something. Go and get Heidi and Tilly, and take them as far away from here as possible. Keep them busy and keep them laughing.'

Reen froze for a moment but Kim pushed her forward.

'Sure,' she said.

Letting out a huge sigh, he walked down to the pub and stood outside, waiting for the girls to be away from their father's side, and safely with Kim and Reen. He knew they would be distracted for a while with ice-creams and lollies.

Once Heidi and Tilly were inside the store, Dave shoved his hands in his pockets and slowly walked over to talk to

Chris, who was standing with his brother and some other onlookers.

'Can you come with me for a moment?' he asked. From the resigned look on Chris's face, Dave could tell he knew what was about to happen, but the ranger followed him without a word. When they reached the police car, they faced each other.

'Chris Maynard, I'm arresting you on suspicion of animal trafficking,' Dave said.

Tears welled up in Chris's eyes, but he didn't speak.

Dave said, 'Now, mate, I'm going to allow you the dignity of walking out of here without being handcuffed. Just get in the back of the car. No one needs to know any of this just yet.'

Now a broken man, Chris choked out: 'My girls . . .'

'I'm sorry.' Dave didn't know what else he could say.

'Ask Jacob and Eliza to look after them,' he whispered. 'Until I'm back. He's my brother. My family. Don't let welfare get involved. Please,' he begged.

'That will be okay for the time being,' Dave answered. He knew that at some stage welfare would have to be involved, but, for the moment, those little girls would be with two people who loved them. And not only that, the whole town would gather them to their hearts and love them.

Epilogue

Weeks later, Jacob drove into Blinman with Eliza in the passenger seat, and Heidi and Tilly in the back. The girls had been very sad and quiet since Chris had been taken away to await trial, but Jacob hoped that with him, Eliza and Reen giving them love and support, and the endless stream of visitors, including Mary and John, they would be okay. Eliza had just had the last of her physio sessions. Her arm might never move as well as it had, but she hoped it would heal enough to allow her to do all the things she wanted to do.

'Look!' Eliza said, a laugh in her voice. 'Reen's got the welcoming committee out! There's Mary and John. Oh, and Stacey and Stu! And Dave and Kim!' She stopped, the lump in her throat almost too big for her to continue. 'And Dessie.'

The girls didn't tumble excitedly out of the car as they once had, but they threw themselves into Mary and John's arms with the same gusto.

'It's good to see you all again!' Mary's voice was husky with emotion.

'Lunch at the pub is on us,' John said. 'Reen, you'll have to shut the shop for the rest of the day.'

'What a fantastic idea. This is a day for celebrations!' She put her arms around Heidi and Tilly. 'What do you say, Fire Engines all round?', referring to the lemonade and raspberry cordial drinks that had become the girls' favourites since their father had been arrested.

Heidi and Tilly chorused yes.

Jacob put his arm around Eliza. They started to walk to the pub, but Dave stopped them.

He said to Eliza: 'You were right in a lot of the things you said to Dominic that day in the caravan. His sister being asked to run the family business certainly hurt his pride.

'Basically, he was just a small-town gangster. I think he was under the impression he was running a top organised crime group. He wasn't. It was very small time, but it did involve poaching wildlife. There were other things he was involved with too—drugs and firearms.'

'How did he get into smuggling wildlife?' Eliza asked.

'That's not clear yet, but I do know how the chain worked.' He indicated they should sit down on the store's verandah. 'The Taggarts were transporting the animals across the border.'

'Chris's in-laws?' Jacob asked, shocked.

'They would turn up here three or four times a year, and Chris would have the animals, or eggs, or whatever the orders were, ready for them.

'They'd stash everything in their caravan and drive back to New South Wales. It was a pretty good set-up. Nobody would expect grey nomads to be doing something like that. It was the perfect cover.'

'I still can't believe it,' Jacob said.

'How did Chris get to be involved in this?' Eliza asked. 'Because that doesn't make any sense to me. He loves animals, he loves that park.'

'In his confession, he said that his wife used to do it, until she left. He'd had no idea what she was involved in.

'When she left, his in-laws threatened him. They said they'd begin proceedings to take the kids away from him, citing he was an unfit father. They weren't prepared to give up the money they got from smuggling because their daughter was no longer involved. Chris was terrified of getting mixed up in drawn-out legal proceedings, and the effect that might have on his girls, and didn't know enough about the law to realise the Taggarts didn't have a leg to stand on. He was planning to put money away the for the girls' education. Private boarding schools are pretty expensive but he wanted them to have every possible opportunity.'

Eliza looked over at Jacob and saw his eyes were full of tears. She reached over and put her hand on his knee. The whole business was just so awful, and to hear it detailed out loud was even more upsetting.

A lone crow swooped down and landed in one of the cypress pines. It cawed long and low. Eliza shivered at the haunting cry.

The pub door flew open and Heidi called out to them, 'We're ordering. Are you coming?'

'Be right there,' Jacob answered.

The three of them stood up and started to walk over.

'How strange is it that Dominic was the one behind all this and I've ended up here in Blinman?' said Eliza.

'Well, in my job,' said Dave, 'fact is usually stranger than fiction. But I've got to admit, the links between you and Blinman, and Dominic and Chris, have been on the bizarre side.'

'Bizarre doesn't seem to cover it,' Jacob said dryly.

'So, what now?' Eliza asked.

'Court for all of them,' Dave answered. 'Jail for Dominic, without a doubt. We've found Simon's body, so not only will we have him for the poaching, we'll get him for murder and assault too.

'I don't know about Chris: if he'll get jail time or if the judge will be lenient under the circumstances. A good lawyer might be able to work a miracle.'

'What about the girls?'

'They can stay with you for the moment. If you'll have them.'

'Of course we will,' Eliza said. 'We love them as if they're our own.'

They walked into the pub and she looked around. Despite all the awful things that had happened, she knew how lucky she was.

Heidi came over and hugged her, then told Jacob what she wanted to eat.

Eliza beckoned to Mary, John and Dessie.

They came over to her, and she held out her arms. 'Thank you for being my family,' she said.

Tears filled Mary's faded blue eyes and she pressed her lips together, as if she were trying to think of something to say. John reached out an arm and wrapped it around Eliza's shoulders as he took Mary's hand in his.

Eliza lay her head on John's shoulder, and smiled into his shirt, which smelled like sun and clean air. They were the best grandparents any girl could hope for.

She could see Dessie out of the corner of her eye. He nodded and closed his eyes briefly. She was sure he was giving a quick prayer of thanks. Eliza reached out to grasp hold of his hand.

'Thank you,' she mouthed.

Dessie didn't say anything. He didn't need to. His face was full of tenderness as he watched her.

'Excuse me. What about me?' Reen had put her arms around the three of them and was looking at them all, her face soft.

Gulping hard, Eliza gave her a watery look. 'What *about* you?' But she hugged her too.

'Actually, you all seem to forget that's my job,' Jacob said as he pulled Eliza to him, his hand resting on her waist, and looked down at her, his face filled with love.

'Ugh. Do you have to kiss her *again*?' Tilly asked in a bored tone.

'Yes, I do,' Jacob answered, reaching down to press his lips to Eliza's. 'I like kissing her.' He looked over at the girls and wiggled an eyebrow at them, which set off another chorus of groans.

Eliza blushed and looked down. Then, just as quickly, she lifted her head and looked at everyone in the room.

'I am so lucky,' she said. She reached out to the girls, who came and stood next to both of them. Heidi looked up at her.

'We're the lucky ones,' she commented. 'Where would we be if you hadn't been here?'

'Yeah,' Tilly added. 'We like being with you and Uncle Jacob.' She paused. 'Even if you do kiss so much.'

Laughter filled the pub and everyone began talking again.

Eliza took her wine and sauntered over to the window, to look out on the quiet street. From the fear and sadness she had felt when she'd arrived in Blinman, she had emerged a strong and independent woman. She had gone from not having anyone, to having a whole town, not just a family. A place to belong and people who loved her.

In a phone call, while Eliza had been in Adelaide for surgery, Kim had said: 'It takes time, but so often, tears turn to smiles, smiles turn to laughter, and laughter turns to kisses. Days turn into weeks, weeks into months, months into years. And, suddenly, you forget what life was like before. That, my darling girl, will happen to you.'

Standing there in the pub, with her 'town', Eliza understood what Kim had meant. She was beginning to forget what life had been like before. Now, she had other people depending on her, and she would be there for them, every step of the way.

Acknowledgements

The last twelve months have been incredibly challenging.

Firstly, to my sister, Suz. I wouldn't have finished *Indigo Storm* if it weren't for your persistence, support, phone calls, plotting and general nagging. How you did all this with a brand new baby, I'm not sure.

To my beautiful friends, who have stood steadfastly beside me and held my hands, during my darkest times and my happiest: Amanda, Ann, Carolyn and Aaron, Em and Pete, Heather, Jan and Pete, Robyn and Tiffany.

Catherine (what a lucky find you were!), Gina, Anna, Kath, Scottish, Shelley, Jenny, Marie, Kelvin, Mel, Maree, Lauren, and Graham and Kate. All at the Rotary Club of Esperance Bay.

I am so blessed to have the best tribe in the world.

Rochelle and Hayden—I love you both so very much. You are the lights of my life.

To my beautiful, gentle soul, Garry. Thank you for always

being there, never wavering in your belief in me and also understanding my chaos!

To mum and dad, Nicholas and Susan, who love me when I'm unlovable, and to my beautiful nieces and nephews Ned, Lexy, Mac, Elijah and Chloe—you are precious jewels.

Richard Moore. Appreciated your help and knowledge.

Dave Byrne. Wow. This is the seventh book you've been in and helped with! How lucky I was to find you when I was writing *Red Dust*. From the bottom of my heart, thank you. None of these books would have been the same without your help, knowledge and friendship. By the way, we still haven't managed that beer yet!

My agent Gaby Naher, publisher Louise Thurtell, editors Sarina Rowell and Sarah Baker, thank you for your understanding and patience. I promise to deliver my next manuscript by the deadline!

To Kelly Waite, who asked me the hardest questions to get me back on track—thank you . . . I think!

To my wonderful readers, I'm so incredibly lucky to have you. After all, without you both the story and the characters within these pages would be absolutely nothing.

Please feel free to contact me. I love hearing from you all and I do my best to respond to everyone!

Facebook: https://www.facebook.com/FleurMcDonaldAuthor/
Twitter: @fleurmcdonald
Website: www.fleurmcdonald.com

Here's to a brand new era with nothing but love, laughter and happiness.

Author's note

The Flinders Ranges are a part of Australia I love very much. The scenery and wildness are amazing; there simply aren't enough adjectives to paint you a proper picture. Firstly, I have to confess that I've made many changes to the landscape and also invented places, even though I have also used some real places as settings. I did this to bury the bodies (so to speak!) where they needed to go!

Blinman is a township 511 kilometres north of Adelaide. I'm sure that nothing like the events in this book have ever happened there. Well, if they have, I don't know about it! To suit the story, I've used some poetic licence with the natural features of the national park.

The Kanyaka ruins, the Wilson cemetery and Blinman all feature in *Indigo Storm* as they are not only steeped in history but also wonderful spots to visit. They are not far from where I grew up, but I've only seen them in all their glory during the last twelve months. I just knew I had to set a book in this area.

Plus the crime writer in me could see so many places to dump a body where it would never be found . . .

Thanks to Dick Thorp for his suggestion that we visit the Kanyaka ruins on our trip away. The creative juices started flowing the minute I saw those crumbling buildings.

I've consulted Lesley Slade's *Blinman: A concise history of Blinman*, and Tony Bott's *On the Line* to get a 'feeling' for the area's history.

If you ever get the chance you should visit!